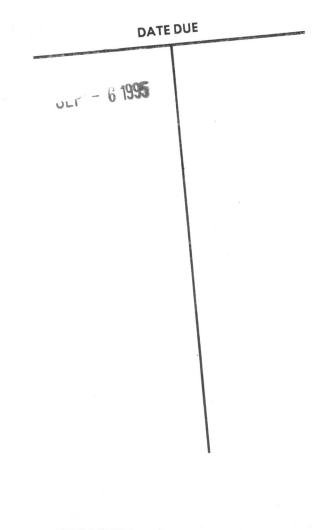

A MATTER OF CONSCIENCE

A MATTER OF CONSCIENCE

A NOVEL

PALMA HARCOURT

BEAUFORT BOOKS
Publishers • New York

For Audrey and Alastair

Library of Congress Cataloging-in-Publication Data

Harcourt, Palma.
A matter of conscience.

I. Title.
PR6058.A62M3   186   823'.914   85-9162
ISBN 0-8253-0305-2

Published in the United States by Beaufort Books Publishers, New York.

Printed in the U.S.A.   First American Edition

10 9 8 7 6 5 4 3 2 1

Seeing nothing, the old man stood at the long window and looked down into the square which was slowly coming to morning life. It was still very early but he had been unable to sleep. Ironically, today was his birthday; he had achieved the Biblical three score years and ten. And this morning, not unreasonably, his thoughts were on death—though not his own.

He was a handsome man, despite his age, with a shock of white hair and arrogant features belied by gentle brown eyes. Personally, he no longer cared if he lived or died. If at that moment an assassin had entered the salon he would have accepted the bullet with equanimity. Indeed, he knew he would have embraced it gladly if by so doing little David Gorey could have been brought back to life.

It was absurd, he thought angrily, that he should care so much about the child's death. Quite absurd! In the past he had killed, and sent others to kill, knowing full well that innocents might suffer in the process. The possibility had never bothered him before. But now, because a ten year old English boy whom he'd never seen had drowned, he was overcome by guilt. There was no sense to it.

Yet, sense or not, he couldn't ignore it. Heaven knew, he'd tried—told himself it was accidental, incidental, told himself he was not responsible, told himself it was the will of God. But he no longer believed in God. Or did he? It made no difference. The boy continued to haunt him.

He had at last thrown away the clipping from *The Times*. After a week in his wallet, constantly inspected, it had become torn and dog-eared—and unnecessary. He no longer needed it to visualize the picture of the small boy, dark haired, dark eyed, in grey flannel shorts and a white shirt, holding a model

5

yacht in loving hands. *David Gorey, dead after an explosion on his grandfather's boat,* the caption had read, and the small face had stared out at him, so like his own son at that age that the old wound had been reopened and grief renewed.

Both dead, he thought bitterly, both victims of circumstance. But there the similarity ended. His own David had been killed in a legitimate war, a soldier fighting for his country. The war in which little David Gorey had become unwittingly involved was of a different character, undeclared and unrecognized. Nevertheless, it was war, and war implied casualties. So why should he blame himself? If anyone were to blame it was surely Sir Reginald Gorey.

Suddenly becoming aware of the figures and vehicles in the square below—from this height as unreal as toys—the old man turned away from the window and began to pace the room. He had no doubts about the general's death, but he could not believe that, had the Englishman known how much he was at risk, he would have hazarded his grandson. And that was the crux of the matter.

As far as the old man was concerned there was no question of betraying his own comrades. That was impossible. He had never thought of such a step, and never would. On the other hand, could he contemplate the death of another David Gorey without making some effort to prevent it?

The old man paused at the far end of the room and picked up the silver-framed photograph that stood on the grand piano. For a full minute, his face pinched as if the pain were physical, he stared at the likeness of his own son, dark haired, dark eyed, handsome. He had been nineteen when he was killed, soon after the photograph had been taken, but the resemblance to the much younger English boy was strong.

At last the old man set down the photograph and, as if it had helped him to resolve his problem, strode purposefully to his desk in a corner of the room. He sat and drew a piece of paper towards him. He wrote quickly, without pausing for thought. When he had finished he folded the paper and placed it carefully in a plain envelope.

The next step wouldn't be difficult. He knew what had to be done and whom he could trust to do it. He also knew there

6

could be many a slip before his ultimate end was achieved, and even that would be only a compromise. But it was the best he could do, a reparation for young David Gorey and, he hoped, a salve for his own troubled conscience.

ONE

Keith Dayton was scared; always honest with himself, he was prepared to admit it. Twice his nerves had forced him to draw up on the hard shoulder of the Autobahn between Frankfurt and Cologne, get out of the BMW and urinate against a tree beside the motorway. At the last stop he had produced a mere trickle but now, only a few kilometres on, he felt the need again. He shifted uncomfortably in his seat. He was sweating too, though the night was cool, and he loosened his tie.

His tension was increased by his surprise at being so unexpectedly and unusually unnerved. Earlier in the day he had brought off a multi-million pound deal with a German firm – a deal that could be self-multiplying. He was a businessman, and a bloody good one; Rossel's were lucky to have him. Doubtless his boss, John Rossel, who had started the electronics firm that bore his name, would get his desired knighthood in due course, but it was he – Dayton – who would have done a great deal to earn the honour for him.

The trouble of course was this other – occupation, could you call it? They hadn't exactly leant on him, but the sense of his obligation had been heavy, or so he had believed. Now, biting his lower lip, he wished he had refused them, told them to go to hell. He had in fact made an effort, urged that there was a limit to his indebtedness. But they had persisted, and he'd been weak.

It wasn't as if he were a coward, or as if this were the first time he'd helped them. By now, he was a pretty experienced courier. The thought reassured him. Suddenly conscious that he was driving very fast and would be early for the rendezvous, he eased his foot from the accelerator.

It would be simple, he told himself. All he had to do was meet Ernst Bauer, collect whatever Bauer had brought and memorize any oral message there might be. He'd done it before, and there had never been trouble. Once he'd been stopped going through the 'green lane' at Heathrow, but the customs officers had been looking for drugs, and hadn't been really interested in him. It was part of their technique, to stop the occasional prosperous, well-dressed character amongst the hordes of jeans and rucksacks. Nevertheless, he'd been horribly conscious of the film sewn into the lining of his jacket.

Checking his watch against the quartz car clock, Dayton drove even more slowly. It was well after midnight and, apart from the occasional heavy articulated truck that thundered past, there was little traffic on the moonlit Autobahn. He reached his destination five minutes before the appointed time. It was a small *Parkplatz* several miles south of Cologne – one of the many lay-bys that were scattered at regular intervals along the highway.

Dayton climbed out of the BMW, relieved himself yet again and stretched. Momentarily he was feeling less nervous. He waited, wishing that the moon were not so bright. True, there were plenty of trees and bushes around the *Parkplatz*, but darkness offered more protection.

Bauer was late. Dayton got back into the car. He yearned for a cigarette, but he'd given up smoking some months ago to please his wife, Irena, and had none with him. Deprived, he bit at his thumb like a small child. It gave him little comfort. He cursed Bauer silently.

Then in the distance he heard the unmistakable sound of a powerful motor-cycle. He felt himself cringe inwardly. It could be Bauer, of course, but never before had Bauer arrived on a motor-bike. Bauer always drove big, expensive cars, usually Mercedes. Dayton held his breath, waiting for the bike to roar past, but it slowed, and turned off the road.

Keeping low in the driving seat, he watched the motor-cyclist dismount and take off his helmet. With relief he saw it was Bauer. Scrambling out of his car, he went to meet him.

'Hello, Ernst. I thought you were never coming,' he said. He spoke in English. Dayton's German was excellent but Bauer liked to practise his fourth or fifth language. 'I wouldn't have waited much longer.' He was pleased that at least he sounded reasonably calm, under control.

'I'm sorry. I couldn't help it.'

Bauer came close and peered up into Dayton's face. A square, stocky man, he looked even more square and more stocky in his motor-cycling gear. His voice was hoarse with nervousness. Dayton, tall and thin by contrast, regarded him with distaste and involuntarily took a step back. The German's breath smelt of stale beer.

'What's the matter?' Dayton asked. 'Is something wrong?'

'I think so, yes, but I'm not sure. Anyway, this is the last time, you understand. You tell your masters. *Ya?*'

'Sure I'll tell them. But they'll want to know why.'

'My contact is dead. Knocked over in the street. Killed. It was an accident perhaps—but perhaps not. Anyway, I'll have no more for you.' Bauer spoke quickly, his words tumbling over each other. 'This is the last time. Positively.'

'Okay. I'm not arguing.' Dayton tried to sound reassuring, but it required an effort; the German was beginning to annoy him. 'But let's talk about now. Have you got something for me?'

'*Ya!*' Forgetting his worries, Bauer was suddenly triumphant. 'Have I ever something! Names! Britishers, all of them – and all of them in danger for their lives.' Unzipping his leather jacket, he fumbled for his wallet and produced a piece of paper. 'It is priceless, no?'

'Maybe.' Dayton held out his hand for the paper. By the light of the moon he saw clearly that it was a photocopy of a handwritten list of names. 'Where did you get this? Why are they in danger? Who's after them?'

Bauer gave him a sly glance. 'You have the money for me?' he countered.

'I've got the money. Here.' Dayton held out a wad of notes, and Bauer put them carefully into an inside pocket. 'Now, what does this list mean?'

'They are people of importance, of influence in different areas – spheres of public life, you would say, and . . .'

The German paused, his eyes widening in fear. A large car – an Audi – had swept past the *Parkplatz*, but had then braked sharply. Now it was reversing into the exit. Even before it stopped, a man jumped from it, a pistol in his hand. Bauer ran for his motor-cycle, but it was obvious he would have no time to manoeuvre the heavy machine back on to the highway. He paused and threw himself to the ground by Dayton's BMW. He drew a gun of his own, and fired first.

Dayton watched in amazement as the man from the Audi stumbled and almost fell. Almost simultaneously there was a second shot, an echo of Bauer's. But the man's aim was poor. The bullet, if meant for Bauer, went wide. Dayton felt its impact under his shoulder as it spun him round. Then he was lying on the ground, more astonished than afraid, but for the moment without pain.

There were more shots. Bauer was firing from the shelter of Dayton's car, while his opponent had been joined by the driver of the Audi and between them they were trying to take Bauer from two sides. Dayton, seizing his chance while they were occupied, began to crawl towards the trees and bushes that surrounded the *Parkplatz*. As he reached them he heard Bauer scream.

The sound galvanized Dayton. He was on his feet and running, dodging between the trees, stumbling through the undergrowth, regardless of the brambles that tore at his clothes and face. He had no clear idea where he was going, but at least he was getting away from Bauer and his assailants; he had no qualms about leaving the German to his fate. At the back of his mind was the thought that he must try to keep parallel to the Autobahn.

He knew the road quite well and he retained a vague memory of a *Tankstelle* – a service area – a few kilometres ahead. It was most unlikely that anyone would be about at that time of night. The restaurant would be shut, and the petrol pumps self-serve – and it was some distance away. But still, later there would be more traffic, and if he could find somewhere to lie up beside the road . . .

Catching his foot in a root, Dayton fell on his face and lay, gasping. It was only then, as he tried to struggle up, that the pain hit him. For a moment he blacked out. When he came to, he found his hand pressing against his shoulder. Slowly, as he brought himself to take it away, he became aware that his fingers were warm and sticky. It was as if his hand had been dipped in tar, though he knew that it was blood.

His first thought was of Irena, his wife, and what she would do if he died, alone, beside a German motorway. Caro, his daughter, would be all right, but Irena . . . His second thought was of the list that Bauer had brought. He managed to search through his pockets and was glad to find that, in the midst of the excitement, he'd had enough sense to thrust it inside his jacket. He had no idea of its provenance or its importance, but he had been told that information from this contact was usually accurate and of great significance, and clearly he had to relay it to the UK. He was just a middle-aged businessman, and he'd been the world's worst fool to get involved in these affairs. But since he had, he supposed he must do his best to see it through.

Carefully Dayton got to his feet. To his surprise he didn't feel too weak. Light-headed certainly, and with a sense of unreality, but able to walk. He walked. For a while he was sure he was lost. And, in harmony with his wandering steps, his mind also wandered.

'Forty-six,' he murmured aloud. 'Twice married, one child.' He stopped, puzzled again. 'Where am I? What am I doing here?'

As if against his will he returned to the present. The pain in his shoulder stabbed, and he leaned against a tree. As the spasm passed he saw to his surprise that he was staring at a conglomeration of buildings and a floodlit forecourt, and he realized that somehow he had managed to reach the *Tankstelle*. He must have been lucky, and cut across a curve in the Autobahn. Suddenly he felt incredibly, overwhelmingly, tired.

But the sight of the service area gave him hope. At least it was a sign of civilization. Someone might be napping in the car park. Someone might pull in to fill up. Some of the staff would be sure to arrive in a few hours. Meanwhile there might be a washroom open, even vending machines; he was conscious suddenly of a great thirst. And, of course, a phone!

In spite of his condition, Keith Dayton caught himself grinning broadly, wondering why the obvious had escaped him for so long. A telephone! He could dictate the damned list to London. Then, duty done, he could find somewhere to shelter and sleep until help came. He was bleeding hardly at all by now, and what he had to do no longer seemed difficult.

In fact, the *Tankstelle* was deserted, and Dayton had under-estimated the mental and physical effort that would be needed to accomplish even the simplest task. Though he believed he was being efficient, he wandered dazedly through the complex and it was only by chance that he noticed the phone booth the second time he passed it. He went in, leaned against the glass wall and stared stupidly at the instrument. The pain was stabbing again.

Luckily he had some change in his pocket and after a while, when for a brief moment he felt better, he found it and dialled. There was a long pause while he waited, listening to the British ringing tone and thinking nostalgically of London. Then he became anxious. Why the hell didn't someone take his call? He'd been assured that the phone was always manned, and that there was always a responsible officer on duty.

'Hello!' a voice said. 'Hello! Who's that?'

Dayton didn't answer. The words were wrong, not what he had expected to hear, and his anxiety was multiplied by the vague sense that the voice – a woman's voice – was familiar.

'Hello!' the voice said, more peremptorily. 'Who is it? Who do you want? If you do not tell me I will ring off.'

'Irena!'

Overwhelmed with relief, he managed to breathe the word into the mouthpiece. Now he knew who it was: Irena, his wife. He recognized the Polish cadences in her voice, and the fierce tone with which she always tried to cover her insecurity. But why had she answered this phone?

'Keith! Keith! Is it you?'

'Yes, darling. Where are you? In London?'

'No, of course not. You know where I am – at the cottage – that's where you've phoned. What is it, Keith? Darling, what's wrong?' Her voice was sharp with fear.

'I thought you'd be in London,' Dayton said stupidly.

'Not till Friday lunchtime. That's what we arranged.'

'I forgot.'

'Then why – ?' She was obviously puzzled.

Dayton swallowed hard. The pain had receded again and his mind was clear. He knew what had happened. In a moment of aberration he had dialled the wrong number. He must have been thinking of Irena and . . . Should he hang up and dial again? No, he couldn't chance it. His money would soon run out. There was one possibility.

'Irena,' he said. 'I'm still in West Germany, in a phone box. Call me back here immediately.' Frantically he searched for the number. With typical German efficiency, there it was in large figures above the phone.

'Irena,' he repeated. 'Will you do that? Don't forget "010" and the country code. I'll wait.'

He heard her voice say, 'Yes,' as the line went dead.

This time the wait was short. The phone rang almost at once and he lifted the receiver. Irena's voice said, 'Keith? Keith, darling, tell me what is wrong.'

'There's nothing wrong,' he lied.

'Then why do you phone in the middle of the night?' Irena was practical. 'And you sound so strange. Your voice seems to come and go.'

'That must be the line. It's not good.'

Another lie, he thought; he could hear every word Irena said with perfect clarity. But he needed to reassure her. Time was passing and he couldn't stand here chatting. He was conscious of his thirst, and there even seemed to be a taste of blood in his throat. The pain in his shoulder, though not acute at the moment, was dully present and threatening. He was hurt, and there was no use pretending otherwise. He needed help, and as soon as he could get it. The sky was beginning to lighten and he should be back on the highway, trying to cadge a lift while he had the strength. Even now lorries, cars, all sorts of vehicles might be passing. But first the list . . .

'Keith! Are you still there, Keith?'

'Yes. Listen, darling. I want you to do something for me. Have you paper? Pencil?'

'A minute.'

Again Dayton waited, breathing hard. He had pulled the photocopy from his pocket and was holding it in his hand,

15

sticky with blood. He had not yet read it. He willed Irena to
hurry, suddenly impatient, afraid that if she didn't return
quickly he might not have enough strength to explain.

'Yes, Keith. I'm here.'

'Irena, this is a terribly serious matter. You understand that?
I have a list of names I'm going to read to you. You must take
them down and . . . Christ!'

'What is it? What has happened?'

Dayton didn't answer immediately. He had just glanced at
the list, and he was appalled. Not only were most of the ten
names familiar to him, but three of them he knew well, very
well. He wouldn't have described the three as close friends –
he had few really close friends – but they were certainly more
than acquaintances. And, according to Bauer, they were all
said to be in danger! Why? From what?

'Keith! Keith!'

'Take down what I say, Irena. Please, darling. Carefully.'

Dayton began to dictate the names. He read without expression, spelling any he thought she might not know. He
heard her gasp when he came to 'Mayberry', and blessed her
when she didn't attempt to interrupt.

He continued, though the effort was becoming too much for
him. For some reason his wound had started to bleed again.
A red mist of exhaustion and shock came and went before his
eyes. His words didn't seem to correspond with his thoughts.
Twice Irena had to make him repeat a name. The spasms of
pain were beginning to recur. He knew that he might soon
lapse into unconsciousness. Thankfully he came to the end of
the list.

'Darling, I love you,' he said inconsequentially.

'Yes, yes. I know, Keith. And I love you, but – these names.
What do they mean? What do I do with them?'

'Irena, they're important. You must take care. I know you
don't know about me, what I've been doing. I'll explain –
tomorrow – next day – as soon as I get home. Till then don't
tell anyone. Keep the list for – Don't trust anyone – Piercey –
Not anyone – The phone number's – '

But he couldn't remember the phone number, the one he
should have dialled in the first place, and his words were

16

running into each other. He knew he should be giving Irena explicit instructions so that she could pass on the list, and be free of all involvement – God knew, he should probably never have involved her in this kind of operation at all – but he couldn't think clearly enough. The pain was growing again, and he could scarcely remember the meaning of the list himself.

'Keith, you *are* ill. Where are you exactly, darling? Can you get help?'

For a moment Irena's voice, high with fear and apprehension, brought Dayton's drifting thoughts back to the present and the urgent need to be coherent. He drew a deep breath to make the effort, then thought he heard a car.

'I'll be okay. Don't worry. Always – love you, darling,' he managed to say.

There was a clang as he dropped the receiver, pushed open the door of the phone booth and staggered outside. He'd not been mistaken. He had heard a car. In the early morning light he saw a large grey shape cruising between the buildings of the *Tankstelle*. He shouted feebly and waved. He had no strength to run after it.

Either he was heard, or the driver caught a glimpse of him in his rear-view mirror. The car braked. Dayton saw its red stop lights come on, and felt a dim sense of relief as it made a U-turn and sped back towards him. Here, at last, was the Good Samaritan – and soon there would be hospital, doctors, nurses, everything he needed . . .

The car drew up beside him and the driver got out. It was then, as his lips stretched in a grimace of welcome, that Keith Dayton realized what had happened. He made a choking sound that was almost a laugh, and collapsed on the ground.

The driver slowly let his gun drop, but approached the prone figure with caution. When Dayton lay still, he kicked him gently. Dayton groaned, but hardly stirred. The driver, his face expressionless, looked from Dayton to the phone booth. He noted the dangling receiver, the blood on the floor, the seemingly discarded piece of paper by Dayton's outstretched hand.

Taking a laundered handkerchief from his breast pocket he picked up the photocopy by one corner, wiped it clean, gave

17

it a long look and put it in his wallet. Thoughtfully he again regarded the phone booth. The conclusion was obvious and, with an angry gesture, he went across to the phone and replaced the receiver.

This done, he returned to Dayton. He examined the wound before seizing him under the arms and dragging him to the car. Acting quickly now, as if time were precious, he spread a travelling rug on the floor in front of the rear seat. Then, with some difficulty since Dayton though thin was tall and gangling, he manoeuvred the unconscious figure into the back of the car, and pulled the rug over it. He ran round to the front, got in, and drove off.

He drove recklessly and the wrong way down the Autobahn lane, and he was fortunate to meet no oncoming traffic. But in a very few moments he was back at the *Parkplatz* where the shooting had taken place, and where his companion was waiting with the body of Ernst Bauer.

TWO

Slowly Irena Dayton replaced the telephone on her bedside table. Involuntary tears were streaming down her face. She was thinking of her husband with love and longing. Where was he? What was happening to him? She had no faith in his reassurances. Nor could she really believe that he would be home tomorrow – she glanced at the clock – today. He was due at Heathrow about noon. If he didn't come . . .

But could there possibly be any problem? As far as she knew, he had gone to West Germany at the beginning of the week on a perfectly routine business trip for the electronics firm of which he was a director. He often went to Europe on such visits, not only to the West, but sometimes to Iron Curtain countries. Admittedly, then she did worry a little. She had hated it when he went to Poland, afraid that because of her origins – she was by birth a Pole – he might be entrapped, questioned, even arrested. As it turned out her fears had in that instance been foolish, but there was no knowing what a communist regime might try in the future.

This time, as far as she knew, he'd had no intention of crossing the Curtain – for it still was a Curtain, in spite of some communist countries' attempts to rationalize the situation. This time his visit had been only to the West. Tonight he should have been in Cologne; as usual, he had given her a copy of his itinerary. But now she had no idea where he really was, or what he was doing. She only knew that he was in trouble. She had heard the clang as the receiver was dropped. She had shouted Keith's name, but there had been no response – only a thick silence.

'Dear God, let him be all right,' Irena whispered aloud. 'Please.'

She threw back the duvet and slid her naked legs over the

side of the bed. At night she always wore a man's pyjama jacket, not the most glamorous of garments, though it was unmistakably sexy. Keith, she had decided, had seen enough of ostentatious glamour with his first wife. Besides, as she admitted to herself half-ruefully, glamour as such wasn't one of her strong points.

Irena Dayton, born Irena Kalak thirty-six years ago in Warsaw, was not a beautiful woman. Taller than most of her compatriots and black-haired, she had a thin, narrow body and a long face with too prominent features that were redeemed by a fine pair of brown eyes. Keith Dayton hadn't married her for her looks or her fortune; she'd had neither. Nevertheless, theirs had been a happy and satisfactory marriage. But now, when everything seemed to be going well for them, when Keith was prospering in his business and she was beginning to make a name for herself as a portrait photographer, suddenly, without warning, some catastrophe had befallen them. What? Almost the worst part was not knowing.

After a few minutes Irena pulled on an old Viyella dressing-gown, thrust her feet into slippers, took the list of names her husband had dictated to her and went downstairs. The cottage was small – two little bedrooms and a bathroom upstairs, and below one fair-sized all-purpose room and a kitchen. They had bought it only six months ago and it still needed a lot of work. The garden remained a wilderness. But there was a wonderful view of the Sussex downs, and they loved the place. Unlike their London house, which incorporated her studio and was used to entertain Keith's business acquaintances, this was their own private retreat which they intended to share with no one, except perhaps Keith's daughter Caro.

Resolutely Irena wiped away the last of her tears on the sleeve of her dressing-gown. She told herself she would have to wait, to be patient. She put on the kettle to make a cup of tea and, while it boiled, sat at the kitchen table and considered the names she had written down. She assumed they were all in some way connected with Keith's business, for John Rossel, Keith's boss, was on the list – and Sir Peter Mayberry. She knew that Mayberry, who was a Tory Member of Parliament with a safe London seat, had money in the firm, and she suspected it was Mayberry's influence that had originally, in a period of sickening unemployment, got Keith his present job. At the time she hadn't much liked the idea. She had nothing against Sir Peter himself, except that he was rather a stuffed-shirt character. But she saw no reason why Keith should owe anything to Patricia Mayberry – the former Mrs Dayton, and Caroline's mother. The job however had been too rewarding to refuse, and in fact had turned out well. Keith enjoyed it, and had earned himself a directorship in the firm.

The kettle began to sing. Irena warmed the pot, made the tea, fetched milk and a mug and returned to her seat. While she waited for the tea to stand she considered the other names. Hector Coyne she knew too, of course: he was another Tory MP, with a constituency in the Midlands and a junior Government post, but, most importantly, he was engaged to Caro. And she had met Baroness Lecque, having been commissioned to photograph her for the dust-jacket of a book that redoubtable member of the House of Lords was writing. The rest meant nothing specific to her, though some were vaguely familiar. Maybe she had seen them on television, or read of them in the newspapers.

But why did these people matter so much? What was so important about them that Keith, clearly ill or hurt, had made such an effort to phone her in the middle of the night and pass the list to her? And what should she do with it if Keith didn't return when he'd promised? He had been vague, rambling, and because of her concern for him she'd failed to concentrate on his words. Now, as she tried to recall exactly what he had said, she found it difficult.

Sighing, Irena poured her tea and, as the daylight brightened outside the kitchen window and the waking birds began their songs, she forced herself to think. At least she could remember that Keith had told her to keep the list safe and trust no one with it – especially someone called Piercey.

Irena frowned. She had never heard the name Piercey – or was it Percy? Then there was the phone number that Keith had tried – and failed – to give her . . . Suddenly cold, she wrapped her gown tightly round her and drank more tea. It was a long time, she thought, a very long time, since she'd felt so alone and helpless. On the whole she'd been free of such feelings since eight years ago Keith Dayton, in a way she had never quite understood but with the help of the British Government, had persuaded the Polish authorities to permit them to marry and to grant her an exit visa.

★

While Irena Dayton worried and wondered, Hean – the driver of the Audi in which her husband lay unconscious – had reached the *Parkplatz* by the Autobahn. With relief he saw his colleague, Brenner, leaning against the BMW and smoking a cigarette as if taking a break in the course of a long journey.

'You're okay?' Hean said, jumping out of his car.

'A flesh wound in the arm. Nothing serious. I've done what I can for it and it can wait. What about you? Did you find him?' Brenner asked anxiously.

'Yes, but too late. The bugger had cut across country to a *Tankstelle*. He'd almost certainly managed to phone through whatever Bauer gave him. The receiver was off in a phone booth, there was blood on the floor and I found this.' Brenner handed Hean the photocopy. 'I should have gone after him at once.'

Brenner glanced at the paper and swore. 'We shan't be popular when we put in our report,' he said. 'Where's he now?'

'He's in the car. He was wounded and he flaked out, but he'll live – if we let him. Where's Bauer?'

'In the bushes. Dead. He was too far gone. I got nothing out of him.' Leading the way to where Ernst Bauer's body lay beside his motor-cycle, Brenner spoke fast. 'I've done all I could with one arm, but he should be hidden better than this – and his bike. The police patrol'll find him soon enough but even a short delay could be useful.'

Hean looked down at Bauer in undisguised disgust. 'Dirty rotten Jew!' he said viciously, and kicked the body.

Brenner winced. 'Jews come in all shapes and sizes,' he said mildly. 'They're no different from anyone else.'

Hean laughed, a laugh without amusement, but he made no comment and began to drag the body deeper into the trees

22

towards a thick patch of undergrowth. Brenner left him, with an admonition to hurry, and himself went back to the Audi. Here, peeling off the rug that covered the unconscious Dayton, he made a rapid but thorough search of the Englishman's pockets and took another quick look at the wound under his shoulder.

'A Brit,' he said when Hean joined him, 'as I'd already gathered from the stuff in his car. Supposedly some sort of businessman. Keith Dayton by name. We'll deal with him as soon as we can. But not here. You've coped with Bauer?'

'As best I could. The bike was more of a problem.'

Brenner nodded. 'Let's go then. You take Dayton's car – the key's in the ignition – and follow me. I think I know a good place.'

'You can manage with your arm?'

Brenner didn't bother to answer. Time was passing. Already he could discern a lightening in the sky, and there was appreciably more traffic on the Autobahn. With a glance in the back to make sure his passenger wasn't visible, he got into the Audi.

He drove steadily for some kilometres, but left the Autobahn at the first exit and turned south on minor roads. Hean followed at a discreet distance in Dayton's BMW. They passed through a village, apparently still sleeping, and found themselves in a forest. On one side the ground was fairly level; on the other a narrow wooded area concealed a steep drop into a ravine. Brenner slowed and almost immediately found what he hoped was the ideal spot. As the road curved sharply a rutted track led into the woods. He took it without hesitation.

Minutes later Hean had lifted Dayton out of the car and propped him in a sitting position against a tree. Brenner crouched beside him, pleased to see that Dayton's eyelids were quivering as he struggled to regain consciousness. Brenner slapped Dayton's cheeks gently.

'There's some whisky in his bag,' he said to Hean. 'Get it.'

Hean found the whisky and Brenner, supporting Dayton's head, helped him to drink from the bottle. Most of the liquor went down Dayton's chin, but he managed to swallow a little and, as its glow warmed his stomach, he opened his eyes. He had no idea where he was or how he had got there.

23

'Thanks,' he said, not recognizing either of the two men and believing for the moment that he'd found friends. '*Danke schön.*'

His gratitude was short-lived. Brenner clenched his fist and gave him a sharp jab below the shoulder where the bullet had entered. Dayton cried out with the pain and promptly fainted. Brenner cursed and set about reviving him again. This time Dayton was wary.

'Who are you?' he said when he could speak. 'What do you want?'

'Never mind who we are,' Brenner answered in English. 'Tell us about you. You're Keith Dayton – British. Supposedly you work for an outfit called Rossel and Company in London.'

'I do – work for Rossel's, I mean,' Dayton replied. 'You can check, though why – '

'And who else?'

'Who else – what?'

'Who else do you work for?'

'No one.'

'That's a lie, if ever I heard one!' Brenner struck Dayton brutally across the face, causing him to flinch and drop sideways. Brenner roughly pulled him upright. 'Listen, Mr Dayton or whoever you are, we've no time to waste. We want answers, straight answers. Now! Who do you work for? What did Bauer tell you?'

'Who's Bauer?' began Dayton, and Brenner hit him again.

The questions continued relentlessly. Dayton had never thought of himself as brave; he knew he abhorred physical violence. He told them what they wanted to know – more or less. He admitted he was a courier. He gave them names, places, phone numbers. Hean made scratchy notes on an old envelope, peering closely at what he was writing in the poor light beneath the trees. Then they came to the present, and Brenner showed Dayton the photocopied list. Dayton explained his relationship to Rossel and Mayberry and Coyne, but denied any real knowledge of the other names.

'I've heard of them, yes, some of them – but that's all! And I don't know what the list's about. Bauer had no time to tell me. All he said was that – that they were in some kind of

24

danger. God knows why or when or who from.' Dayton's voice rose, willing them to believe.

'But you knew the list was important – vital – didn't you?' Brenner persisted.

'He said that too, yes.'

'Important enough for you to find a phone, though you were wounded, and phone your controllers in London?'

Dayton didn't answer at once. He closed his eyes and groaned softly. There was one thing he must not tell them. He must not involve Irena. He heard his whimper turn into a shriek as Brenner put pressure on his wound. He screamed at them. 'Yes! Yes, damn you! I told London. I read out the whole bloody list.'

He waited, conscious of the warm dampness around his genitals as his bladder emptied involuntarily. He didn't care. He was beyond bothering about such trivia. He felt himself sink through layers of cloud as if into a deep sleep and was unaware that his two captors had got to their feet and were standing a few paces away from him, discussing how best to make his death appear an accident.

*

It was some time later that Brenner and Hean left the rented Audi at Wahn Airport, halfway between Cologne and Bonn, and caught a taxi. The taxi took them to a prosperous town house off the Sachsenring, a couple of kilometres south of Cologne cathedral and the centre of the city. Here the door was opened to them by a pleasant-faced woman in her fifties. She greeted them without surprise, though she had never seen either of them before.

'My husband has gone to his office, but you are welcome,' she said. 'He left instructions. Whatever you wish.'

'Thank you, *mein Frau*. We're grateful. You are alone at present?'

She bowed her head, acknowledging the thanks. '*Bitte. Bitte schön.* Yes, I'm alone. My cleaning woman doesn't come today.'

'*Gut.* Then, first, for me, a telephone. It's imperative I make a long-distance call. Afterwards we'd enjoy some breakfast and a chance to shower and change our clothes.'

'Certainly. I'll show you to my husband's study. His business requires that he telephones a great deal, to all over the world. An extra call won't be noticed.' She paused. 'But – your arm?'

'Later perhaps, if you have some antiseptic and a dressing. It's only a flesh wound.'

Once again the woman showed no surprise. 'I'll attend to it when you are ready,' she said practically.

Brenner nodded his appreciation, and followed her to the study. It was a beautiful room, expensively furnished and lined with books, but he scarcely noticed his surroundings. Only waiting till the door was closed he sat himself at the long mahogany desk and dialled a number. His call was not unexpected, and there was only a minor delay before he was making his report.

'. . . and, as I said, sir, I'm sorry, but we were too late. The list has gone to London. I blame myself.'

'No one can achieve the impossible. It's unfortunate, but . . .' A sigh travelled down the line. 'Tell me about the – er – loose ends, and I'll take it from there.'

'Bauer will be found within forty-eight hours at the outside, I would say, sir. We took his money and valuables and did our best to hide him and make it look like a robbery, but I doubt if that scenario will hold up. It was all we could do in the time available.'

'And the Englishman? Where did you leave him? Not with Bauer, I hope.'

'No, sir. Way off the Autobahn and quite a few kilometres further south. When we'd finished with him, we put him in his car, sprinkled a little petrol around and pushed it over the side of the road. It bounced down a nearly sheer slope, hitting a few trees and finally bursting into flames. We didn't wait to see, but after the petrol tank exploded there can't have been much left of Dayton.' Brenner did his best to speak without emotion. He didn't like some of the things he had to do, and it was worse when it was a matter of covering previous mistakes. He waited through a lengthening silence.

Then, 'Right. You know where to go.'

'Yes. Thank you, sir.'

The line went dead and Brenner grinned ruefully. He'd not received the expected reprimand, but he'd certainly gained no bonus points, which was fair enough. He'd not prevented the list reaching London and he'd had to leave two corpses behind. He swore aloud, softly, and realized he was still speaking in his accented Russian – the language in which his phone conversation had been conducted. Telling himself to be more careful, he went in search of his hostess.

Hean had already showered and changed. When Brenner reached the room that had been allotted to them he was packing their guns, his dirty clothes and his passport into a small bag; this would be left behind to be disposed of. Brenner stripped and added his own garments and papers. In a short while, refreshed, his arm expertly bandaged, he joined Hean for breakfast.

And later in the morning they left the house, separately, though they both checked in at Wahn Airport. They were no longer called Brenner and Hean. They had different names, different legends, and they travelled by different routes. Their ultimate destinations, however, were identical. They were going to a safe house in Zurich to await further orders.

*

The man who had been speaking to Brenner sat for some minutes after he had replaced his receiver, considering his course of action. His problem was two-fold. He had, if possible, to undo the damage that had been done, and he must protect the old man.

He had no doubt that the old man, who was incidentally his own father-in-law, was responsible. He could even comprehend why the old man had decided to act as he had, contrary to what had been agreed, contrary to the oath that had been sworn. He could imagine the old man's agony of conscience before taking his decision, and to some extent he could sympathize. He didn't regard his father-in-law as a traitor. But he knew that some might.

Fortunately the old man had been cunning and had covered

27

his tracks well. It was chance that had first betrayed, not him, but what he hoped to achieve. He would inevitably be suspected – he'd never been whole-heartedly with the rest of them – but to prove his guilt, if one could call it that, would be far from easy. Of course there was a possibility that no one would try – if the damage could be limited or mitigated.

After a while the man reached a decision. It could do no harm, he thought, and at least it was worth a try. He pressed the button on the intercom and, when his secretary answered, said, 'Put me through to our embassy in London, please. I need to speak to the Cultural Attaché. It's urgent.'

THREE

The flight from Wahn arrived at Heathrow on time. The passengers went through immigration control, collected their baggage from the carousel and eventually emerged from the customs hall. There was the usual crowd waiting to greet them at the barrier – friends, relations, business acquaintances, hotel representatives, drivers holding notices with names on them. Among this crowd was Dermot Piercey.

Piercey was thirty years old, of medium height and reasonably attractive. He was wearing an inconspicuous grey flannel suit, and easily merged into the background of the crowd around him. He might have been there to meet a girlfriend, a sister, a favourite uncle. He watched the exit with the same interest and anticipation as everyone else. He was waiting for Keith Dayton.

The trickle of arrivals increased to a flood, and then subsided again till it seemed to cease. But after a minute or two a flustered elderly lady appeared; she was accompanied by a porter pushing a trolley and it was clear from her comments that her delay had been caused by the loss of one of her bags. Even later came two men, complaining angrily at the unfairness of the customs officers.

Piercey continued to wait. The people around him changed as a new flight was expected, but the general character of the crowd remained the same, and they all continued to watch the exit doors with equal anticipation. The passengers they were awaiting, however, were quite different from those who had come from Germany. This group were sunburnt and wore the lightest of summer clothes, though it was a cold and drizzly day in London.

A fat lady pushed past Piercey to embrace a young couple. 'And how was Spain, dears? Have you had a marvellous time? You both look wonderful,' she declared.

Piercey continued with his vigil. Dayton was a seasoned traveller. He usually appeared among the first of the passengers on any flight and, during the time he had acted as a courier, had never failed, in the absence of a prior warning, to arrive at the appointed time. Still, it was always possible that on this occasion he had been delayed either before or after leaving the plane; so many minor events can cause delay.

Half an hour later Piercey went up to the British Airways executive lounge, showed his membership card and explained to the girl that he'd been expecting an important business colleague on the Cologne/Bonn flight. 'Could you possibly check if a Mr Keith Dayton was on the aircraft?' he asked with a deprecating smile.

Dermot Piercey was rarely refused. The girl pointed out that the enquiry might take a few minutes, and suggested a pre-lunch drink while he waited. Piercey helped himself to a whisky, collected a newspaper and found a comfortable chair. He wasn't worried, merely mildly irritated. Dayton's mission, his meeting with Bauer, had been completely routine, and there was no reason to suppose that any disaster had befallen him.

Piercey was deep in an article on the National Front and the spread of neo-Nazism in Europe when the girl came across to him. He looked up hopefully. 'Any luck?'

'I'm afraid not, sir. Mr Dayton was on the passenger list, but he just didn't show at Wahn though he was paged repeatedly as the flight was boarding. He hadn't reconfirmed in Germany, so they had no contact number for him.'

'Ah well. Too bad!' Piercey finished his drink and got to his feet. 'I expect he'll turn up sometime.'

He thanked her for her help and hospitality and went. There was no point in hanging around Heathrow all day; Dayton might arrive on any one of innumerable flights, not even necessarily direct from Wahn. They would have to meet later, probably over the weekend, he thought resignedly. Dayton would phone if he had anything of importance to report.

Piercey had a quick sandwich and a cup of coffee in an airport snack bar, then collected his car and drove back to Central London. It was just after three o'clock when he was ready to report to his master in the tall building south of Westminster Bridge.

'Yes, go right in. The General's been asking for you for the last couple of hours.'

Pamela Sherwood, personal secretary to the Chief of the Secret Intelligence Service, shook her immaculate grey head reprovingly at Piercey. She liked the young man, but she had worked for the General for twenty years, and she mirrored what she believed to be his feelings. She was rarely wrong.

'Where the hell have you been, Dermot?' demanded Major-General Sir Christopher Weatherby, retired, as Piercey came into his office.

Piercey explained. Unlike Miss Sherwood, he had worked directly for the General for less than a year. Weatherby, to the dismay of some of his immediate subordinates, was inclined to by-pass the normal bureaucratic process. He hand-picked a personal staff, which was employed on special tasks and reported directly to him. In other, less exotic parts of the civil service to be chosen for such a staff would have marked one out as a 'high-flyer'; in the SIS, as far as Piercey had been able to tell, it merely meant highly irregular hours and particularly trying chores. Weatherby seemed to expect not only initiative, extreme efficiency and absolute devotion to one's work, but also an almost mystical understanding of events.

'Damn!' Weatherby said, his shaggy eyebrows meeting in a frown. 'This could be serious. You don't know, but we were expecting some very important material out of East Germany. I was hoping Bauer and Dayton would be the channel.'

'What sort of material, sir?' This was the first Piercey had heard of any such expectation – any reason why Dayton's latest trip should be more important than his previous ones.

Weatherby regarded him, his almost colourless eyes without expression. 'I haven't the faintest idea,' he said. 'But you'd better get on the end of a phone right away, and find out what's happened to the courier.'

'Yes sir,' Piercey said.

'And, Dermot,' Weatherby added as Piercey was about to open the office door. 'Be casual about it. Don't show how interested we really are.'

31

'No sir,' Piercey said. As he shut the door gently behind him, he wondered how he was expected to obey these two conflicting orders.

*

The Daytons' original plan had been for Irena, having spent some days during the week of Keith's absence at the cottage, to drive back to London on Friday to meet her husband at their Hampstead house and to keep an appointment for a photographic sitting late in the afternoon; they would spend the night in London, and return to the cottage for the weekend on the Saturday. But after the extraordinary phone call she'd received from Keith so early that Friday, Irena wasn't sure what to do.

She spent the morning at the cottage in a mood of miserable uncertainty and finally, having had an early lunch, decided to go to London rather than cancel her sitting. She drove faster than usual, eager to get there now that she'd made up her mind, but the traffic was heavy in the suburbs and it was mid-afternoon before she drew up in front of their house. Seen through the heavy drizzle, it looked miserable and uninviting.

The telephone was ringing as she fitted her key in the lock. She hurried desperately but the moment she got into the hall the ringing ceased. Certain that it had been her husband Irena swore aloud, unconsciously in Polish.

'And what did all that mean?' asked a laughing voice behind her.

Irena swung round. 'Oh, Caro! I didn't hear you. It was the phone,' she added. 'But I was too slow.'

'I know,' said Caro. 'I heard it too while I was packing, but I couldn't get here in time either. Does it matter?'

'N–no. Probably not,' said Irena. Then she stopped. How to explain? But she smiled warmly at the girl; she was very fond of her step-daughter.

When Patricia Dayton had divorced Keith some ten years ago she had been given custody of Caroline, but neither she nor Peter Mayberry, her new husband, had really wanted to be bothered with the child. Caro, sent to a boarding-school,

32

had spent most of her holidays with her father, and when Keith had subsequently married Irena, Caro had accepted her step-mother without hesitation.

Putting an arm around Irena's thin shoulders, Caro hugged her. 'Are you okay?' she said. 'You look a little peaky to me. Nothing's the matter, is it?'

'No. I'm just annoyed, I suppose. I might have missed a client.' Irena was surprised how easily she lied.

Caroline laughed – an ingenuous, happy laugh. 'Irena, now you're becoming famous, you must have an answering service – or at least one of those machines. Incidentally, when are you going to do me? A one-off, just for Hector. It's to be my engagement present to him.' She glanced at the expensive diamond ring on her left hand and said, a little defensively, 'He says that's what he wants.'

'And why not?' Irena said.

Hector Coyne was a lucky man, she thought. Admittedly he was rich, and a rising star in the political firmament. One of London's most eligible bachelors, he'd had his choice of girls. But anyone who married Caroline would be lucky. At twenty-two – sixteen years younger than Coyne – she had her mother's beauty without Patricia's calculated selfishness, her father's warmth and dependability without his self-doubts. On balance, Irena believed, Hector Coyne was getting more than he was giving.

She said, 'Let's go along to the studio and have a look at my book. If you're not too busy with all the wedding preparations, we'll make a date for next week.'

'That would be splendid. It's the perfect excuse because Ma can't object.' Caro pulled a face. 'You know, Irena, if I'd known what a circus she was going to make of this wedding, I'd have insisted we elope.'

Irena laughed, but she didn't comment and together they went along to the studio. It was because of its obvious potential that she and Keith had bought this Hampstead house. Red-brick and Victorian, it had originally been little more than a cottage – the sort of cottage in which respectable Victorian gentlemen had kept their mistresses, Keith had insisted – but a former owner had added two small wings at the back. One

33

of these had been adapted as an admirable photographic studio and darkroom; the other they had later converted into a flatlet for Caro, where she could come and go as she pleased. It was an arrangement that suited everyone.

Now, while Caro admired some of Irena's prints pinned to a cork board on the wall, Irena found her appointments book. They agreed on a time, and discussed what Caro should wear and what kind of photograph would appeal to Hector Coyne.

'It's got to be fairly conventional,' Caro said. 'Hector really wants something he thinks his friends will admire.'

Irena looked up with surprise at Caro's frank comment on her fiancé and was about to speak when the phone on the desk rang. Snatching up the receiver, she said, 'Hello,' quickly, hopefully. At once she was disappointed. It wasn't Keith.

'Mrs Dayton?' a man's voice enquired.

'Yes. I'm Mrs Dayton.'

'Mrs Dayton, it's your husband I want to speak to. I was scheduled to have a business meeting with him today, but he failed to turn up. I wondered – perhaps you could tell me if he's back from Germany.'

'No – I mean, he – ' Irena stumbled over her words. 'Who is that speaking?' she asked finally.

'Oh, sorry! My name's Dermot Piercey. I suppose Keith's not at home, is he?' There was a pause, so long that Piercey said, 'Mrs Dayton, are you still with me?'

'Yes, Mr Piercey, but someone here was speaking to me.' By now Irena had herself under control. 'My husband's not at home. I suggest you try his office.'

'I've done that, or I wouldn't have bothered you. You are expecting him today?'

Irena could see no reason for not replying honestly. 'Yes, I am,' she said.

'Then perhaps you'd be kind enough to ask him to phone me the moment he gets in. He knows the number. Will you do that, please, Mrs Dayton?'

'Yes. Very well, I will. Goodbye, Mr Piercey.'

Irena didn't bother to wait for his response. She replaced the receiver and leant against the desk. She felt physically ill. Keith should certainly be at his office by now – because of

Caro she'd not had time to check – but apparently he wasn't, and this man Piercey, against whom Keith had warned her, was already making enquiries about him.

'Irena, are you all right?'

'Yes.' Irena nodded; she had completely forgotten the presence of Caro.

'You've gone dreadfully white. Come and sit down.'

'It's nothing. A moment's faintness. It happens occasionally.'

Caroline looked at her step-mother anxiously. 'Shouldn't you see a doctor? Does Dad know?'

'It's nothing, I tell you.' Irena spoke with unusual sharpness. 'I must make a note to tell Keith to phone this Mr Piercey.' She pulled a piece of paper towards her, and realized she didn't know how to spell the name. She said, 'Have you ever heard Keith mention someone called Piercey, Caro?'

'No. I expect he's one of Dad's business chums.' Caroline dismissed the subject. She was still anxious about Irena, but she didn't want to fuss. She looked at her watch. 'Heavens, I must fly! I'm meeting Hector. We're going down to his parents' place for the weekend. Back on Monday.'

She gave Irena a quick kiss and made for the door. Over her shoulder she said, 'Give Dad my love when you see him.'

'I will,' Irena promised.

But when will that be? Irena asked herself as the studio door closed behind Caroline. The first thing to do was try his office. Maybe they'd heard from him and not been prepared to tell a casual caller, if that's what Piercey was. She dialled and asked for John Rossel. She got Beryl Ackley, Rossel's secretary, whom she knew slightly.

Mr Rossel had already left for the weekend, Miss Ackley said, but anyway he couldn't have helped. He'd himself expressed some surprise at Mr Dayton's non-return and the absence of any message. 'But you know what travelling's like these days, Mrs Dayton,' she concluded cheerfully. 'Mr Dayton could easily have got caught up somewhere. I'm sure there's no need to worry.'

Irena thanked her and said goodbye. She collected the bag she'd dumped in the hall when she arrived, and took it upstairs to their bedroom. She tidied herself, returned to the studio and prepared for her sitter. She had decided she must go on as usual, follow her normal routine – and hope and pray. There was no alternative – at least for the moment.

★

For his part, General Weatherby had come to much the same conclusion, though he wasn't long on either hope or prayer. Piercey's enquiries had got them nowhere. Of necessity, the enquiries had been circumspect, but as far as could be ascertained the facts were these.

Keith Dayton had been alive and well the previous day – Thursday. He had telephoned the hotel he always used in Cologne, and told them he would be arriving that night. He expected to be late, possibly very late, but they should keep him a room as he would need a few hours' sleep before leaving for London. The hotel had done as he asked, but he hadn't arrived. The room had remained empty and there had been no further message from him.

'We can assume he met Bauer, or went to meet Bauer,' the General said, 'but after that it's anyone's guess.'

'He's got our phone number if he does turn up.' Piercey tried to be helpful. 'And I left a message with his wife.'

'Yes.' Weatherby was thoughtful. 'You say she sounded a little strange?'

'She seemed nervous or tense, and she was definitely short with me,' Piercey said.

'Probably irrelevant.' Weatherby sighed. 'I'll get in touch with Maurice Fenton in Bonn and tell him to keep his ears open. Otherwise, I don't think there's anything to be done for the present. If we've had no news of Dayton by Monday, we'll reconsider.'

★

But there was one man in London that Friday for whom Keith Dayton's name meant action. This was the Cultural Attaché, who earlier in the day had received an urgent international call

36

from his home department – a call that had nothing to do with culture. An accredited diplomat, he was clever, well-read and interested in the arts, as one would expect from someone in such a post. But like many such attachés around the world, his main duty was collecting information – intelligence, military, economic, social, that could be useful to his country.

This time the request he had received was unusual, and the problem had required much thought, some research and a certain amount of telephoning. The result was that at six o'clock that Friday evening he was sitting in a corner of the Saloon Bar of a pub off the Tottenham Court Road. On the table in front of him stood a vodka and lemon – a drink he disliked – and beside him on the banquette was a black Samsonite briefcase. He sipped his drink and waited patiently.

'Evening, Mr Mirov. Nice to see you.'

'Hello.' The diplomat answered though, in fact, Mirov was not and never had been his real name. He signalled to the newcomer to sit beside the briefcase. 'What will you have, Mr Hardcastle?'

'Double whisky, please.' The voice was educated, though the man was shabbily dressed. 'Better make it two, Mr Mirov.'

When the whiskies came he drank the first at a gulp and made a face as if it had been bitter medicine. The second he sat and stared at, without touching it. Then he said, 'You have a job for me, Mr Mirov?'

The man he knew as Igor Mirov explained. As he mentioned neither name nor address the explanation was brief. But he did mention a price.

'Who, where, when? The price will depend on all these, Mr Mirov.'

They haggled for a few minutes. It was a matter of principle as much as anything; both knew the outcome. As always, the bargain they struck was no different from what had been offered in the beginning. But Hardcastle was able to finish his second whisky and decently accept a third.

'Cheers!' he said, lifting his glass.

'Good luck! Though you'll scarcely need it,' the diplomat said. 'It's a simple job. But important. There could even be a bonus in it.'

'Really? Splendid! I'll hold you to that.' The voice was steady in spite of the whiskies, and there was a hint of amusement behind it.

'Nevertheless,' the other continued, 'if anything goes wrong you would, of course, be held responsible. So – don't get any clever ideas.'

The threat was naked. There was silence between the two men. Then the Cultural Attaché rose, leaving his briefcase behind him, nodded his goodbye and went out of the pub without a backward glance. He didn't expect to see Geoffrey Hardcastle again, ever.

FOUR

For Irena Dayton, full of anxieties, the weekend progressed in fits and starts. On Saturday morning she hurried out to buy groceries and hurried home again, hopeful that Keith might have arrived, fearful that she might have missed a phone call. She had a sandwich for lunch and left it half eaten when the telephone did ring. But it was only John Rossel asking if Keith had returned.

She did her best to sound casual, as though Keith were in the habit of staying on in Europe after a business trip without bothering to notify either his boss or his wife, but she knew that Rossel wasn't deceived. As soon as she put down the receiver she wondered if she should have told him more. But Keith had been positive: trust no one.

In the afternoon she tried hard to do something constructive, but she couldn't concentrate. She was reduced to tidying out one of the cupboards in the studio when the phone rang again. This time it was Dermot Piercey asking if Keith was at home.

Irena avoided positive rudeness, but she was as short as she could be, suggesting that Piercey should wait till Monday and contact her husband at his office. But the call upset her. She found her hand was shaking as she put down the receiver. She made up her mind that if there was no further word from Keith by Monday, she would indeed go and see John Rossel and appeal to him for help; she could always twist the truth a little and not mention the list of names that Keith had dictated.

But Monday was a long way off, and in the meantime she yearned for someone in whom she could safely confide. By nature and circumstance she was a solitary person with no close friends, and most of the people she knew she had met through Keith. Except, of course, old Cas.

Her friendship with Casimir Sabik dated back to the time

before she left Poland. One day he had been a professor at the University of Warsaw; the following day he had disappeared. This was not altogether unusual, and it was wiser not to ask questions. But on this occasion the unasked questions had been answered: the next time Irena saw Cas he was pushing a laden trolley through a supermarket in Hampstead village.

Astounded, she had called after him. At first he had pretended not to hear his name and made off hastily towards the exit, but when she persisted he stopped. She hadn't seen him for six or more years, but he'd not changed. Greyer, perhaps, and more stooped, but still bright-eyed and inquisitive, reminding her, as always, of a particularly intelligent squirrel.

He had made some specious excuse about failing to recognize her, and in the end they had had coffee together. After that it had been easy to pick up old threads, renew the old friendship. She visited him in his small basement apartment not far away, and she had introduced him to Keith. But there had been an unexpressed antipathy between the two men – for some reason they hadn't got on well together – and Cas preferred not to visit what he called her 'big house'.

Cas, Irena thought, would at least listen to her, and understand the fears she couldn't put into words. On the other hand, though he would give her sympathy, any practical help would almost certainly be beyond him. What was more, there was Keith's warning: trust no one. All she could do for the moment was wait.

Somehow, Irena endured Sunday. She thought of a long walk on the Heath to tire herself and make sleep more likely, but she dared not leave the house. She drank innumerable cups of tea, ate odd snacks and wandered aimlessly from room to room. At one point, staring from an upper window, she noticed, without really realizing it, a shabbily-dressed man that she'd seen in the same place the day before. He was strolling apparently idly along the street, though if one looked closely one could see that he was taking in every detail of his surroundings.

When evening came at last Irena forced herself to cook a modest supper. Sitting at the kitchen table, surrounded by dirty crockery, she eventually finished the bottle of wine she had opened. She felt exhausted, and accepted that she was a little drunk.

She left the dishes and went upstairs, got ready for bed, took two tranquillizers and lay down. She was asleep almost at once, snoring gently, the duvet pulled over her head. She slept heavily for several hours. Then, suddenly, she was awake.

She lay, eyes shut, body tense. Carefully she pulled down the duvet and strained to listen. She had been dreaming, and she wasn't sure if the bang, the crash, whatever it was that had woken her, was part of her dream or part of reality. The house creaked, as old houses will, and she clenched her fists. She could feel her heart beating against her rib-cage.

She told herself not to be stupid; there was no one there. Burglaries were common in Hampstead, but most thieves weren't fools. They usually took care to make sure that houses were empty of occupants before they entered them.

She had almost convinced herself and was about to snuggle under the duvet again when there was a loud squeak from downstairs. Immediately she sat up in bed. She knew that sound. There *was* someone. The door at the back giving on to the passage from which the two wings branched had been opened; she'd been meaning to oil it for days. It couldn't be Caro, who wouldn't be back till Monday. Could it conceivably be Keith?

Cautiously Irena slid out of bed. She went to the window and drew the curtain aside, so that she could look down on the small paved garden at the rear of the house. The studio had a partially glazed roof and, as she watched, she saw a light, a narrow beam from a pencil torch, flickering about the room. Not Keith. Not Caro. Whoever it was seemed to be looking for something. Her cameras were valuable, but . . .

More fascinated than scared, Irena continued to watch. Then the light disappeared. A minute later she heard the passage door squeak again, and knew that whoever it was had returned to the main part of the house. She ran for the bed and jumped in. For the first time she thought of the phone, but she was fearful that if she lifted the instrument beside her a ping on the extension in the hall might alert the intruder. Instead she covered herself with the duvet. If he came upstairs

41

she must pretend to be asleep. She forced herself to breathe slowly and regularly.

Irena counted to one hundred, two, three, four, five. She thought she heard another soft noise, but couldn't be certain. At five hundred she stopped counting and listened to the silence. When she felt sure the intruder had gone, she sat up again, switched on her bedside light and debated whether to call the police. Something made her decide to investigate first.

She slipped into a Viyella robe – the twin of the one she kept at the cottage – and ran downstairs, switching on lights as she went from room to room. She hurried because she was still a little afraid, but no one was there and as far as she could see nothing was missing; a portable television, a video recorder, a silver bowl that had been the Mayberry's wedding present to herself and Keith, some ivory carvings – they were all in their places.

Irena hadn't bothered to put on slippers and, as she passed near a window in the sitting-room, she felt a dampness beneath her feet. Looking down, she saw a stain on the carpet. Immediately, her gaze travelling up, she found herself staring at a vase of mixed flowers that was hopelessly disarranged.

What had happened was self-evident. The intruder had entered – and presumably left – by this window, which was at the side of the house and sheltered from view. He had blundered into the table, upsetting the flowers. The carpet had broken the fall and the glass vase hadn't shattered, but there had been enough noise to wake her. She saw now that the window was unlatched, and she shivered as she imagined him crouching there in the dark waiting to see if his clumsiness had raised an alarm.

But nothing had been stolen from the downstairs rooms and the intruder hadn't attempted to go upstairs. In fact, he seemed to have made straight for the studio. Irena followed. She stood in the doorway and looked about her. Everything was normal, untouched, as she had left it the previous day, her cameras and equipment where they always were.

If the vase hadn't been knocked over, Irena thought, she might never have known that anyone had been in the house. She would have blamed the unlatched window on her own carelessness. As it was, there was no doubt. Someone had broken in, but had stolen nothing. It made no sense, and because it made no sense, she associated it with Keith and his recent strange behaviour.

Miserable, Irena made herself a hot drink and took it back to bed. She didn't think she would sleep again, but the wine and the pills were still having their effect, and she didn't wake until nearly ten. It was a lovely day, the sun streaming through the window where she had failed to draw the curtain properly after watching the light darting round the studio, but she got out of bed reluctantly.

*

While Irena Dayton was dressing that Monday morning, a flight from Paris landed at Heathrow. On board was the man who had wounded Keith Dayton, interrogated him and subsequently arranged for his death. His passport had changed yet again – it was now Swiss and proclaimed him to be an art dealer from Zurich – but his name was once more Manfred Brenner.

He had no trouble with immigration or customs, and took a taxi to central London. He checked in at a small hotel in the West End and, even before he unpacked his briefcase and his bag, he telephoned his embassy. He asked to speak to the Cultural Attaché.

'Hello,' a voice said. 'Herr Brenner?'

'Yes. Brenner here.'

'Good. Your visit's well-timed. I've just heard that the pictures have been delivered, so all that remains is the payment. You'll deal with it personally? Good. The sooner, the better.'

'Yes. I have the necessary – er – cheque.'

'And all the information you need – regarding the payee?'

'Yes. I've been briefed.'

'Right. Then I've nothing more to say, except to wish you luck.'

'You want to know when the transaction's been completed?'

'Of course. Leave a message with my secretary.'

'Very well.'

Brenner grimaced as he put down the receiver. He'd never met the man to whom he'd been speaking, but he knew his kind – the kind that never did the dirty work. Instead, they sent for people like himself, as if he weren't human too. Brenner grimaced again and yawned; he seemed to have done nothing but travel for the last few days, and his arm ached.

He unpacked, washed his face in cold water, made sure he had everything he would require and went down to the bar. A quick drink and he caught a taxi to Harrods. He went in one door and out another. He'd once spent a year in London and knew where he was going. From Harrods it was only a ten minute walk.

The flat Brenner was seeking was unpretentious, the first floor of what years ago had been a private house. The main door was locked, but it took him only a moment to use a plastic card to force it. He ran up the stairs and rang the bell of No. 3.

'Who is it?' a man's voice demanded.

'Special delivery, sir. From Mr Mirov.'

'What?'

The door opened, then made to close, but Brenner had thrust his foot in the opening. He heaved with his shoulder and burst into a narrow hall. 'You're Geoffrey Hardcastle?'

'Yes. I'm Hardcastle. And who the hell are you?'

'Messenger from Mr Mirov, sir.'

As he spoke, Brenner acted. From one pocket he pulled a thick pad which he clamped over his own mouth and nostrils, from another what might have been a child's toy pistol. Without hesitation he directed it straight at Hardcastle's face and pulled the trigger. Hardcastle gasped, choked and collapsed on the floor. He was dead almost instantaneously.

'You all right, Mr Hardcastle?' a woman's voice called from further inside the flat. 'Something the matter?'

Brenner turned to flee. He'd been told that the man lived alone, but he'd been tired and not thinking straight; he'd not foreseen the possible presence of someone else. Startled, he stumbled and fell against the edge of the door, hitting his wounded arm. The gas pistol spun out of his hand and skittered across the floor. Footsteps sounded in the corridor.

'Mr Hardcastle?'

Brenner ran, down the stairs and out of the building, forcing himself to a walk as soon as he reached the street. No one followed him. He was safe. But he was furious with himself. He'd bungled the job, like any amateur. He'd eliminated Geoffrey Hardcastle, but he'd lost the gas pistol, and there was now no chance that Hardcastle's death would be taken for a heart attack.

★

'Beryl? John Rossel here.'

'Hello, Mr Rossel. Where's here?'

'Heathrow, dearie! Why don't you take a look at my engagement book occasionally! You should know I'm on my way to Brussels. Back some time Thursday. For God's sake, take your finger out!' Rossel had adopted the bullying tone that came naturally to him when he was harassed. 'What I want to know is, any news of Dayton?'

'You're not the only one, Mr Rossel.' Beryl Ackley wasn't prepared to respond equably to Rossel's mood, and she spoke curtly. 'Mrs Dayton was the first. Wanting you, she was. Very worried about her husband.'

'So he's not home yet.' Rossel spoke half to his secretary, half to himself. 'Where the hell can he be? If he'd had an accident we'd have heard by now.'

'That's what I told Mrs Dayton, but she didn't seem to think it much consolation. She says she can't go on sitting and waiting and doing nothing. She said you were her husband's boss, you'd sent him to Germany, and it was – '

Rossel cut her short. 'Okay, Beryl. I've got the message.'

He guessed that Beryl had put her own interpretation – exaggeration, perhaps – on what Irena Dayton had actually said, but even so the affair was worrying. He couldn't have the Polish bint going off at half-cock; not now. There couldn't be a worse time to have his affairs put under a magnifying glass.

He changed his tone. 'Listen, Beryl,' he said earnestly. 'Call Mrs Dayton back. Tell her I've gone to Europe for three or four days and while I'm there I'm going to make enquiries about Keith. Someone must know what's happened to him, and I'll find out. Tell her to try not to worry and I'll be in touch.'

'Right. I understand, Mr Rossel.'

'Good girl. I'll bring you a nice gift from Brussels.'

'Thanks, Mr Rossel. I'll do my best to keep Mrs Dayton happy, but what shall I say to this man Piercey? He phoned again this morning. He's very persistent.'

'We've still no idea who he is, have we? He didn't say – '

'No. I can't find any reference to him in the files. And he wasn't giving anything away. I tried some tactful questions, but he just turned them aside.' Beryl Ackley paused. 'You know he's been bothering Mrs Dayton too. She's no idea who he is either. She says her husband's never mentioned him.'

'Damn!' Rossel swore. 'Look, if he phones again, tell him that we've discovered Dayton's been delayed on business, and that I've gone to the Continent and won't be back till the end of the week. That ought to hold him.'

His flight was boarding now, and John Rossel hung up the phone hurriedly. He still had another call to make. He dialled, waited, biting his lip with impatience. To his annoyance it was Patricia Mayberry who answered.

'Patricia, John Rossel here. Listen, I'm in a desperate hurry. I'm about to miss my plane. I was hoping Peter – '

'He's not at home. You'll have to make do with me, John. I'll pass on any message.'

Rossel drew a deep breath and spoke fast. The situation was slightly embarrassing, but he knew that Patricia, for all her faults, could be relied upon, especially when her own interests might be at stake. He blessed her for listening without interruption, said a quick goodbye, and ran for his aircraft as the voice over the loudspeaker made a final call for him by name.

*

Rossel was not to know, but Lady Mayberry had lied to him. Sir Peter was indeed at home, but he was in his bath, and he had a rooted objection to being disturbed there. Nor was

46

he best pleased when he emerged from the bathroom to be confronted by Patricia, beautiful and elegant as always. She relayed John Rossel's message with total accuracy and waited, her expression showing nothing of what she felt.

'Damn your ex-husband!' Mayberry said, more viciously than he had intended. Though he'd slept till mid-morning he was still tired; the House had sat late the previous night, thanks to a Labour attempt at a filibuster, and the Whips had been on the watch, so that he'd not got to bed till after three. 'What do you think he's been up to?'

'I haven't the faintest idea,' Patricia shrugged, 'but somehow Rossel implied it could be – unfortunate, for the firm and for us.'

'If Dayton's had an accident or been taken ill, his wife would have heard by now. He must have carried some identification.' Mayberry pursued his own train of thought. 'He can't have just vanished – not unless he wanted to. You don't think – '

'What? That he's gone off with some woman?' Patricia sounded amused. 'Very unlikely. He's besotted with Irena.'

'No. That he's taken himself off to Russia. He was always bloody left wing and he often goes to Commie countries on business. He must have made a lot of contacts there who'd be interested in the technological information he's acquired by now.'

'You're not serious, Peter?' Patricia was startled by the suggestion. She stared at him, violet eyes wide. 'Is that what Rossel was suggesting? That Keith's defected? Surely not. Not Keith. That would be ghastly.'

'It would indeed.' Mayberry was busy dressing, discarding one tie for another. 'Dayton's not only your ex, my dear. He's also Caroline's father – Hector's father-in-law to be – and he works for Rossel's, of which Hector Coyne and I are both directors. So we'd all be heavily involved.'

'It would ruin the wedding.'

'It would ruin a great deal more than that!'

For a moment they were both silent, considering the implications, though their thoughts were quite different. Patricia's were wholly selfish; insofar as she considered anyone else – Caroline, Peter, John Rossel, Keith – it was merely in relation

47

to herself. Peter Mayberry's thoughts were of wider scope; he would have called them statesmanlike. But they were much less assured than his wife's, much more fearful, for he knew a great deal of which Patricia was unaware.

At length he said, 'I may have jumped to the wrong conclusion. We'll have to wait and see. Meanwhile we'd better do what Rossel asks – stop Irena making a fuss, if possible, and find out who this chap Piercey is. Can I leave Irena to you, darling?'

'Yes. I'll go round there before lunch. I can always make Caroline the excuse.'

'Good girl!' Mayberry was hearty. His red face was paler than usual as he crossed the room to put his arms round his wife – a gesture she accepted rather than reciprocated. 'I'll try and cope with this chap Piercey. Let's hope he's not a security dog – one of Sir Rupert's MI5 boys, for example. The last thing I want is those people poking into my affairs.'

Patricia nodded her understanding, but, as Mayberry knew, she understood only half of what was going on.

FIVE

Patricia Mayberry pressed her finger on the doorbell, and kept it there. She had driven from central London – the Mayberrys' town house was off Knightsbridge – to Hampstead, at some inconvenience to herself. The weather was humid, the traffic heavy and the journey had taken longer than she had expected. The Daytons' car was in the garage, she was sure that Irena was at home and she had no intention of returning without seeing her.

To demonstrate her determination Patricia began to press the bell in irritating bursts. Long, short, short. Long, short, short. The sound stretched the nerves and it was only a few minutes before Irena flung the door open. Patricia gave her a dazzling smile.

'Irena, my dear! You *are* here. I'm so glad. I was beginning to despair.'

Irena made no reply. Her face was puffy, her eyes bloodshot from crying and black-circled from lack of sleep. She looked desolate. A kind friend would simply have hugged her, but Patricia wasn't particularly kind. She walked past Irena into the hall as if she owned the house, while Irena watched silently.

Over her shoulder Patricia said, 'I really came to see Caroline. There are so many preparations to be made for the wedding, decisions to be taken, things to be done – and she leaves it all to me. What it is to be a mother!' When Irena still didn't speak, she continued. 'She's not in her flat; I've tried there. Do you know where I can find her?'

'She's spending the weekend with Hector Coyne's parents,' Irena said. 'She told me she'd be back today.'

'Well, she's not back yet.' Patricia allowed herself to sound aggrieved. 'But perhaps you could help, Irena. You're an artist. You must have an eye.'

49

As if unaware of what she was doing Patricia had moved into the sitting-room. Irena followed her, wondering why Patricia had come and what she really wanted, wishing she would go, scarcely listening to her.

'An eye?' she queried absently.

'Yes, an eye,' Patricia said. 'It's so important that everything *looks* right at a wedding. For instance, you simply can't have one dumpy bridesmaid when the others are tall and slim, no matter if the dumpy one is an old schoolfriend or something.'

Patricia continued to chatter, seemingly oblivious of Irena's lack of interest. Then abruptly she stopped. She peered into Irena's face. 'My dear,' she said with apparent concern. 'Something's wrong. You look ghastly. What is it?'

Of all the people in whom Irena might have confided Patricia Mayberry was the last. 'Nothing,' she said firmly.

'Don't be silly. Of course there is.' Patricia was equally firm. 'You've been crying. I should have noticed before. That's why you were so long answering the door. It's Keith, isn't it? You're worried about him?'

Irena's every instinct urged her to deny that she was in the least worried about her husband, but over the years she had acquired a certain understanding of the way Patricia's mind worked. She was sure that the sudden change of attitude and the quick reference to Keith were not spontaneous. Patricia knew about Keith; that was why she was here.

Picking her words carefully Irena said, 'Patricia, why should you think I'm worried about my husband?'

'Oh, John Rossel had to speak to Peter this morning on some business matter; he happened to mention that Keith hadn't returned from Germany yet, and there was no news of him.'

'I see.'

'Have you heard from him, Irena?'

The doorbell saved Irena from the need to lie. She frowned. She wasn't expecting anyone this morning. 'Excuse me,' she said absently, and went into the hall. Patricia followed.

'Good morning,' Dermot Piercey said as Irena opened the front door. 'Mrs Dayton? Mrs Keith Dayton?'

'Yes. I'm Mrs Dayton.'

'Mrs Dayton, my name is Dermot Piercey.' He noticed the

50

widening of her red-rimmed eyes, her lips parted as if she were about to take a deep breath, her instinctive withdrawal, her careless dress. 'We've spoken on the phone a couple of times, and I expect your husband's mentioned me.'

'No,' Irena said. 'Keith's never mentioned you, Mr Piercey.'

Lie number one, Piercey thought, interested. 'Really?' he said with obvious disbelief; Weatherby had told him to lean on the wife a little. 'You surprise me, Mrs Dayton. However . . .'

He turned and introduced the man he had brought with him. 'My colleague, Ian Farling.' Farling had red hair, blue eyes and a round, innocent face that had deceived many people in the course of his career. 'Good morning, Mrs Dayton,' he said.

Irena paid him no attention. 'My husband's not here,' she addressed Piercey abruptly.

A new voice spoke for the first time. 'He's in Europe and he won't be back till the end of the week.' Piercey noted the startled expression that flicked across Irena's face as she heard this comment from the elegant woman who had come to stand at her shoulder. He smiled, said nothing, waited.

'The – the end of the week?' Irena failed to hide her surprise and hope. 'But before you – '

'That's what John Rossel says, and he should know.' Patricia lied again without effort. 'I'm Lady Mayberry,' she added for Piercey's benefit. 'My husband's a director of Rossel's. You have business dealings with the firm, I gather, Mr Piercey. And Mr Farling too?'

'Why no, Lady Mayberry.' Piercey was amused. 'Whatever gave you that idea? Any business we have is with Mr Dayton personally.'

'I've told you he's not here,' Irena intervened.

'I know, Mrs Dayton. But right now we've not come to see him. We've come to see you,' Piercey said patiently. 'May I suggest you invite us in. It's a little difficult to hold this sort of conversation on the doorstep.'

Irena ignored the request. 'Me? Why me? Why should you want to see me?'

'And who *are* you exactly?' Patricia demanded. 'Whoever

51

you are, you're making a nuisance of yourself. I think we should ask you to leave these premises.'

'That would be extremely unwise!'

Piercey's words, like a slap in the face, carried an authority that stopped even Patricia Mayberry. She recovered sufficiently to demand to see some identification, some credentials, but seemed satisfied by the coloured laminated cards, complete with photographs and fingerprints, that the two men produced. Minutes later they were all in the sitting-room; Piercey was seated opposite the two women and Farling had faded into the background. Piercey had suggested tentatively that Lady Mayberry might like to leave them to speak to Mrs Dayton alone, but she refused. Unexpectedly, since Piercey had sensed a certain antipathy between the two women, Mrs Dayton supported her, and he didn't persist. Now they faced him, both aggressive, and Irena obviously fearful.

'Mrs Dayton, as you saw from our ID cards, we represent a department of the Foreign Office, and we're a little worried about your husband,' he began. 'But perhaps I should first say that what I'm going to tell you is in the strictest confidence. You understand?'

'Yes.'

He glanced at Lady Mayberry, and she nodded. He had no hope that either of them would respect the confidence, but he'd made his point. More importantly, he'd distracted them from making enquiries about exactly which department of the FCO he and Farling represented.

He continued, in accordance with his plan. 'Mrs Dayton, I'm sure you're aware that during your husband's frequent trips to Europe for his firm he sometimes performs small commissions for the Foreign Office.'

Irena ran her tongue over dry lips. 'No,' she said. 'No, I didn't know that.'

'Oh, come – ' Piercey began, when Patricia interrupted. 'You mean he's been spying?' she said. 'For us?'

'Spying, Lady Mayberry?' Piercey laughed. 'Good heavens, no. Nothing as exciting as that. It's merely that from time to time he would deliver a letter or a packet, or collect one and bring it home. It's as simple as that.'

'A sort of messenger boy?' Patricia sounded disappointed.

Piercey shrugged. 'Yes, if you want to put it like that. But it's a valuable service, if routine. Many businessmen do it for us.'

'And it's dangerous,' Irena said suddenly.

She made it a statement, an accusation, rather than a question. Piercey regarded her curiously. He could have sworn that Dayton's activities as a courier had come as a surprise to her, but he was equally sure that she'd lied when she'd denied that Dayton had never mentioned his name. And she was not only fearful, she was wary and antagonistic. It was an entirely subjective feeling, but Piercey sensed that for some reason her antagonism was directed against him personally.

'Oh, Mrs Dayton,' Piercey responded deprecatingly, 'I wouldn't say that. However, we know Mr Dayton intended to return to England last Saturday, and we can't help wondering why he didn't send a message if he was delayed. But Lady Mayberry's story is that your husband will be home at the end of the week. If so . . .'

'It's not *my* story,' Patricia interrupted sharply. 'It's what John Rossel told me. I suppose I might have been mistaken. It was on the phone and he was in a hurry.'

'And you've had no communication with your husband yourself, Mrs Dayton?' Piercey turned to Irena who was staring at Patricia as if puzzled by what she'd just heard her say. He didn't wait for an answer. 'Strange he should have contacted Mr Rossel and no one else, isn't it?' he remarked casually. 'I think Lady Mayberry must have been mistaken.'

'Possibly.' Patricia looked at her watch. She had learnt a good deal from her visit, more than she'd expected, and she didn't want to commit herself to definite statements she might later want to refute. She judged it was time for her to go; she could depend on the Foreign Office men to do her job for her and stop Irena making any kind of fuss. She stood up suddenly, taking everyone by surprise. 'I must fly. I've got a luncheon date. Goodbye, my dear.' She bent and kissed Irena on the cheek. 'Try not to worry. Goodbye, Mr Piercey, Mr Farling.' She smiled graciously at each of the men in turn.

Piercey let Lady Mayberry go without protest. Though he'd

found her reactions interesting, it was Irena Dayton who was important at the moment. He began to interrogate her gently. How long had she lived in England? Did she have any family still in Poland? Had her husband seemed under any strain before he left on his last trip? Occasionally Farling threw in a question. Irena answered carefully, never volunteering more than she was asked. As far as Piercey could judge from what he already knew, she answered truthfully, but her caution intrigued him.

He changed his tactics, though he still spoke gently. 'Mrs Dayton, you're hiding something from us, aren't you?'

'I've got nothing to hide, Mr Piercey.'

'You were surprised when Lady Mayberry said your husband was expected home at the end of the week. Had she told you something else before we arrived?'

Irena hesitated. Then, 'She said – I understood her to say – that John Rossel had had no news of Keith.'

'Right. Thank you, Mrs Dayton.' Piercey got to his feet and he saw the relief flood over Irena Dayton's face. Then he added, 'There's just one thing. Would you mind if we had a look around your house? Perhaps Mr Dayton has a study . . .'

Again Irena hesitated, as if struggling to understand what Piercey had said. Then, when its meaning dawned on her, she shook her head violently. 'No!' she said. 'No, Mr Piercey. I've answered all your questions, but no, I'm not having you snooping round my house.'

'We've no intention of snooping, Mrs Dayton.' Piercey let his voice grow cold and formal. 'We hope to find something among Mr Dayton's papers that would help us to locate him. Surely – '

'No!'

'Mrs Dayton, you must appreciate there's a chance your husband could be in trouble – and we are on the same side, you know!'

'Are we?' Irena seemed to ask the question almost involuntarily.

Piercey glanced at Farling and raised his eyebrows. 'I hope so,' he said. 'I sincerely hope so.'

Irena met his gaze, and he could see once again the fear,

the near-despair, beneath her antagonism. Nevertheless, her attitude had made him determined to get his way. As he was wondering how best to proceed there came the sound of the front door opening, quick footsteps in the hall and a clear voice calling Irena's name. Caroline Dayton came into the sitting-room.

'Hello,' she said, smiling from Irena to the two men. Then her expression changed. 'What is it? What's wrong?' She went to Irena and put her arms around her step-mother. 'Darling, what is it? What's happened? Is it Dad? Has he had an accident?'

'He – he's not come home. No one seems to know where he is.' Irena motioned towards Pierccy and Farling. 'They're – they say they're from the Foreign Office. They say Keith was – was doing something for them.'

'What sort of something?' Caroline asked. 'I'm Caro Dayton. Keith's my father.'

Farling smiled in acknowledgement and gave a small bow. Piercey grinned at her. 'Dermot Piercey,' he said, 'and my colleague, Ian Farling. We're a little worried about Mr Dayton's non-appearance on Saturday.'

'I see,' Caroline said slowly. 'So what can we do to help?'

Irena said, 'They want to look through Keith's papers and things, but I won't allow it.'

'Why ever not? If they think it might help, then of course they must,' Caroline said at once. Suddenly she smiled. 'You can trust Mr Piercey, Irena. I know all about him and I'm sure he's dependable.'

Piercey was startled. 'What do you know about me?'

Caroline laughed. 'Well, for one thing you stopped a runaway horse when you were twelve and nearly got killed in the process.'

'How on earth – ' began Irena.

'He's Dermot Piercey. I was at school with his sister, Deirdre. She used to tell me lots about him. She thought he was wonderful. She was always showing us snaps of him.'

Piercey avoided Farling's eye as Irena said, 'So – what's this got to do with Keith?'

'Nothing directly,' Caroline said, 'but it means I can vouch for Mr Piercey – at least to some extent. You must let him

55

look through Dad's papers if that's what he wants. After all Dad's got nothing to hide, Irena, and if it might help to find him . . .'

Irena still hesitated. Keith had warned her against Piercey; he'd told her to trust no one – specifically not Piercey. But that had been about the list of names he'd dictated, and the list was quite safe. She'd copied it on to the smallest possible piece of paper and sewn it into the lining of her bra. Then she'd destroyed her hurried, scribbled original.

Perhaps, she thought, since everyone was so insistent, it would be best to let the Foreign Office men look through the papers in Keith's corner of the studio. It might quiet their suspicions, stop them trying to discover whatever Keith didn't want them to know. And there was nothing really private in Keith's desk or filing cabinet. If Piercey liked to study the details of their mortgage and their household accounts, good luck to him.

'All right,' she said abruptly. 'Come along.'

Irena led the way, followed by the two men and, slightly to her annoyance, by Caroline who was asking Piercey about his sister. When they reached the studio she went straight to the far end, only to find herself alone with Farling. Caroline and Piercey had stopped for Piercey to admire a row of portrait photographs hanging on the wall.

'That's Dad,' Caro said, pointing. 'You have met him, haven't you?'

'Yes, several times,' Piercey said gravely, 'and that's a splendid photograph.' He studied Dayton's intelligent, sensitive face, and thought that Irena Dayton was a fine artist who understood her husband and had brought his strengths and weaknesses into brilliant focus. 'A splendid photograph,' he repeated.

'Mr Piercey!' Irena was impatient.

'I'm sorry,' Piercey said. 'I was just admiring your work.'

Ignoring the compliment, Irena pointed to the desk and filing cabinet. 'This is where my husband deals with family matters,' she said. 'I doubt if anything here will interest either of you, but look at what you like. Anything else would be at his office.'

56

'Thank you,' Piercey said meekly.

Piercey and Farling were conscious of the two women watching them, but they exchanged no words as they commenced a systematic search. To start with, it looked as if Irena was right. Fortunately Keith Dayton was an orderly and businesslike man, and it took little time to search the desk. It yielded nothing worthwhile, though they learnt a fair amount about the Daytons' personal and financial affairs.

They began to go through the filing cabinet with equal care. Piercey was the first to find something of interest. In a file neatly labelled 'Income Tax' he came across a photocopy of what looked like a list of military electronic stores; Piercey, though no expert, could identify a battlefield radio transceiver and some ECM equipment. Each item had figures beside it. He studied it, frowning as questions chased through his mind. Not only had the photocopy been filed incorrectly – and by an apparently meticulous man – but it bore no relation to anything else they had seen. Certainly it didn't come under the heading of family matters. He showed the paper to Farling, who gave an almost imperceptible nod of satisfaction, then handed it to Irena. 'Have you seen anything like this before, Mrs Dayton?'

'No,' Irena said doubtfully. 'What is it?'

Caroline took the photocopy from her. 'It looks like something Dad brought home from the office.'

'Possibly,' Piercey agreed. 'I'm sure you won't mind if we take it with us when we go.'

'But why?' Irena demanded. 'What's it got to do with you, or the Foreign Office – or anyone else?'

'Irena!' Caroline protested.

While the two women muttered together in some sort of argument, Piercey and Farling finished with the files in the top drawers of the cabinet. They found nothing further of interest, but in the bottom drawer they discovered a black Samsonite briefcase. It was locked, and Piercey concealed Farling with his body as the latter deftly opened it.

With a silent whistle Farling presented it and its contents to Piercey. As in a doctor's bag, the components were each buried in their soft resilient plastic resting places. Piercey gave no evidence of surprise. He merely felt a great regret.

57

'Is this yours, Mrs Dayton?' he asked.

'No,' Irena said blankly. 'It's obviously photographic equipment, but I've never seen it before.'

'Miss Dayton?'

'No. It's not mine and I've never seen it. What is it?'

Piercey said without emphasis. 'Mrs Dayton's quite right. It *is* photographic equipment – the kind that's used to reduce documents to a very small size – to make "mircrodots", if you like.'

For a long minute there was silence. Piercey and Farling watched the expressions that skittered across the women's faces. Their reactions weren't identical, but Piercey was certain that initially his blunt statement had shocked both of them. Then Irena, Dayton's wife, grew still, totally withdrawn. Caroline, Dayton's daughter, became furiously angry.

'Damn you, Dermot Piercey,' she exclaimed. 'How dare you suggest my father's some kind of spy – communist spy, I suppose. He's the last man to do anything like that. Why, you said he'd been working for you. He's a fine, honest man!'

'I'm not suggesting anything,' Piercey said mildly, thinking how attractive Caro Dayton was when flushed with anger. 'But we've found things in this house that need explanation. Mrs Dayton, I shall have to take this briefcase as well as the paper I showed you. I'll give you a receipt, of course.'

'You've no right – ' Irena began predictably.

'This is England!' Caroline said. 'It's not a police state – or it's not meant to be.'

'I'm sorry,' said Piercey. 'I really am. But in the circumstances we've every right. Now, Mr Farling will stay here with you while I telephone – '

'For help – against two women?' Caro was sarcastic.

Piercey looked at her. 'Off the record I'd like to say, "Don't be so bloody stupid", he said, momentarily matching her anger. Then, seeing the mild surprise on Ian Farling's face, he controlled himself. 'I realize it's a difficult situation, but you can make it easier for yourselves.' He turned to Irena. 'For instance, Mrs Dayton, I'm afraid it will be necessary for the police – plain clothes officers – to search this house. Will you give your permission, or must we get a search warrant? I assure you we shall have no trouble in getting one if we have to.'

Irena had sat down, her hands folded across her breasts as if to ward off a physical attack. She was pale and somehow seemed to have diminished in size. She was lost in thought, and Piercey had to repeat his question.

'Do what you like,' she said wearily. 'You will anyway. Why bother to ask?'

'A warrant,' Farling said to Piercey.

Piercey nodded. Ian Farling was his junior and not in the habit of proffering advice. He guessed that Farling thought he'd shown too much sympathy for the two women – especially Caroline. He smiled wryly. Farling maligned him; his judgement was unlikely to be warped merely because Caro was attractive and had known his sister.

'I'll be as quick as I can,' he said. And he left the studio without a glance at either Irena Dayton or Caroline.

SIX

General Weatherby was on the phone, talking to the British Embassy in Bonn. Across the desk from him, waiting for the call to end, sat Dermot Piercey and Ian Farling, and on the desk in front of the General were the black Samsonite briefcase and the photocopied document that they had removed from Dayton's house. Piercey was thinking of Caro Dayton; Farling was considering his chances of promotion in the near future. Weatherby was wholly concentrated on his conversation.

'Yes. A short, square type. No possibility. I understand.' He listened for a moment to Maurice Fenton, the man at the other end of the secure line. 'Right,' he said finally. 'Well done, Maurice! You'll keep on trying, of course. And I'll be sending someone over to brief you fully and back you up.' He put down the receiver and stared through Piercey and Farling, his thoughts elsewhere. Then he said, 'They've found Ernst Bauer.'

'Dead?'

'Yes, Dermot. Shot, sometime early Friday, in a lay-by on the Autobahn a few miles out of Cologne. He was armed, and there had probably been a fight of some kind. In any case, there was a lot of blood on the ground. And the German police, being their usual thorough selves, want to know the blood group of our missing businessman.'

'Why, sir?' Farling asked. 'Aren't they certain of the identification?'

'Of Bauer? Yes. Fenton says they seem sure, even though he was robbed and his papers taken. But the police aren't entirely happy about passing the affair off as simple assault, and naturally our enquiries about Dayton – pointing to the same general area at about the same time – have roused their curiosity.'

'What of Dayton himself, sir?' Piercey said. 'I take it there's no sign.'

'Not unless some of the blood in the lay-by was his.' Weatherby was grim. 'First thing tomorrow, Dermot, I'd like you to go to Germany and put Fenton fully in the picture. We may need his help. At present he's working half-blind. Then find out what you can about Bauer and try to trace Dayton's movements. Ian here will get his nominal business itinerary from Rossel's for you.'

'Right, sir.' Piercey felt vaguely regretful; at this point he would have much preferred to stay in London.

The General turned his attention to Farling. 'Ian, as soon as we've finished here, I want you to cut along to Rossel's and get that itinerary. You'll find Special Branch already there; I suggested they should do the office as well as the house. You can let me know if they've had any luck. Tomorrow you can look into Dayton's vettings. See if you can find any holes in them – in the light of these.' He indicated the briefcase and the paper before him.

'Yes, sir.' Unlike Piercey, Farling was pleased with his assignment but he said tentatively, 'Sir – '

'What is it, Ian?'

Farling studiously avoided looking at Piercey. 'I have to admit, sir, there's one thing that worries me. While I agree with Dermot that the wife and daughter gave every appearance of being completely innocent, I can't understand why Dayton should have left that briefcase in an unlocked cabinet and the photocopy so readily available unless he had reason to trust them.'

'Trust them to do what?' Piercey interrupted. 'Not to pry? And if they came across the things by chance to accept them as "just office stuff"? Anyway I never suggested Irena was totally innocent. She knows something she's determined to keep from us, but if it's relevant to the briefcase or the photocopy why didn't she hide them more securely – even dispose of them – as soon as Dayton went missing?'

Weatherby intervened. He said mildly, 'You do realize, don't you, that we're all assuming Dayton's guilty?' and waited for the younger men's reaction.

'You're suggesting the stuff might have been planted, sir,' Piercey said at once, and Weatherby nodded.

For some minutes they continued to question, to surmise, to argue, but the discussion got them no further. Finally Weatherby called an end to it. Piercey went off to arrange his travel, and Farling left for the offices of Rossel & Company.

*

Meanwhile the Daytons' house, including the wing in which Caroline lived, was being searched. The men were expert, thorough and careful. Going into the kitchen to make coffee and sandwiches for herself and Irena – they'd had no lunch – Caro was astonished to find one of the search team earnestly sifting flour and another examining the contents of the freezer. They grinned at her when she told them they must be crazy, but they made no reply.

Hurrying over her task, she returned to the studio, surprised to find herself near to tears. Irena still sat unmoving, staring into space. Caroline put down the tray and drew a deep breath. She accepted the need to be calm and sensible, but by now her tears had turned to anger and she yearned to scream, to shake these men who were violating her family's privacy so inexorably, to attack the woman plain clothes officer who watched and listened, so that she couldn't even talk openly to Irena. Dermot Piercey had been bad enough, but at least he'd been human. These people . . .

She passed a mug of coffee to Irena and offered her a plate of sandwiches. Sounding falsely cheerful, she said, 'Come along, darling. We must eat. God knows how long we'll have to put up with this lot, but as soon as they'll let us I'll contact Pa and Hector. They'll know what should be done.'

'No!' Irena pushed away her plate. She had taken only one bite from a sandwich, but she wasn't hungry. 'No!' she repeated. 'It's not right to involve them, or you, Caro. You must keep out of this as much as possible.'

'Irena, are you mad? How can I keep out? It's my father they're accusing. You're not suggesting Dad's guilty, are you?'

'Of course I'm not, but . . .'

'But what?'

Irena shook her head hopelessly. She couldn't explain her doubts and her fears. She couldn't confide in Caroline, not when the names of Peter Mayberry and Hector Coyne were on the list that Keith had entrusted to her. That damned list! If her mind hadn't been so consumed by it, she might have mentioned the strange intruder who had broken into the house on Saturday night and stolen nothing. How right she'd been to associate him with Keith, she thought bitterly, and how wrong in her guesses about his purpose.

Too late now, too late once that briefcase had been found, to rectify her mistake. No one would believe her; they'd merely assume she'd invented the story to protect Keith. No, she must say nothing, just wait – wait for Keith to return. And if he didn't, if he were dead, then what happened to her would no longer matter, and she could think about that list again.

'Mrs Dayton!'

Conscious that this wasn't the first time her name had been spoken, Irena glanced up into a square, expressionless face. 'Yes,' she said.

'We've finished, Mrs Dayton. The search is complete. Everything is as it was, but if you'd care to look around, make sure you've no cause for complaint – '

'No, that won't be necessary,' Irena said.

'Did you find what you were looking for?' Caroline asked coldly.

Momentarily the man hesitated. 'And what might that have been, miss?' he said. Then his mouth tightened as if to conceal a smile, and he added, 'No, Miss Dayton. We found nothing – untoward.' He gave a small bow. 'We'll be going now. Good afternoon.'

'Good afternoon,' Irena said automatically.

'And you mean we're free to do what we like?' Caroline mocked.

'Yes, Miss Dayton.'

The woman officer had hardly followed him out of the studio when Caro said, 'I bet they've bugged the phone, Irena. I'm off to find Pa and Hector, whatever you say, and I propose to tell them everything. We need help, darling.' She put an arm round Irena's shoulders. 'Why don't you come with me?'

'No.' Irena was firm. She reached for a sandwich; suddenly she was hungry. She began to eat ravenously and, ashamed of her appetite, smiled at Caroline. 'But you go if you must, Caro. I'll be all right. Don't worry about me.'

'Are you sure? We could get them to come here if – '

'No. Please.'

'Okay.' Caroline left reluctantly. She didn't understand the change in Irena since all the officers had gone. She couldn't know how relieved Irena was that there had been no question of personal searches, and how thankful she was to be at last alone in her own home.

*

If Caroline failed to understand Irena's reactions, she understood those of her step-father and her fiancé even less. She was expecting sympathy and support, assurances of help for Irena and herself and, not least, for Keith. Instead, as she entered the drawing-room of the Mayberry's Knightsbridge house Peter Mayberry and Hector Coyne broke off their earnest conversation to turn on her. Patricia, lying on a sofa, watched the scene in silence.

'Keith – any news?' Mayberry asked abruptly.

'Have you come from Hampstead? What's going on up there?'

It was not so much the questions as the way they were asked, with animosity as well as anxiety, that took Caroline by surprise. She looked at the two men and thought how alike they were, and how odd it was that she'd never noticed the resemblance before. They were both tall and solid, with round heads and strong features, fair hair and blue eyes, and they shared the same arrogant air. They could never have been mistaken for each other, but they were the same type. They might have been brothers, Caroline supposed – Hector, whom she was going to marry, the younger by a mere six years.

Caroline suppressed her feelings and began to explain.

'There were two men from the Foreign Office – Piercey and Farling – '

'We know that,' Peter Mayberry interrupted. 'Patricia met them this morning. Piercey's in Intelligence. I found that out quite easily. He works for General Sir Christopher Weatherby. I guess Farling's in the same racket.'

Patricia intervened suddenly from the sofa. 'Your father's been spying for them. Did you know that?'

'He sometimes acted as a courier, I know. That's hardly spying,' Caroline corrected.

'And now they suspect him – of working for the other side,' Coyne said. 'I suppose they're searching his house. We know they're going through Rossel's offices with a fine-tooth comb. They won't find anything to incriminate him there, though. The house is clean too, I hope.'

Caroline looked up sharply as she took in the implications of Coyne's remark. It went against the grain, but she knew she had no alternative but to elaborate. Quickly she explained, keeping the statement as brief as possible. The storm of questions overwhelmed her.

'For God's sake,' she said. 'It's no use asking me. I don't know what the briefcase means. I don't know what Dad's done or why he's done it, but – but I'll tell you something: Dad's no – no traitor!' Her voice broke.

'I could kill him,' Patricia said quickly and viciously, as if Caroline hadn't spoken. 'He's ruined everything. What are we going to do about the wedding? Postpone it? Or cancel it?'

Caroline didn't bother to answer her mother. She glanced at Hector Coyne, expecting him to refute Patricia's suggestion without hesitation, but he merely looked pensive.

'We mustn't panic,' he said. 'That would be disastrous. After all, I can't really believe that Dayton's an important defector. There could be sympathy for him if it turned out he was put under pressure because of his wife.'

'Yes – that damned Pole,' Mayberry agreed.

Caroline fought to control her anger, digging her nails into the palms of her hands. Her voice was tight. 'You both seem to forget you're talking about my father and my step-mother – people I love,' she said.

'Caro, you don't understand,' Coyne protested, but he spoke absently. 'We're just trying to think what's best for – for everyone.'

'You mean for yourselves,' said Caroline defiantly.

Patricia sat up. 'Darling, don't be silly,' she said. 'Hector's thinking of all of us, how to mitigate the scandal. The publicity could be appalling. Reporters pestering; cameramen, TV all over the place. We shan't have a moment's peace – and none of our friends will want to know us any more.'

'We have a choice,' Mayberry addressed himself to Coyne, as if Patricia hadn't spoken. 'Either go on as usual, or lie very, very low.'

Coyne made the decision. 'We go on as usual, but it might not be a bad idea if Patricia and Caroline took a quiet holiday in the country – just till we see the way the wind's blowing.'

'What about Irena?' Caroline demanded, though it seemed to her that now they were talking about something completely different.

'The sensible thing to do about Irena is keep away from her,' Coyne said bluntly. 'If your father's gone over to the communists it'll be because of her influence. Oh yes, I know,' he added as Caroline opened her mouth to argue, 'but half the central Europeans who supposedly fled to the West to escape communism are undercover agents, many of them sleepers, happy to enjoy the prosperity they didn't have at home – till the time comes to help destroy it.'

'That's absolute rubbish – about Irena, I mean,' Caroline said heatedly. 'What's more, it's libellous.' She looked at Coyne in disgust.

'Maybe, but Hector's right.' Mayberry supported Coyne. 'So the first thing you must do is get out of that flat of yours, my dear.'

'Excellent advice,' Patricia said.

'I'm damned if I will!'

Tempers blazed and died down again. As Hector Coyne said, the situation was far too serious for them to quarrel. In the end, they compromised. Mayberry and Coyne would use their influence to find out all they could about the accusations that might be brought against Keith Dayton and, conceivably, against Irena. Meanwhile, preparations for the wedding would go ahead, Caroline would stay in her Hampstead flat and they would all behave normally – until or unless the police and the media made this impossible.

She shouldn't have hoped for more, Caroline told herself as later that evening she drove back to Hampstead. They'd been shocked by what she had to tell them, and you couldn't blame them for that. Nor could you blame them for their reactions. They were conventional people with a lot at stake, and they'd behaved conventionally. None of them had ever pretended to be fond of Irena, but somehow she'd expected that Hector, at least, would have been more understanding, more – more loving –

When she reached her destination, she parked the car and let herself into the main house. A light was on in the sitting-room, but there was no sign of her step-mother. Calling Irena's name, Caroline went from room to room, her anxiety growing. Eventually, having discovered that Irena's car was missing and decided that there was nothing more she could do, she went to her flat. Here she spent a couple of difficult hours, thinking hard, until she heard the crunch of wheels on the gravel drive.

She didn't go in to say good night to Irena.

*

Lady Weatherby was in the country looking after a sick friend, and the General had dined late at his club. Afterwards he went along to the smoking-room, helped himself to coffee and settled down in a comfortable armchair with the evening newspaper. He was alone; on a Monday evening the club was always empty. Putting his feet up on a table, he determined to relax. It had been a trying day, and he feared that the days to come might well be more trying.

Idly he turned the pages of his paper. There was a scarcity of hard news, unless you happened to be interested in sport or the Royal Family or the latest strike, or even a debate in the House of Commons on the sale of fertilized embryos. But one story on an inside page caught the General's interest, and made him sit up, remove his feet from the table and emit a low whistle.

67

The story was really worthy of page one, unless it had reached the newsroom late, or the authorities had dropped a hint about playing it down. In some ways it was surprising they hadn't issued a 'D' notice, the General thought. A Mr Geoffrey Swanson Hardcastle had died that morning in strange circumstances in his Kensington flat. According to his daily cleaning woman, a Mrs Mavis Browne, Mr Hardcastle had gone to answer the doorbell. She had heard voices and then a loud bump as if someone had fallen. She went to investigate and found her employer lying on the hall floor. She had immediately telephoned his doctor – and the police.

'My first thought was that he'd had a heart attack or something,' Mrs Browne was quoted as saying. 'But I heard running footsteps and realized the door was wide open. Then I saw a gun under the hall table so I knew something was wrong.'

'Good for you,' Weatherby muttered to himself as he continued to read.

The doctor and the police had arrived simultaneously. The cause of death appeared to be heart failure, but the presence of the gun, which was found to fire gas capsules instead of bullets, complicated the situation. Enquiries were under way, and an early arrest was expected.

Weatherby grunted. He had little faith in an early arrest, but he was intensely interested. Though he had never met Geoffrey Hardcastle, he knew a good deal about him. He knew for instance that Hardcastle was not averse to undertaking illegal commissions, often for foreigners. He guessed that Hardcastle had been eliminated, either because he'd fallen down on some such job or learnt too much in the course of one. Weatherby would have dearly liked to know what the job had been.

The method – the gas gun – was also intriguing. Not so long ago an eminent member of the House of Lords had died of heart failure in what might have been similar circumstances. The peer had been on the point of leaving his London residence when he collapsed. His butler, hurrying after him with some papers he'd forgotten, caught a glimpse of a man on the steps outside the open front door, and swore later that he'd smelt a whiff of some kind of gas. But, in his lordship's case, there had been no hard evidence.

68

General Weatherby shook his head. He couldn't imagine any connection between Hardcastle and the noble lord, and anyway it wasn't his problem. He had enough on his plate at the moment, he thought grimly, without looking for more. He folded the newspaper and prepared to go home.

Then another member came into the smoking-room in search of coffee – and company. He was an economist called Clarkson who had a finger in a good many pies, and he was known in the club as a talker. Usually Weatherby did his best to avoid him, but now he had no chance. Clarkson sat himself down opposite the General and began to chat.

Weatherby listened, letting the words flow over him without giving them any real attention. After ten minutes, as Clarkson showed no sign of ceasing his monologue, the General looked at his watch and got to his feet.

'I must be off,' he announced.

'Oh, not yet, old boy,' Clarkson said at once. 'Not till you've told me about this man of yours – what's his name? Dayton – that's it: the chap who's gone over to the Russians.'

Weatherby, who disliked Clarkson, disliked being called 'old boy' and disliked surprises, subsided slowly into his chair. His smile was thin, his almost colourless eyes without expression. 'Dayton?' he said blandly, frowning as if he'd never before heard the name. 'What's this all about?'

'That's what I hope you're going to tell me.' Clarkson leant forward so that Weatherby could smell the liquor on his breath. 'It seems Dayton's one of those businessmen always travelling to foreign parts to boost our exports. He was meant to be doing a bit of spying for us, but they say that, in actual fact, he was on the other side – and now he's done a bolt.'

'Really?' Weatherby raised his shaggy eyebrows. 'And who are "they"?'

'What?'

'You said *they* say.'

'Oh, I was at a party earlier at the American embassy, and that was the buzz going round. The Yanks aren't too pleased, as you can imagine.' Clarkson gave Weatherby a sympathetic smile – a gesture the General failed to appreciate. 'They feel they can't trust us anymore, and who can blame them? We

Brits have been a sieve for secrets recently. But you know that as well as I do – better, I expect. So tell me about this character Dayton. In strict confidence of course. You know I wouldn't breathe a word.'

Weatherby got to his feet again. 'My dear chap,' he said, half drawling his words. 'I'd certainly tell you if I knew anything, but I don't. What you're saying is news to me. And it's only a rumour, isn't it? If I were you I'd be careful how far I spread it. I wouldn't be surprised if it turned out to be completely false.'

'You wouldn't?' Clarkson was interested, eager.

Weatherby didn't deign to reply. With a wave of his hand he strode from the smoking-room. He'd forgotten Geoffrey Hardcastle. His mind was once more concentrated on Dayton, and on the rapidity with which his story had become public property. Someone, he thought, could have blown it on purpose. But who? And why?

SEVEN

Piercey's breakfast the next morning was interrupted by a startling item on the radio news. The report gave no names, but it was clear that the mention of a 'missing British businessman' almost certainly referred to Keith Dayton. The bulletin was scarcely over before Piercey's phone rang.

'Weatherby here. Your flight's not till mid morning, is it?'

'No, sir.'

'Office, then. As soon as you can get there.'

'Yes, sir. Er – have you been listening to the radio?'

'About our friend? Of course. There's a paragraph in *The Times* too. And there were rumours about town last night; I heard one in my club.'

'I see, sir.'

Piercey's words were cut short by a sharp click as the receiver was replaced at the other end of the line. He hurried to finish packing, grab his bag and briefcase and find a taxi. He met the General in the lobby of their office building and they went up in the lift alone together.

'How have the media got hold of it so quickly, sir?'

'Someone told them,' Weatherby said laconically. But he saw Piercey's expression, and relented. 'There are three possible sources, as I see it, Dermot. One's a leak from the security boys for reasons of their own, and another's a leak from Dayton's family. Neither seems awfully likely, in my opinion. The third possibility is that it's part of an attempt by someone or some outfit to discredit Dayton – '

'He – or they – would have to know that Dayton's disappeared, and also that we've a reason to suspect he might have gone over.' Piercey was thinking aloud. 'That narrows the field a bit, sir.'

71

'Indeed,' said Weatherby, 'but it doesn't help us to understand why.'

The lift stopped, and as they got out Weatherby gestured to Piercey to follow him. They went through Miss Sherwood's office with an exchange of good-mornings. In the inner sanctum coffee and biscuits appeared almost at once.

Weatherby said, 'This leak's interesting, but it's not the main reason I wanted to see you before you go to Germany. There's been a development you should know about. After Special Branch left the Dayton's place yesterday the girl, Caroline, went off to the Mayberrys, which was not unexpected. But later Mrs Dayton also left the house, and she went to visit her old Polish friend, Casimir Sabik. She was there several hours, and she probably had supper with him.'

'And was that unexpected, sir?' Piercey asked as Weatherby paused to drink his coffee. 'As you say, they are compatriots. She could have wanted to talk things over with someone she knew would be sympathetic.'

'I grant you that.' Weatherby bit into a digestive biscuit. 'However, Sabik was an unfortunate choice. What you don't know is that we've had a file on that particular individual for quite a time. You could say he's a kind of minor Soviet agent. He picks up unconsidered trifles and passes them to an embassy contact. We've used him once or twice – without his knowledge, of course – for low-level disinformation operations, but we've not thought him important. We could be wrong.'

'Because of Irena Dayton? There's never been anything against her, has there, sir?'

'No. But I've not finished yet.' The General held up a monitory finger. 'By chance Irena was slow starting her car when she left Sabik's, and our man saw the Pole slip out of the building right after her. He had a choice and he followed Sabik, who took a taxi to a private club in the Holland Park area, stayed there three-quarters of an hour and then went home. And here's the crunch, Dermot. Ten minutes before Sabik left the club a Third Secretary from the Soviet Embassy came out of the place and got into a black limousine that was apparently waiting for him. What do you think?'

'The whole thing seems a bit amateurish on their part, sir.

It might be a coincidence. Anyway, I wouldn't say it necessarily condemned Mrs Dayton.' Piercey hesitated. 'What are you going to do about it, sir? Pull in Sabik? And Irena Dayton?'

'Not immediately. I propose to play a waiting game, and hope that a few of the pieces of this puzzle will soon begin to fit together.' Weatherby finished the last biscuit and drained his cup. 'What we need, Dermot, is a slice of luck.'

★

Luck, Piercey thought as his aircraft taxied to its stand at Wahn airport, was a commodity in seriously short supply that day as far as he was concerned. He was over an hour late, his flight delayed by the omnipresent 'technical difficulties' that attend air travel. He smiled to himself without humour.

But as Piercey came through customs he found Maurice Fenton waiting. He was driven to a pleasant house half way between Bonn and Bad Godesberg, where drinks and an excellent lunch were ready. Mary Fenton made him welcome, and then tactfully mentioned a golf commitment and left him and her husband alone together.

Fenton was a small, sandy-haired man who seemed to have perpetual trouble with his contact lenses, because his eyes were always red and sore. He was no one's idea of an intelligence officer, though in fact he had a brilliant mind and his physical appearance was often an asset. He wasted no time on preliminaries.

He said, 'My German opposite number in the BND is getting angry, though he doesn't show it — yet. He's made it clear to me that whatever's going on is none of their business, and they wish we and others wouldn't play games in their back yard.' He gave a resigned smile, and added, 'Naturally I pleaded innocence, but he didn't believe a word of it.'

Piercey considered. The BND was the centralized West German civilian intelligence service, as opposed to the BfV, the internal security authority.

'Did *you* believe *him* – that the BND regard it as none of their business?' Piercey said finally. 'And what about the BV? Do they feel the same?'

'Don't ask me. I wouldn't know. My liaison's strictly with BND. And on the whole, yes, I did believe my contact. But my guess is that the German authorities are fully prepared to take a hand if it suits them, or if they think their own interests are involved. Are they?'

'What?'

'Are West German interests involved?'

'God knows.'

'Doubtless. But suppose you tell me what Weatherby knows. Or, rather, what he wants me to know.'

'I'll do my best. And don't think you're being kept in the dark. That may have been true at the beginning, but now – '

They moved to the table and, while they ate lunch, Piercey talked. Fenton was a good listener, and his questions were germane, though there were few that Piercey could answer with any conviction. After the briefing they sat in silence for a minute or two.

Then Piercey said, 'It would help a lot – a hell of a lot – if we knew who was on whose side.'

Fenton nodded. He said, seemingly inconsequent, 'Let me explain what I've arranged for you.'

A car had been rented in Piercey's name and was waiting in the Fentons' driveway. A room had been booked in the Cologne hotel where Keith Dayton always stayed, and where he had failed to arrive the previous Friday night. The police had been told of Piercey's arrival. They would cooperate by informing him of any progress they had made in their investigations, and, should he wish, he could visit the morgues in the area and view any unidentified bodies.

'Sounds jolly,' Piercey said.

Fenton grinned. 'You'll have to look suitably anxious. As far as the authorities are concerned, the cover story is that you're a cousin of Dayton's, acting on behalf of the family as his wife's not fit to travel. It was the best I could do at short notice. You had to be close enough to justify your enquiries, but not too close, in case Dayton's really in the shit.'

'Thanks. That's as much as I could expect. In any case, I guess my cover doesn't matter much as long as the authorities

74

are prepared to be reasonably cooperative. I'll go and tackle them now. Thanks to Mary for the lunch.'

'What are we here for? But don't let this thing get out of hand. Keep me informed. You know – long-term relations with the Germans and all that.'

'Sure.'

Shortly afterwards Dayton said goodbye to his colleague and drove back to Cologne. He checked in at the hotel where Fenton had reserved a room for him, and asked to see the manager. There was no delay, and he was immediately shown into an inner office where a stout and beaming German offered him afternoon tea or coffee, or anything he might prefer.

In accented but fluent English he said that Herr Piercey was doubly welcome. Herr Dayton had been a valued client, and whatever they could do for his cousin would give them much pleasure.

As the manager reminded himself of the sad circumstances of Herr Piercey's visit his broad smile was replaced by a suitable expression of funereal solemnity. Piercey, setting his face in similarly mournful lines, expressed his gratitude. Then, though he already knew the answer, he asked when the hotel had last heard from Keith Dayton.

'Last Thursday morning. By chance I took the call myself and Herr Dayton seemed, as you say, in fine form.' Momentarily the manager permitted his smile to return. 'He joked with me. He said he might be late, but he would arrive eventually and he wouldn't expect to find anyone else in his bed, however attractive.'

Piercey smiled in return. 'So you kept his room, but he never came.'

'That's right, Herr Piercey. We were worried – not about the room, but about Herr Dayton himself. It had not happened before. Herr Dayton was always a most punctilious man.' The manager sighed. 'When we heard nothing from him, and the British Embassy made enquiries, and then the police, we naturally became more and more worried. And now that his car has been found – '

'I didn't know that,' Piercey said quickly. 'When? Where?'

75

'It was an accident, some way south of Köln in a country area. I myself was only told this morning. The agency for the car is in the hotel, you understand, and we arranged the rental for Herr Dayton. I fear the car was a total wreck and burnt out. That's why it took so long to identify.'

'And Herr Dayton himself?'

'No, no, Herr Piercey. There was no one in the car. Naturally I asked.' The manager was reproachful. 'There were just the remains of what had apparently been a small bag and a brief-case. That was all. Of course the police may have more information by now.'

'Yes, I must go and see them,' Piercey said, eager to be on his way.

At police headquarters his welcome was noticeably less warm than it had been at the hotel. He was received politely but formally by a man in a business suit who introduced himself as one Herr Wetzel. Piercey admitted that he spoke some German, but they both agreed they would be more comfortable in English. Almost at once Piercey found himself answering questions rather than asking them.

'You do not wish to view the body of Herr Bauer?'

'No. Why should I, since it's clear he's not my missing relative?'

Piercey's continuing insistence that he was related to Keith Dayton received a pitying smile from the German. 'So you have never met Herr Bauer?'

'No, mein Herr. I've told you – '

'But Herr Dayton knew Herr Bauer. They were associates, were they not?'

'You mean Herr Bauer had business dealings with Rossel's, the electronics firm Herr Dayton worked for?' Piercey did his best to sound surprised. 'I really wouldn't know.'

'Did Herr Dayton work for the British Government?'

Purposely Piercey misunderstood. 'I imagine Rossel's have some government contracts. But why do you ask?'

'And you yourself, Herr Piercey? Do you work for the British Government?'

'That, if I may say so, is none of your damned business! What's the point of all these questions? I came to you hoping

76

you would help me trace Herr Dayton. Some great misfortune may well have befallen him, and you . . .'

Dermot Piercey had decided the time had come to take the offensive. He let his temper flare, but his reaction had no apparent effect on Herr Wetzel, who remained totally impassive. However, he probably rang a hidden bell, Piercey thought, because as his tirade came to an end there was an opportune knock at the door and an attractive girl in the green uniform of a German police officer came in.

'The report on the shooting, mein Herr,' she said. She laid a file on the desk and went out without a glance at Piercey.

'What shooting?' Piercey demanded as the door closed behind her. 'You're not still talking about this man Bauer, are you? What the hell's he got to do with my cousin?'

'Permit me.' For a minute or two Herr Wetzel made a pretence of studying the file while Piercey looked irritably about the dull office. Then, shutting the file cover, he said, 'Herr Piercey, I'll try to reconstruct for you what I think happened in a *Parkplatz*, a small lay-by, on the Autobahn some distance south of Köln in the early hours of last Friday. I could, of course, be wrong, but . . .'

As Wetzel continued it became quite obvious to Piercey that, in spite of his deprecatory words, the German was in his own mind sure of his facts. And indeed, had Brenner and Hean been present, they would have been horrified at the accuracy of the reconstruction. Piercey listened in silence, comparing what he knew of Dayton and Bauer and their likely meeting with this account. Almost everything seemed to fit and he waited, fearful of what was to come.

'. . . and that's where the mystery begins. Herr Dayton had found his way to this telephone booth in the *Tankstelle* – the service area, presumably to call for help . . .'

'How do you know it was Keith – Herr Dayton?' Piercey interrupted. 'Why should he have been there at all? It makes no sense to me.'

'I'll come to that later, mein Herr,' Wetzel said patiently. 'The mysterious thing is that the man in the telephone booth – whoever he was – then disappeared. He must have been badly wounded, so he probably could not have moved far without assistance. Where did he go? Where was he taken? By whom? And why? So many questions.'

'But you've got the answers.' Piercey couldn't prevent an element of sarcasm from creeping into his voice.

The German looked up sharply, but refused to be disconcerted. 'Some of them, yes, Herr Piercey. As you know, the car rented by Herr Dayton has been found – a burnt out wreck – but there was no sign of a body, either Herr Dayton's or anyone else's.'

'So?'

'Listen, Herr Piercey, please. There was a second accident that night, though at the time we had no reason to connect the events. You must understand that Herr Dayton's car plunged from a minor road down the side of a steep ravine. On the far side of this ravine – where the terrain is not so steep – is another minor road, and it was here that the second accident occurred. You visualize the scene?'

Piercey nodded, and Herr Wetzel continued. 'Now, the details of the second accident. A motorist, rounding a corner, hit a man who he says was wandering in the middle of the road. The man was taken to hospital unconscious and has so far remained unconscious. He had no means of identification on him. His wallet contained only a mixture of German, American and English money – mostly Deutschmarks. His clothes were various – and he wore no shoes.'

'No shoes?' Piercey exclaimed involuntarily.

'No shoes, Herr Piercey – and that interested me. If someone is thrown from a car with great force it sometimes happens that he loses his shoes. It was one of the reasons why I connected the two accidents in my mind. Unfortunately I did not receive a full report on the second incident till yesterday, but as soon as I did I compared the description of the gentleman in hospital with that of Herr Dayton provided by the British Embassy. I think we may at least hope that the unconscious man is indeed Herr Dayton.' He smiled thinly.

You know damn well it's Keith, Piercey thought. Aloud he said, 'But – but is it possible? To survive so much? To be thrown clear from a car crashing down a ravine, to – to crawl what I assume was some distance up hill to a road, to be

78

knocked down by another car? And live?' He shook his head in disbelief.

'I assure you stranger things have happened. Indeed, I feel certain that on this occasion they did happen.' The German's smile had become sardonic. He leant towards Piercey, his elbows on the desk, his hands cupping his chin. 'Let's not forget Ernst Bauer, mein Herr. Or the man who was shot but managed to drag himself to the telephone – the man who then disappeared. Let's not forget I said that the coincidence of the two accidents was but one of the reasons I had for hoping our unconscious friend is Herr Dayton.'

Piercey gritted his teeth. He wondered about the man sitting opposite him. Certainly he was no ordinary police detective, of whatever rank. He was almost certainly from West German intelligence or security – BND or BfV. And, whoever he was, he knew too much. Piercey said, 'I've not forgotten anything, Herr Wetzel. Tell me your other reasons.'

'There's really only one, Herr Piercey. It was discovered in the hospital that the victim's many injuries included a bullet wound. Luckily for him it was a clean wound. The bullet had passed through the body without damaging any vital organ, but Herr Dayton – if I may call him that – had lost a lot of blood. Remember the blood in the lay-by and the telephone booth, Herr Piercey. I have not as yet checked, but I would stake my reputation on some of those samples being identical with the blood of the man in hospital, the man who seemingly managed to escape from Herr Dayton's car. Would you not agree?'

Piercey made no direct reply. Instead he demanded. 'Where is he? When can I see him?'

The German held up a hand. 'Not so fast, Herr Piercey. You and I must talk a little more. Meanwhile, rest assured that your – er – cousin is in good hands. He's been transferred to a large hospital right here in Köln where the equipment and staff are excellent. And, of course, he's absolutely safe.'

'Safe?'

'Under guard. Remember again, Herr Piercey. There was a shooting incident – and a dead man. It remains a police matter, mein Herr.'

'I realize that, but . . .'

79

'Herr Piercey, what does the name Liz mean to you? Or should it be Lise? Short for Elizabeth, say.'

'In connection with Keith Dayton? Nothing, Herr Wetzel.'

The German regarded Piercey sceptically. 'Not another relation?'

Piercey kept his temper. 'Not that I know of. Herr Dayton's wife – his present wife – is called Irena. His first wife was Patricia. His daughter's Caroline.' Piercey shrugged. 'Why?'

'A mistress, perhaps?'

'Perhaps, but I've not heard of her.'

'Strange. It's the one name – the one word – that the unconscious man has uttered.'

Piercey made no response and abruptly the German changed the subject, returning to the question of Ernst Bauer and his association with Keith Dayton. Piercey stone-walled, pretending complete ignorance and offering only blank denials. Together they wasted time until eventually the German pushed back his chair.

'They'll be expecting you at the hospital, Herr Piercey,' he said. As the policewoman returned to the room, he came around the desk and offered his hand. 'I hope we may talk again after you have seen Herr Dayton – assuming it is Herr Dayton.'

He laughed, and Piercey was forced to laugh too, sharing the joke, but thankful the interview was at an end.

*

Keith Dayton lay on his back in a private room, a neat narrow mound in a neat narrow bed. His face was pale, paler than the tube which passed up his nose. His breathing was shallow, and only the slightest stirring of the sheet that covered him to the chin showed that he was still alive. A nurse sat beside him, attending to the oxygen supply and the intravenous drips, and watching for any signs of returning consciousness.

Outside the door the police officer on duty came to attention as a doctor approached along the corridor with Dermot Piercey. The doctor let Piercey go ahead of him into the room, to stand beside the bed.

The nurse, who had risen at their entry, shook her head and said in German, 'No change, Herr Doktor. He mutters from time to time, but no words are intelligible. Just the same name, over and over.'

'Do you recognize him, mein Herr?' the doctor asked Piercey.

'Yes. He's an Englishman called Keith Dayton. He was in the Federal Republic on business for his firm. How is he?'

'Ill. Very ill, mein Herr. But he has a good constitution. He should live.'

'I'm thankful to hear that and I'm most grateful to you and the hospital for looking after him so well,' Piercey said formally. 'I myself have to return to England tomorrow, but if there's anything he needs a Herr Fenton of the British Embassy in Bonn will – '

Piercey had turned away from the bed, but the nurse had kept an eye on her charge. She interrupted. 'Look! His lips are moving. He's trying to speak. He's asking for Liz – Lise – whatever the name is.'

'Such a pity, mein Herr, that you don't know who she might be,' the doctor said. 'It could be of great help to the patient if . . .'

But Piercey was paying him no attention. He was leaning over the bed, his face close to Dayton's, blocking the view of the two Germans. He was about to speak when suddenly Dayton's eyes opened. Either it was chance, or somehow the injured man's subconscious recognized Piercey as a friend, but Dayton seemed to strain himself to make an extra effort to be understood, and Piercey caught the word he had been trying to say.

It wasn't Liz or Lise or any other man or woman's name. The word was 'List'. And, as Keith Dayton sank back once more through clouds of consciousness, he mouthed another word which Dermot Piercey interpreted as 'Danger'.

EIGHT

'This was a peaceful country once, but not any more.' The driver of the staff car that had met Dermot Piercey at Heathrow was a talker. He pushed his cap back and scratched the bald spot on his head. 'A couple of days ago a chap was killed by a gas gun of some kind as he opened his own front door. Just like that. No apparent reason. Then yesterday . . .'

He stopped, momentarily distracted from his monologue. 'Look at those thugs!' he said indignantly, pointing at two youths in black leather suits who were shouldering their way along the pavement regardless of other pedestrians. 'They'll be at this "Britain First" rally in Hyde Park next Sunday, I bet. They've got National Front written all over them.'

Piercey grunted and the driver continued. 'As I was saying, yesterday some rich Jew called Kaufmann got himself shot in Hampstead by a guy on a motorbike. In broad daylight, too. Supposedly he was mistaken for that Rabbi Richler who's always on the box about the increase in anti-Semitism in Britain. Not that I hold with anti-Semitism, mind you. Whoever threw that fire bomb into that south London synagogue a few months ago deserves what he gets.'

'If he's ever caught,' Piercey said absently.

'Sure.' The driver nodded. 'But it's not right to call us Brits anti-Semitics when our own Foreign Secretary's a Jew, is it, sir?' For a moment he was silent, negotiating the traffic. Then he added, 'I saw the girl his son's going to marry the other day, and is she ever beautiful!'

Piercey grinned. He knew Rebecca Sonberg, the daughter of the Israeli Ambassador in London – indeed, he had been invited to the wedding reception – and he wholeheartedly agreed with the driver, but he had too much on his mind to attempt a conversation.

After an indifferent meal on the aircraft, most of which he had left uneaten, Piercey could have done with a drink and a couple of sandwiches when he reached the office. But Weatherby was waiting with Farling, and he had to settle for the coffee and biscuits that Miss Sherwood served.

Weatherby's first question, after he had listened in silence to Piercey's report, was, 'You're positive Dayton said "list"?'

'As positive as anyone could be in the circumstances, sir.'

'Right. Now, let's accept Herr Wetzel's reconstruction of events and let's accept that this "list", whatever it may be, represents – or is related to – the important information we've been hoping to get out of Germany. Given all this, there are a number of immediate problems. Did Dayton manage to phone anyone from that service area and pass on the list? And, if so, who did he phone?'

Piercey said, 'It's possible he tried to pass the list on to us but collapsed before he got through.'

'That assumes he's in the clear,' Farling replied. 'He's still got to explain the incriminating stuff we found in his house and the fact that his wife consorts with a known agent.'

'At least we know he's not defected,' Piercey said quickly.

Weatherby looked from Piercey to Farling and back again before he intervened. 'So the present position is that Fenton's holding the fort in Cologne. He won't be able to show too much interest – no more than a normal consul in a normal British subject. And there's no knowing when Dayton may recover consciousness and start talking. My view is we've got to get Dayton back here in the UK as soon as possible. I'll get on to Fenton right away and try pulling some strings. I think we can persuade the Germans to cooperate. They may even be glad to get rid of him.'

Piercey, remembering his second session with Herr Wetzel that morning, looked doubtful, but he didn't argue the point and Weatherby continued, 'In the meantime, Dermot . . .'

★

'They're no damned good,' Irena said, surveying the line of prints she had taped up on the studio wall. 'They're not you, Caro. They've got no life, no sparkle.'

83

Caroline shrugged irritably. 'They're not quite what I'd hoped for, I admit, but I'm sure they'll please Hector well enough.'

'I'm sorry. They don't please me. We'll have to try again.'

'It's not your fault. It's me. I'm worried about Dad and – ' Caroline stopped. She couldn't explain about Hector, about how things had changed in recent days, how she didn't seem to understand him any more, how she was no longer sure she was in love with him. 'You've done a splendid job on old Red Biddy there,' she said accusingly.

Irena regarded the row of photographs at which Caroline was pointing. 'Yes. I like most of those. Lady Bridget's got a wonderful face and bone structure – '

'She's a bloody red! She makes no secret of it.' Suddenly Caroline's pent-up emotions exploded. 'For God's sake, Irena, when Dad's in the kind of trouble he is, why do you have to mix with known communists? Can't you see it could make it worse for him?'

Irena stared at her. She said coldly, 'I never ask my sitters about their politics.'

She might have added that this particular appointment had been made some weeks ago, and that she hadn't thought to cancel it. She'd made herself continue with her work because it helped to pass the endless hours. Without it, she felt she could have lost her sanity. Nights, with the help of wine and sleeping pills, were not too bad, but the days grew less and less bearable as time went on.

The doorbell rang, loud in the silence between the two women, and distracted them from what might have been an incipient quarrel.

'I'll go,' Caroline said.

Irena followed her, apprehensive as always now when either the telephone or the doorbell rang. She found Caro letting Dermot Piercey into the hall, obviously with some reluctance. She wanted to ask if he had news of Keith, but the words stuck in her throat.

She said, 'Please come into the sitting-room, Mr Piercey.'

'Thank you.' Piercey sat in the chair she indicated. It had

84

been a long and tiring day, and he hadn't been pleased to be saddled with the coming interrogation.

'Mrs Dayton,' he began. 'I'm sorry to disturb you in the evening like this, but I've one or two questions I must ask.'

'What a surprise!' Caroline murmured sarcastically.

Piercey ignored her. 'They're important, so please answer carefully. First, take your mind back to last Thursday. You were at your country cottage, you said. Were you staying there alone?'

'Alone? Yes.'

'Did your husband know that's where you'd be?'

'Yes. I'd said I'd be going back to London on Friday, as I did.'

'Did you have any visitors that Thursday, or on Friday before you left?'

'No.' Irena was puzzled. 'Not if you mean friends. The milk was delivered, and someone came to mend the fence. That's all.'

'What about telephone calls – either day?'

Irena's hands were clasped in her lap, and Piercey saw them tighten convulsively until the knuckles were white. He watched her swallow before she spoke, and knew she was preparing to lie.

'No, Mr Piercey.'

'None?' He expressed surprise. 'Your husband didn't ring you?'

'No!' Irena repeated firmly, too firmly.

Piercey turned to Caroline. 'What about you, Miss Dayton?'

'What about me?' she regarded him with amusement. 'Do you mean, did I have any phone calls? Lots and lots. I lead a busy social life. Would you like a list?'

Irena, who had relaxed as Piercey's attention shifted to Caroline, drew a short, sharp breath which she tried ineffectually to change into a cough. Caroline, startled, looked at her, and to cover her embarrassment Irena said, 'Mr Piercey wants to know if Keith called you, Caro.'

'Say, late Thursday night or early Friday morning? He might have phoned here or to your flat,' Piercey pressed, addressing Caroline but watching Irena.

85

'If he did, I wouldn't know,' Caroline said. 'I wasn't around. I spent the night with Hector – Hector Coyne, my fiancé.' She smiled sweetly at Piercey. 'I often do.'

Piercey refused the challenge. He said, 'If Mr Dayton were in some kind of difficulty, who else might he phone? Lady Mayberry, your mother, for instance?'

'Heavens, no. She'd be the last,' Caroline said at once. 'I'm not sure. I'd have thought Irena, but – '

Irena interrupted. 'Mr Piercey, you know something – something about my husband. What is it? Tell me, please. Is he – is he dead?'

'No, Mrs Dayton, I'm glad to say he's alive. All I can tell you now is that he was involved in a car accident in West Germany, and he's in hospital there. He's been unconscious for some days, but he's improving and the doctors expect him to live.'

Irena's face was radiant though tears rolled down her cheeks; momentarily she was lost in a private world. 'Thank God,' she whispered to herself. 'Thank God!'

'Why didn't you tell us at once instead of all that nonsense about phone calls?' Caroline demanded angrily. 'And where is he?'

'Yes, where is he? I must go to him,' Irena said.

'I'm afraid that won't be possible.'

'Why not?'

Piercey replied with brutal simplicity. 'It's a security matter. As the wife of a suspected enemy agent, Mrs Dayton, you wouldn't be allowed to leave the country.'

'And what about me – the so-called traitor's daughter?' Caroline demanded.

'I wouldn't advise you to try, Miss Dayton.' Piercey spoke coolly. 'The West Germans, in whose jurisdiction he is, have excellent reasons to suspect Mr Dayton of espionage, but we're doing our best to persuade them to let us bring him back to the UK.' Suddenly he relented, and added gently. 'If they agree, as we hope they will, perhaps your father may be able to prove his innocence. In any case it's surely best at this point to keep everything in as low a key as possible and avoid any unnecessary scandal.'

'Best for you, you mean, and whatever little outfit you work for.' Caroline was scathing.

'Best for all concerned, Miss Dayton, including your father and yourself and . . .' Piercey hesitated. He'd tried to be friendly, to offer helpful advice, and she'd as good as spat at him. He couldn't resist the temptation. '. . . and for Mr Hector Coyne,' he added.

*

Hector Coyne rose from the green leather-covered bench and, with a bow to the Speaker, left the chamber. There would be a division later, so he'd have to stay in the House. Meanwhile he didn't have to listen to interminable speeches about the safety of the individual and the growth of violence throughout the country, about lawlessness and police brutality. Much of what was being said was poppycock, and the rest was propaganda. None of it was original. He'd heard it all before, and he'd other things on his mind.

He went into one of the Members' bars and ordered a whisky before strolling out on to the terrace. He leant on the parapet and stared across the darkening river at the County Hall and St Thomas's Hospital on the far side. Tower blocks further away looked like giant's playthings, outlined against the evening sky. Beneath him a tug went by, hooting mournfully as it approached Westminster Bridge, and in the distance the siren of a Thames River Police launch pierced the constant roar of London traffic.

Coyne's thoughts were of Caroline and their forthcoming marriage. He was in love with Caro, but he'd been in love before and he was cynical enough to guess he would be again. He was only thirty-eight, and it was unlikely that Caro would satisfy him for the rest of his life. But he'd expected it to be a suitable marriage, on every level. Now – silently he cursed Keith Dayton.

Patricia had telephoned earlier to say that, according to Caroline, Keith had been found and was in a West German hospital. Details were meagre, but at least Dayton hadn't gone over to the other side. Nevertheless, the situation was difficult.

There was still the possibility of a trial, with its accompanying publicity. If only the damned man would die, Coyne thought viciously. Then a lot of problems would be solved.

Not all, of course. He hated the idea of security men nosing around Rossel's. He trusted John Rossel, but – Coyne's mouth set in a grim line. There had been too many mistakes lately, too much had gone wrong. A breeze came off the river and he shivered.

'Hector!'

'Hello, Peter.' Coyne turned and gave Mayberry a resigned smile. 'Don't tell me. There's more bad news.'

'No. On the contrary. Some silly chap tried to question me about Dayton in the middle of a TV interview I've just been taping. You should have seen his face when I told him Dayton was in hospital recovering from a car accident.' Mayberry spoke with satisfaction. 'The interview's going out after the BBC news this evening and it'll put an end to the rumours – at least for a while.'

'For a while, yes.' Coyne was still sour.

'Cheer up!' Mayberry said. 'I've been talking to John Rossel too. He's flying back from Brussels tomorrow. He thinks he may have found the man we need. He won't come cheap, but he's a real top-flight professional.'

NINE

A Member of Parliament for twenty years, Sir Peter Mayberry was by now a polished performer on television. He came over well – perhaps a little pompous, but nevertheless honest and straightforward, the sort of legislator on whom a viewer could depend. His opinions were orthodox and unoriginal, but he answered questions with apparent sincerity and he was prepared on occasion to admit to error or even ignorance.

As the interview came to an end Patricia switched off the set and nodded her approval. Peter had dealt admirably with the sudden questions about Keith. He'd been calm and unflustered, and had given better than he'd got. Sitting by herself on a sofa in their elegant drawing-room, and fingering the diamond clasp that had been Peter's latest present to her, Patricia Mayberry smiled with satisfaction.

Not everyone involved was equally pleased with the programme. Not everyone involved even saw it. Caroline had insisted on taking Irena out to dinner to celebrate the news that Keith was alive. General Weatherby had been forced to attend an official reception. Ian Farling was at the theatre with a girlfriend. Dermot Piercey, though he was at home, was watching a video of a foreign movie. But Casimir Sabik, who had been instructed to keep his eyes and ears open for any information relating to Keith Dayton or his family, had followed the broadcast with the greatest interest. As it ended he at once tried to telephone Irena, only to be disappointed when there was no reply.

And two other men in London, amongst the hundreds of thousands who saw the programme, reacted immediately to what Sir Peter Mayberry had said. When he told his interviewers that Keith Dayton had been involved in a serious car accident in West Germany, but had survived, they were each appalled.

In his hotel room Brenner went to the bottle of whisky he had bought earlier in the day, poured a stiff measure into his tooth glass and drank it neat. He told himself that the story couldn't be true, that it was some attempted ruse on the part of the British. There was no way Dayton could be alive, not after what had happened to him. Then he began to consider the situation.

The phone rang as Brenner finished his drink. He put down the glass on top of the dressing-table, sat on the edge of the bed and picked up the receiver. He was sweating.

'Yes,' he said. 'Brenner here.'

The man at the other end of the line didn't give his name, but the voice was unmistakable. Brenner swore silently. He'd not been prepared for such a quick response. He'd expected the Cultural Attaché to be out for the evening or entertaining at home, not watching television.

'You heard what was said about our – late friend? Is it conceivable that it could be true?'

Brenner answered without hesitation. He could have gained time by saying he had just come in and didn't know what his controller was talking about, but he was too well trained. He said, 'I heard. Though I find it extremely difficult to believe, it is – I suppose – just possible.'

'Thank you. I shall do what is necessary and be in touch.'

Brenner was about to answer but the call had already been terminated. Slowly he put down his own receiver. He pictured the Cultural Attaché as single-minded and without compassion. Maybe this was quite wrong, but it was irrelevant. The facts of the matter were that he and Hean might well have bungled an important mission. Now the position had to be retrieved. To the best of their ability they would have to repair the damage – whatever the cost to themselves. He accepted that without question. And so would Hean – still presumably awaiting orders in Zurich.

Collecting the glass and the bottle of whisky Brenner pulled up a comfortable chair beside the telephone and settled down for a long wait. By the time the phone rang again the level in the bottle had fallen appreciably. He picked up the instrument on its first ring.

His orders had come through. He was to remain in London

and set up the next two on the list – a senior civil servant and a well-known television personality – so that he would be fully prepared when action was required.

The Cultural Attaché made no mention of Keith Dayton and Brenner drained his glass with a sense of relief, thankful that it was someone else – probably Hean – who had drawn the short straw.

★

For his part, Hean was unhappy, driving through the night from Zurich to Cologne. He had hoped to join Brenner in London, and the sudden change of plan was unsettling. The new assignment, apparently forced on them by necessity, was hurriedly conceived and seemed to him to be suicidal. He had no wish to die, but it had never occurred to him to refuse to do as he was told.

He got rid of his rented car at Wahn airport, leaving it, keys in the glove compartment, in the return car park. It was paid for and would be collected automatically and without question. Then, as he and Brenner had done the previous Friday morning, he took a taxi to a spot near the town house off the Sachsenring.

He was expected. The same middle-aged woman opened the door to him. She was politely welcoming, but gave no sign of recognition. Her husband had not yet left for his office and she showed Hean into the study.

'You have eaten, mein Herr?' she asked in German.

'Nein.'

'Then I shall get you some breakfast while you talk.'

The man who sat behind the long, mahogany desk waited impassively until she left the room. Then he said, 'We've done our best but we've had very little time. When we heard what was required my wife telephoned around, pretending to be the – er – patient's sister, just arrived from England and unsure which hospital he was in. So we located him. It wasn't difficult. Innocent people will believe any story.'

'How is Dayton?'

'Improving. They've been able to move him from down south to a hospital in Köln. It's a big place, on the other side

91

of the city, beyond the Hauptbarnhof; I'll give you all the details later. Apparently he has periods of consciousness, but he's not talking yet. Unlike the nurse on night duty.' He permitted himself a sardonic smile. 'She even let slip Dayton's room number.'

'Good.' Hean waited for the bad news.

'We know the hospital fairly well, and can describe it for you. As we remember it, the room is likely to be at the end of a corridor and somewhat isolated.'

Hean nodded. 'Easy to guard?'

'Yes, I fear so. Do you want a pistol, any weapon?'

'No. An unconscious man should present no problem, and otherwise I must rely on bluff.'

'I wish you luck,' the man said formally.

Something more than mere luck was needed, Hean thought, as he entered the hospital. His briefing had been detailed, but he had been able to make no preparations, other than to ensure that he carried no means of identification. It was shortly after eleven the same morning, and visiting hours for patients in private rooms had just commenced. There was nothing to distinguish him from other people who had come to see relatives or friends. He even carried a small bunch of flowers.

In the event, luck helped. Hean was standing, waiting for a lift, when he saw two men, deep in conversation, go through a door marked 'Private'. A minute later they emerged. Each was wearing a long white coat and one had a stethoscope round his neck. They were unmistakably doctors.

Hean seized his chance. He was ready to explain that he had mistaken the place for a toilet available to anyone, but fortunately this wasn't necessary. The small dressing-room was empty, and he saw what he wanted immediately. On a line of pegs hung a white coat, a stethoscope protruding from the pocket. When he emerged, the flowers abandoned, he too had become a doctor. And in a large hospital the presence of an unfamiliar face was unlikely to be remarked.

He entered the lift purposefully and got off at the third floor, where he strode along as if he owned the place. A pretty nurse smiled at him and he nodded a greeting. Then he saw a small procession approaching; he took it to be a specialist with senior

92

nurses and medical students in attendance. Hastily he turned aside to pick up one of the wall phones that were scattered at intervals along the corridor; he began to conduct an imaginary conversation.

The little procession passed without comment, but somehow the incident had unsettled Hean. He almost missed the side corridor he was seeking, and he had to make an effort of will to approach the room that he knew to be Dayton's. Not only was the number right, but the uniformed police officer seated outside was a final confirmation.

'*Guten tag.*'

The man came to attention. '*Guten tag, Herr Doktor.*'

Hean entered the room quickly. He expected Dayton to be alone, and at most semi-conscious. The actual killing should be simple. A quick blow across the throat to break his gullet, and the Englishman would die at once, and silently.

But as Hean shut the door behind him he realized that the reality was different. Only minutes before Keith Dayton had regained full consciousness, and for the first time he was holding something approaching a coherent conversation with his nurse. Brenner and Hean had been part of his recurrent nightmares, and he recognized Hean instantly. His eyes widened in terror. He opened his mouth and screamed. It was a high, thin, warning sound.

The nurse was also a fully-trained police officer, and her reactions were immediate. She swung round and, as Hean in three strides reached the bed, the hard edge of his hand raised to strike the fatal blow, she flung herself across her patient and chopped the killer's arm aside. Hean was taken by surprise. He had intended to silence Dayton, then deal with the woman, but she'd been too quick for him.

Out of the corner of his eye Hean saw her jab her thumb on a red button – a panic button. Behind him the guard burst into the room, pistol in hand. Hean knew he was beaten. His chance of killing Dayton was gone, and his one thought now must be of escape.

Without hesitation he charged the guard, catching the man off balance and knocking him to the floor. The gun went flying. Then he was out of the room, momentarily safe. The nurse, intent on protecting Dayton, had made no attempt to stop him.

Outside the door he paused fractionally. He had no hope of reaching the main corridor before the guard was after him, but a nearby bathroom offered at least temporary shelter. He reached it, he believed unseen, and shot the bolt. He could hear voices and running footsteps, but he paid them no attention. He made straight for the window and opened it.

Below, beyond a wide sill, was a sheer drop to a concrete path. Above there was nothing. To one side, however, was the iron grill-work of a fire escape. It looked a long way off, but Hean measured the distance with his eye and decided that a jump might be feasible. Carefully he climbed out of the window on to the sill. Fists began to pound on the bathroom door. A voice demanded to know who was inside. Hean jumped.

*

Casimir Sabik had failed to talk to Irena the evening before, but he telephoned early that morning. Irena was pleased to hear his voice, and guilty that he had had to learn the news of Keith from the television screen.

'I'm sorry, Cas,' she said. 'I should have called you at once, but we were so excited and Caro took me out to celebrate. Come and have lunch with me. I'll expect you about twelve-thirty. We'll drink to Keith.'

For the first time since the small hours of Friday when Keith had horrified her with his incomprehensible call from Germany, Irena was happy. Keith was alive and safe. Soon they would bring him home. He would explain that damned list of names, confront Dermot Piercey, and surely be able to clear himself of all those incredibly stupid accusations. Then, once he was well again, they would be able to go back to their ordinary, sane lives together.

Sabik arrived exactly on time, a bunch of roses in one hand, and two bottles of wine in a carrier bag in the other. He was worried, though he tried not to show it. Earlier, while he was doing his shopping, his suspicions that during the last few days he'd acquired a team of watchers had been confirmed. He guessed it was the British, but he wasn't sure. Anyway, he didn't like it.

He wiped the frown off his face as Irena opened the door and greeted her with a wide smile. 'Wonderful news about Keith, my dear,' he said as he kissed her. 'I'm so happy for you.'

'Thank you, Cas.' Irena took the roses that Sabik presented to her with a small formal bow, and led the way to the kitchen, where she put the flowers in water while he opened the wine. 'It *is* wonderful, isn't it? They're going to fly him home as soon as he's fit enough to stand the journey.'

As always she found Cas relaxing. The other evening when she had been so upset by Dermot Piercey and the search of the house, she had gone to him to pour out her troubles, and he had been infinitely kind. He'd asked no prying questions, but she'd told him everything – or almost everything. Mindful of Keith's words she hadn't mentioned – even to Cas – Keith's phone call, or the list of names she had been given.

Sabik poured two glasses of wine and offered one to Irena. Then, while he sat at the kitchen table, keeping their glasses filled, and she cooked their lunch, she told him about her last encounter with Dermot Piercey.

'I see,' said Cas slowly. 'But I still think it's dreadful they won't let you go to Keith. Surely they can't suspect you? You've cooperated with them. You've held nothing back. Or do they think you have?'

The last question was carefully thrown away, as if the mere suggestion were ludicrous, but Irena smiled wryly, and Sabik seized his opportunity. Suddenly serious, he said, 'You're not, are you? Holding something back from them, I mean? Are you in trouble, Irena? Because if so, you know you can rely on me. I may be old and stupid, but I'd do anything I can to help.'

'I know you would, Cas.' Irena was touched. She went to him and, bending over, kissed him on the cheek. Sabik patted her hand.

'Don't tell me if you'd rather not,' he said.

'There really isn't anything to tell, Cas. It's only – Well, Keith telephoned me after his accident. Of course at the time I didn't know he'd had an accident. He didn't explain. He just sounded ill and incoherent.'

'He phoned you? Somehow he got to a phone box? Oh, my dear! How terribly worrying for you.' Sabik hesitated, but it was an obvious question and it would be odd not to ask it. He shook his head in bewilderment. 'But I still don't understand. Why keep it secret from the authorities – from this man Piercey and the Foreign Office people? And even from me?'

'Because . . .' Irena stopped and shrugged, irritated with herself. She really hadn't meant to tell Cas about Keith's call, but he'd been so kind, so sympathetic – and somehow it had slipped out. Now she'd have to tell him more, but perhaps it didn't matter with Keith coming home. Anyway, she couldn't think of an adequate lie. 'Keith told me not to mention it to anyone. He said he'd deal with the problem – whatever it is – when he got back. He just wanted me to take down a list of names. I think he knew he was badly hurt and was afraid he might forget them.'

Sabik poured himself some more wine. His hand shook and some drops spilt on the table. He mopped them up quickly with his handkerchief. He had no idea of the significance of what he had just heard, but he thought – guessed – that it could be of immense importance. He waited for Irena to continue. When the silence lengthened, he said carefully, 'And this list he gave you? You've kept it?'

In spite of his care he may have spoken too sharply, too curiously. Irena, though she couldn't have explained why, was regretting her confidences. She had no intention of showing Cas the list.

'No. He never managed to give it to me,' Irena said. 'He started to. He mentioned John Rossel's name, and Hector Coyne's, and what could have been Peter Mayberry. He was in a bad way. I could hardly hear him. To be honest, I'm not even sure he knew himself what he was saying or doing. Poor Keith.' Memory overwhelmed her and she was silent.

'No one else? No other names?'

'No. No. Come on, Cas. Lunch is ready. Let's eat.' Irena became nervously energetic. 'It must be something to do with the firm – with Rossel's, but I don't know what. Anyway, Keith will be home soon, I hope, and he'll explain everything.'

'Of course, my dear. Of course. Let's hope it's very soon.' Sabik stood up. He knew he would learn no more now. He put an arm round Irena's shoulders and gave her a brief hug. 'What can I do? Lay the table?'

During the meal they talked of their shared homeland, of the Poland they had known and the Poland of today, of Lech Walesa and Solidarity, of the conflicting powers of State and Church. As always it brought them closer to each other. Nevertheless, Sabik left early, pleading that he had promised to visit an old compatriot for a game of chess.

Sabik walked for some distance after he left the Daytons' house, and he soon spotted the dark blue Ford that was now following him. He knew at least one man would be ready to jump out and trail him on foot. He also knew his tradecraft was adequate and he could lose them, but it might be obvious and time could be important; he'd already wasted enough. He decided to play the innocent.

He caught a bus that took him down the hill to Hampstead Village and went into the Post Office. There were three telephone booths, all of them occupied, but as he approached a girl came out of one at the end, holding the door back for him. He thanked her and went in. In the next booth he could see through the glass an elderly lady, talking volubly. He dialled his emergency number.

He watched the door of the Post Office, and he was soon rewarded. A couple came in. They were followed by a woman with two children, and then a man. The man looked about him before walking to the shelves holding a collection of telephone directories. He took one down and began to rifle through the pages. It was so obvious as to be laughable, thought Sabik.

Having located his watcher, Sabik turned his back. His number had answered. He identified himself and spoke rapidly. He told the man at the end of the line everything Irena had said.

'And you are sure,' he was asked, 'that all she knows is just those three names – Rossel, Coyne and possibly Mayberry – and she believes the list has something to do with her husband's business? And that she's told no one but you about the matter?'

'Absolutely sure,' Sabik said, unaware that by this positive assertion he was saving Irena's life.

TEN

'I understand,' Brenner said. 'I'm to forget the previous order. For the moment the client has lost interest in the pictures you marked before. In their place he wants action on numbers seven and nine.'

'That's correct. Rapid action.'

'Yes.' Brenner hesitated. He had no wish to mention names, but he must avoid any error. 'Numbers seven and nine,' he repeated. 'That is "R" and "C"?'

'Right. And I regret to say you'll have no help. The assistant we hoped to provide for you won't be available.'

Brenner yearned to ask why Hean wouldn't be available. Had something gone wrong with Hean's attempt to eliminate Dayton? Had Hean been captured, killed? Brenner knew he was guessing. He wasn't even certain that it was Hean who'd been assigned to the completion of the task they'd failed to accomplish together. Without warning he shivered, suddenly cold. It wasn't as if Hean had been a close friend – you didn't have friends in this business – but he'd been a good, competent, reliable partner. Sharply he concentrated on the telephone conversation, realizing that he had already been thinking of Hean in the past tense.

'I'm sorry about that,' he said steadily. 'These two pictures – is there any question of priority?'

'No. Whatever's convenient for you. But speed is essential, before the news gets round and they become . . .' The Cultural Attaché gritted his teeth; he wondered how dependable Brenner was, and what difficulties might arise if the Brits succeeded in having a straight talk with Dayton. 'These two could, as far as we're concerned, become – unbuyable. They could disappear from the market.'

Brenner interpreted the Cultural Attaché's carefully chosen words. He knew nothing of Casimir Sabik, but he understood

98

that the British had been warned, and that would complicate the problem. The operation was becoming more and more complex.

'Only those two?' he said.

'A possible third. But let us hope that won't concern you.'

Brenner didn't query this enigmatic answer; he was used to taking orders. 'How long do I have?' he said finally.

'Let me see. Today is Friday. Shall we say, within a week? You're the expert and I leave it to you. But I would suggest the sooner the better.'

'I understand,' said Brenner again. 'Thank you.' But, he thought, two assassinations within a week were too much. Either they were growing desperate at home, or they'd decided he was expendable. He sighed. 'I'll get on to them right away,' he promised.

★

General Sir Christopher Weatherby smiled his satisfaction. The affair was progressing. The pieces were beginning to fit together, though much depended upon what Dayton could tell them.

'Of course Fenton's had to play it carefully,' Weatherby said to Piercey and Farling who were sharing his mid-morning coffee. 'He's only been able to pay a couple of visits to the hospital – and then to make arrangements for the ambulance flight rather than to visit Dayton. And when he did see him there were others in the room, and naturally he didn't mention the word "list", in case Dayton responded with a flood of information we'd prefer to keep quiet. He finds it hard to judge whether the man's still too ill to talk sense, or whether he's playing for time; he thinks probably the latter. Anyway, between us we've achieved the important thing. Dayton's being flown back tomorrow, as I told you.'

'I take it I'm to conduct the interrogation, sir,' said Piercey. 'When and where?'

'Not immediately, I think. He's arriving in the afternoon, and he'll be met by ambulance and taken directly to our safe house in Kent. Everything's laid on for him there – doctors, nurses and so on. He'll have the best of care, and we can get our tame

99

consultants in if necessary. We don't want him dying on us.'

Farling grinned, but the General had been serious. 'If he's worth killing to stop him talking – and that attempt in the hospital was a desperate throw – then he's worth preserving so that we can listen. But, to answer your question, Dermot, yes. I'd like you to take charge of the interrogation. Talk to him alone first. A friendly chat. Start by assuming he's perfectly innocent. No hint of what we've found. And I should wait till Sunday morning, after he's had a good night's sleep.'

'Right, sir. So his wife and the daughter are to be kept away from him. Are they to be told he's back in the UK?'

'Not at the moment.' The General bit carefully into a biscuit. 'We'll wait and see what Dayton's got to say.'

Farling said, 'Judging by Irena's past form, if she knew where he was she'd dash off to see Sabik, and there'd be another attack.'

'We don't know she – ' Piercey began.

Weatherby interrupted. 'That attempt on Dayton's life in the hospital was something of a blessing, especially as the attacker managed to kill himself by falling out of that bathroom window. It finally decided Herr Wetzel to let us have Dayton before he found he'd got more bodies on his hands. Mind you, we'll have to keep the Germans informed, and we'll owe them a favour. They'll remind us of it sometime. Meanwhile, we all stick to the story that Keith Dayton was an innocent businessman who one unhappy night got himself involved with some villains. Since he can identify them, they've had every reason to try to eliminate him.'

Both Piercey and Farling were already fully briefed on the case, but Weatherby liked to expound and his two subordinates listened dutifully. Piercey found his thoughts wandering to Caro Dayton as they so often seemed to do nowadays. Farling was deciding that, in Weatherby's place, he'd pull in both Irena Dayton and Casimir Sabik and keep after them till they talked, and he wouldn't waste any time about it either.

The General continued, 'It's unfortunate, but I'll be in the country this weekend – a long-promised visit.' He mentioned the name of one of England's great houses. 'There's no way I can cancel it. Royalty'll be there, and anyway my wife would never forgive me.'

'We can reach you if necessary, sir?'

'Of course. Miss Sherwood will give you the details. But only in a real emergency. You'll have to use your judgement. Otherwise I'll expect a report on Dayton first thing on Monday morning. All right?'

'Yes, sir,' Piercey said, and hoped there would be no crisis over the weekend.

★

It was the evening of the same Friday and Hector Coyne was giving a small dinner party at his London flat in Wilton Mansions not far from the House of Commons. On such occasions he employed a caterer who produced food that merely needed re-heating, and a butler to serve it. He saw to the wines himself.

Although she knew there would be nothing for her to do Caroline arrived more than half an hour early. She let herself into the flat with her key, and called Hector's name. When there was no answer she went into the sitting-room.

Sprawled in an armchair was a young man she had never seen before. He was about thirty, a tall and solid-looking individual who might have been a boxer. But his face with its baby-like expression was unmarked and long fair hair curled to his shoulders. He wore jeans and a T-shirt.

'Hi!' he said. 'You must be Caro.' He made no effort to stand up.

Caroline regarded him coldly. 'I'm Caroline Dayton, yes. Who are you?'

'Steve.' He grinned at her knowingly.

At that point Coyne came into the room, already in his dinner jacket, and with a thick manilla envelope in his hand. He seemed disconcerted at the sight of Caroline. 'I didn't hear you arrive,' he said.

To Caroline it sounded like a reproach. She shrugged. The tension in the air made it clear that she'd interrupted something, though what she couldn't imagine. She couldn't think what Hector and this man Steve could have in common.

Steve rose to his feet and Coyne held out the envelope to him. 'Here you are. This should be all the material you need.'

'Ta. I'll say goodbye then.'

Steve nodded to Caroline and made for the door. Coyne followed him. Caroline could hear them murmuring in the hall, but could distinguish no words. It was several minutes before Coyne returned.

'Who on earth was that?' she said.

'A reporter.' Coyne adjusted one of the studs on his evening shirt.

'A reporter? For what paper?'

'Freelance. He writes acid, gossipy columns about people. Not a very nice character, I agree, darling.' Hector Coyne made an apologetic gesture. 'But we've got to keep in with the media, especially now in the midst of your Dad's rather dubious activities.'

Caroline drew a deep breath. 'He doesn't look as if he'd know a noun from a verb,' she said, and in her own mind at once contradicted herself. There was nothing stupid about that young man. He was astute, arrogant and somehow frightening. She glared at Coyne. 'What the hell do you mean about Dad's "dubious activities"?' she demanded.

'Caro, my dear . . .' Coyne began.

The doorbell saved him. The caterers had arrived. The butler organized the food as it was delivered, but it required Coyne's hovering presence, and there was no opportunity for private conversation between himself and Caroline. He prolonged the domestic details until the doorbell rang again and his first guests appeared. Thankfully he welcomed them.

They were a couple whom Caroline had never met before, though she knew the man well by sight. He was a television personality who was seen frequently on the more intellectual panels and chat shows, airing his views on matters of the day. Politically he was known to be ultra right wing, and Caroline remembered that Keith, after watching one of his appearances in disgust, had once called him 'a fascist thug'.

The Mayberrys came next, followed immediately by a history professor from London University and his pregnant wife, also previously unknown to Caroline. John Rossel and a woman gossip columnist completed the party.

Rossel greeted Caroline warmly. 'So glad your Dad's surfaced again,' he said. 'We were getting quite scared in case he'd scarpered off to Mother Russia with all the firm's assets.'

There was some mild laughter at this, in which Caroline did not join. Suddenly she felt an – an outsider, which was absurd, considering that they were in Hector's flat, and her mother was here, and her step-father. The others weren't important, but they all knew each other and were clearly at home. The television man had found an ashtray for himself. The woman columnist – who was older than she looked – had rather inappropriately curled up kittenishly in a corner of the sofa. The history professor had fetched a footstool for his wife.

He said to Caroline, 'That's the worst of having a reputation, isn't it?'

'I don't know what you mean.'

'Keith – your father – he's something of a Red,' the TV character remarked.

'A communist? He most certainly is not.' Caroline felt her temper rise. She knew that the incident with the reporter, Steve, had affected her mood, and she forced herself to speak lightly. 'Whatever made you think he might be?'

'Oh, I'm told it's common knowledge.'

'Then you're misinformed,' Caroline said shortly, no longer caring if she sounded brusque. The two men seemed to be deliberately provoking her. She looked at Hector for support, but he was busy pouring drinks. 'My father's never been particularly interested in politics.'

Patricia said, 'When he was married to me he used to vote Liberal. I could never make him change his mind.'

'What an admission!' Peter Mayberry laughed.

The pregnant woman said, 'I hope you don't hold left-wing views, Caroline. It would make things so difficult for Hector.'

'Of course she doesn't.' Hector had joined them, unusually hearty. 'You don't think I'd pick a girl who wasn't true blue, do you?'

This time the laughter was louder. Hector put his arm around Caroline's shoulders and drew her close to him. It could have been a signal to the others to stop baiting her, because at once they began to talk of other things: the latest West End play, England's prospects in the next test match, the 'Britain First' rally planned for the coming Sunday, the big Jewish wedding that was to take place on Sunday week – the small change of social gossip, interlaced with politics.

Caroline found herself with little to say. She was still seething with anger, and she was glad when they went in to dinner. Hector had put her at the end of the table as if she were already his wife. She had the historian on her right and John Rossel on her left, but they were prepared to talk across her and her silence wasn't noticed. She ate little and drank less.

It was the gossip columnist who brought up the subject of violence, and the conversation became general. The police should be better armed and properly equipped. The courts should impose stiffer sentences, and when the culprits went to prison they should be made to regret every single day of it. As it was, no one was safe. Assaults, burglaries, muggings, car thefts, pointless violence – the UK was becoming impossible.

'It's the damned foreigners who start all the trouble,' someone said.

'Why blame foreigners? This country's owed a lot to foreigners in the past,' Caroline protested in a sudden burst of irritation.

'Only Europeans, and the people you're talking about were well-educated and well off when they came.'

'And that made them okay? I've never in my life heard such utter rubbish!'

There was a sudden bleak silence broken by Patricia Mayberry pushing back her chair. 'Caroline, don't you think it's time we went to powder our noses and let the men get on with their port?' She rose, and, letting the others go ahead of her, she took Caroline by the arm. It looked like a friendly gesture, but as they left the room together her fingers tightened their grip until Caroline winced. 'For God's sake stop playing the fool!' Patricia hissed. 'Hector'll be furious.'

Caroline glared at her but made no reply, and Patricia released her grasp. The other women were already in the bedroom and Caroline was the last to visit the adjoining bathroom. As she was shutting the door, she heard her mother say, 'It's the influence of that wretched Pole, I'm afraid. Once she's married to Hector –'

The click of the latch cut Patricia off. Caroline leant against the wash basin, almost sick with annoyance and anger. She had no quarrel with much of what had been said at dinner – indeed, who could be in favour of violence? – but she hated nationalist prejudice and arrogance and the assumptions of superiority. She didn't understand how these people whom she instinctively disliked could be such close friends of Hector's. And if they were close friends of his, why hadn't she met them before? As for Patricia, apologizing on her behalf – that was just damned cheek!

Caroline took her time, waiting until she was sure everyone was in the sitting-room. She joined them as the butler was offering coffee and liqueurs. Peter Mayberry smiled at her and patted the sofa beside him. She sat, accepted some coffee and asked for a cognac. The rest of the evening passed pleasantly enough, though she failed to enjoy it.

The party broke up comparatively early, and Caroline was thankful to see it end. She waited for Hector to shut the front door behind Rossel and the columnist, the last of the guests to leave. It had been agreed beforehand that she would spend the night there, but now she had no wish to stay and she wondered how to tell Hector this tactfully.

Coyne gave her no chance to speak. Returning to the sitting-room with long angry strides he poured himself a nightcap and swung round towards her. 'Well, you made a fine show of yourself tonight – and of me! Why?'

Caroline was shocked. 'I don't know what you mean.'

'Don't you?' Coyne said roughly. 'Then you're more stupid than I thought. Those were my friends, especially invited here to meet you. You may not like them. In fact, you made it clear you didn't. But you didn't have to be so bloody rude to them.'

'They weren't particularly nice to me.'

'Who can blame them?' Coyne swallowed half his drink. He hadn't asked Caroline if she would like any. 'Don't you realize how much we need friends at the moment? Your father mightn't have defected, but he's still highly suspect. Oh, sure, with luck there'll be a great big cover-up, but that won't stop the gossip – and gossip can do a hell of a lot of harm to someone like me. What friends in the right places can do is temper the gossip – stress the fact that you're not involved, that you're Lady Mayberry's daughter, that Keith Dayton means nothing to you.'

'But that's not true! I love Keith. I always have, far more

than I ever loved Patricia. He's been a wonderful father to me.'
Caroline was furious. 'I'm damned if I'll turn my back on him
now he's in trouble. Anyway, it'll probably all get straightened
out once he's better and able to explain what happened.'

'The more reason for not flaunting your wretched left-wing
views in front of my friends, then. Couldn't you think of me?'

'That's just what I am doing, Hector. Thinking. Hard,' Caroline said. 'And I don't think I want to marry you.' She pulled off
her engagement ring and put it down on a side table. 'Patricia
will cope with the details of cancelling the wedding, returning
the presents and all that. I'm sure she'll make certain everything's done correctly and quietly. You won't have to worry.'

'Caro – don't be silly. I don't want . . .'

For a while longer they argued. Coyne admitted that he'd
been hasty, apologized, said he loved her. He tried to restrain
her, to persuade her to stay, but finally, when she insisted, he
let her go. 'But I'm not taking this as your last word,' he said
as he opened the front door of the flat. 'Think it over.' He
didn't offer to see her to her car.

The Wilton Mansions car park, including a few spaces for
visitors, was directly behind the block of flats. There were only
a few lamps, but Caroline wasn't a nervous girl, and the moon
in its third quarter gave a fair amount of light. Her mind still
occupied with her quarrel with Hector, she reached her car,
got in and started the engine. It was then that she saw the
figure of a man slip from one shadow to another. She locked
the car doors from inside and sat, watching, waiting.

After a minute or two, when he had failed to reappear, she
thought she must have missed him, but she knew she hadn't
been mistaken. She had seen a man near the space allotted to
Hector's car. It was late for a visitor to the flats, but it might
conceivably have been someone who lived there. Admittedly
there had been a vague impression of furtiveness about the
man's behaviour, but she could easily have imagined that.

She debated going to find the night porter, then decided
against it. If a thief stole Hector's Jaguar she didn't really
mind. She switched on her lights and drove out of the car
park. Manfred Brenner watched her go.

ELEVEN

Hector Coyne woke late the next morning, having unwillingly spent the night alone. He was not in the best of tempers, especially when he realized that he had been roused by the persistent ringing of his front doorbell. Reluctantly he scrambled out of bed, pulled on a gown and went to answer it. 'Coming! Coming!' he called irritably as he padded barefoot into the hall. 'Who is it?'

'It's me, sir. Hodgson,' came the reply.

Hodgson was the day porter. Still bleary with sleep, Coyne struggled with the over-elaborate locks and at last got the door open. 'Yes,' he said. 'What is it?'

'Sorry to bother you, sir, but . . .' The porter was willing, but not always tactful. He eyed Coyne dubiously. 'I thought you'd be up by now, sir.'

'I am up,' snapped Coyne. 'What's the matter?'

'Yes, sir, but I meant dressed, like – and it's your car.'

'What's the matter with my car?'

'Nothing, sir. I was just going to ask you if you'd mind moving it. You see there are new people coming into Number 9, and your car and Mr Meier's are making it a bit awkward for the furniture van.'

Coyne drew a deep breath. It was true that there was little room for manoeuvring by the service entrance in the car park, and one had to be neighbourly, but it was a damn nuisance to have to put on clothes and go out. Besides – he rubbed a hand over his chin – he hated appearing in public badly groomed. Depending on who his new neighbours were to be, someone from one of the papers could easily be around, hoping for a snatched interview or a candid photograph. That was one of the disadvantages of living in a well-known block of this kind.

The porter solved his problem. 'If you'd like to give me the keys, sir, I'll move the Jaguar for you.'

'Oh, all right.' Coyne eyed the man. 'But mind you take care. I don't want any scratches. I've only had the car a couple of months.'

'I can drive, sir.' The porter grinned.

'I hope so.' Coyne fetched the keys and handed them over, then went into the kitchen. He put on water for coffee, and bread in the toaster. He collected some orange juice from the refrigerator and, glass in hand, strolled to the kitchen window – the one that overlooked the car park. Below was a great deal of activity – much of it meaningless, Coyne thought.

A tall, thin man, whom Coyne guessed to be his new neighbour, was waving his arms in an effort to direct the movements of a large removal van. The driver was leaning from his cab, apparently protesting that he couldn't turn in such a small place. Another removal man was standing beside Bernard Meier's car – also a Jaguar – talking to Meier who was sitting behind the wheel. He had started the engine – Coyne could see the smoke from the exhaust – but hadn't attempted to move yet.

Hodgson, the porter, came running, holding up the keys of Coyne's Jaguar. There was some discussion as to who should shift first, and where. Then Hodgson opened the door of Coyne's car and slid into the driving seat.

'Now, careful!' Coyne said aloud, though Hodgson was much too far away to hear him.

Regretting that he hadn't gone down himself, Coyne watched as his car began to edge from its place. Meier's car had begun to move too. Someone shouted a warning and Coyne winced. Behind him the kettle whistled shrilly.

Coyne turned, so that afterwards he was unable to say exactly what happened next. But he heard the thump of the exploding bomb and, though he was on the third storey up, thought he felt the floor shake under him. The glass in his kitchen window – the one that overlooked the car park – cracked.

In two strides Coyne was throwing the window open, leaning out. Below him were smoke and flames and a tangled mass of metal. Bodies lay in unnatural attitudes. As Coyne watched, stunned with horror, the furniture van, hovering on two wheels, slowly toppled on to its side. Someone started to scream.

Coyne's first reactions were routine. He ran for the phone and dialled '999'. When he got the police he gave his name and address and his credentials, and he reported clearly and precisely what he believed had happened. His voice was steady. He didn't start to shake until he had put down the receiver. Who, he asked himself, would want to kill him? Or had the bomb been in Meier's car?

He ran into the dining-room, poured himself two ounces of brandy and swallowed it neat. It made him gasp and choke, but it restored his nerve. The questions could wait; he foresaw a lot of them in a few minutes. Meanwhile there were people outside, almost certainly injured, if not dead.

He returned to the kitchen, turning off the furiously boiling kettle as he passed, and went back to the window. Help, he saw, had already arrived, in the shape of other occupants of the flats. A police car was driving in, and the wail of sirens was growing louder. For the moment he wasn't needed.

Hurriedly Coyne made himself a cup of instant coffee and took it into the bathroom. He drank the scalding liquid before he showered and shaved. He was pulling a sweater over his head ready to go down, when the doorbell rang for the second time that morning.

The Detective Superintendent introduced himself and his sergeant. They were insignificant-looking men in inexpensive suits, but Coyne didn't underrate them. Anti-terrorist officers, he guessed, or perhaps Special Branch. They would be polite but persistent. He greeted them affably and took them into the sitting-room.

'You were one of the first to report the incident, sir. And it looks as if your car was the target. Would you be good enough to tell us what you know?'

'My car, was it? How many casualties were there?' Coyne's reply was nicely calculated.

'You've not been down?'

'I was on my way now. I could see from my window I wasn't needed to help immediately,' Coyne said, though he felt this to be an inadequate response.

So perhaps did the Superintendent, for he didn't wait for Coyne to comment further. 'I expect you were shaken, sir. After all, it might well have been you in the car, and not Mr Hodgson.' He went on without pause, 'You were asking about casualties. The porter was killed outright, and one of the removal men. Mr Jackson, the gentleman moving into the flats, is seriously hurt, and so is Mr Meier. Others are suffering from shock and cuts – the windows nearby were all shattered, but these are mostly just minor injuries. Everyone was very lucky. Now we have to discover who did it.'

'Ghastly!' said Coyne. 'I'll help all I can, but I don't think I know that much.' Coyne told them what he had seen. He admitted there were people who disliked him, and who might bear him a grudge, imagined or otherwise, but this would apply to any Member of Parliament, of the Government. There was no particular reason for him to be singled out. He'd never been concerned with Northern Ireland, for instance. His field, as a Parliamentary Under Secretary in the Department of Trade, was mainly economic, though naturally in his constituency he dealt with a variety of matters.

'Of course it remains a possibility that Mr Meier was the intended victim, sir.' The Superintendent was suave. 'Your cars are similar and a mistake could have been made. Was Mr Meier a friend of yours?'

'No. I scarcely knew him. Just enough to say "Good morning", "Nice day" – that sort of thing.'

'There was that attack last Tuesday on Mr Kaufmann outside Rabbi Richler's house. I suppose there could be a connection.' The Superintendent sounded as if he were talking to himself.

Coyne stared. He was aware of the two police officers regarding him with interest, but momentarily his mind was a blank. 'Connection?' he said foolishly.

'They were both Jewish, sir. You knew Mr Meier was Jewish, didn't you?'

'No. Yes. I mean I never really thought about it. If I had, I suppose I'd have realized it. So – yes. But I doubt if he was a practising one. I've seen him washing his car on a Saturday – if that means anything.'

Coyne stopped abruptly. He was talking too much. He bit

the tip of his tongue to remind himself to shut up, and he tried to relax.

In any case, that was the end of the interview. Later a statement would have to be signed and, when experts had examined the scene and the wreckage, doubtless there would be yet more questions. But for the present the police were content to leave him. Coyne saw them out with relief.

Now, he told himself, he must be practical. He must contact his insurance agent, arrange for the garage to loan or rent him a car, prepare a statement for the media who would soon be clamouring. He must see if there was anything he could do to help Mrs Meier or the unknown Jacksons or, especially, the family of the unfortunate Hodgson. But, first, he must talk to Peter Mayberry.

*

Caroline heard nothing about the bomb until the late afternoon. Unlike Hector Coyne she had woken early. She had a mental picture of Hector and her mother each arriving on her doorstep, the one importunate, the other irate. She was eager to avoid either of them, so she took her car and left the flat. She drove into the country and spent the day walking over the Sussex downs.

She arrived back in London, wind-blown and physically refreshed, but with her problem still unresolved. Did she or did she not want to marry Hector Coyne? Strange as it seemed, she felt she had never before seriously considered the question.

Because of his connections with the Mayberrys she had known Hector since she was a child. Over the years she had continued to meet him, casually and infrequently. But about eighteen months ago he had begun to take a real interest in her and naturally she'd been flattered by this unexpected attention. Beside him, her usual boyfriends had seemed gauche and undesirable. Hector dined and wined her at small, select restaurants, took her to parties, sent her flowers, produced unobtainable tickets for whatever she suggested. And, for his part, the one thing he didn't suggest was that they should hop into bed right after their first evening together: it was several months before they became lovers.

Then suddenly, seemingly without any actual declaration, she found herself engaged to him. Everyone was delighted. A date was set for the wedding, and she accepted what her family and friends told her – that she was lucky to be marrying someone like Hector Coyne. But was she, Caroline asked herself, as she tramped over the springy turf? Would she be happy as his wife? The question was still unanswered when she arrived home.

She parked her car and went into the main house. Caroline heard the television in the sitting-room as she went along the hall. It sounded like the news, but before she reached the room Irena had switched the set off.

'Irena, I'm sorry. I didn't mean to disturb you.'

'You're not disturbing me. I couldn't be more glad to see you. You've been out all day?'

Irena's voice sounded faintly accusing, and Caroline stared at her. 'Yes. I went into the country. But did you need me? Have you been trying to get hold of me?'

Irena nodded. It was hard to know where to begin. She had first learnt of the bomb attack that morning, when Patricia had telephoned, her call closely followed by one from Hector himself, seeking Caroline. Since then she had watched the news, listened to the radio, even gone out to buy an evening paper. Clearly Caro had heard nothing of the outrage.

'Irena, what is it? Is it Dad? He's not . . .'

'No. There's been nothing more about Keith. I don't think there will be till Monday. Mr Piercey and his friends wouldn't want to interrupt their weekend.' Irena was bitter. 'Caro, it's Hector. He's all right, but . . .' She told the girl what she knew.

Caroline shook her head in hopeless bewilderment. She didn't know what to say, what to do. She would have been distressed if a mere casual acquaintance had been involved in such a horrifying experience. Because it was Hector she would have expected her distress to be multiplied many times. In fact, she felt nothing but a vague sense of guilt.

She said, 'Are they sure it was meant for Hector? Why not

this Mr Meier? He was parked beside Hector, you say, and he drives a Jag too.'

'According to the man on television the police say the thing was under Hector's car.'

'But whoever did it might have made a mistake. Remember that poor Mr Kaufmann.' Unknowingly, Caroline was echoing the Detective Superintendent's words.

'Yes, I suppose it might have been a mistake,' Irena said hopefully. 'Anyway, he's unhurt, Caro. You must try not to worry about it.'

'I shan't!' Abruptly she added, 'We had a row last night and I broke off our engagement.'

Irena was practical and sympathetic. She produced a bottle of white wine and listened to what Caroline had to say, but she was unwilling to give advice. 'I was lucky myself,' she said. 'With Keith, I had no doubts. I knew he was for me. I'd have hoped, Caro, that you'd feel the same about whoever you planned to marry. But it's for you to decide.'

Caroline nodded, though she had scarcely heard Irena's last few words. Recalling how she had marched out of Hector's flat and sat in the car park controlling her anger, she remembered the shadowy figure she'd seen near Hector's car. If only, she thought – if only she'd reported it to the night porter, then perhaps . . . 'I must go and see Hector,' she said.

*

Brenner yearned to punch the smooth, pink face with its unctuous expression that was mouthing words at him from the television set in his hotel room. The words, as well as the face, made Brenner want to vomit.

'. . . monster who could perpetrate such an act. I voted for the restoration of hanging at the last Parliamentary free vote. I would do the same again, especially for crimes of pure terrorism like this abomination . . .'

Brenner shook his fist helplessly at the screen. He wasn't a monster; in his own mind he wasn't even a terrorist. Certainly he committed acts that could be judged illegal, but there was no way he could consider himself a criminal. What he did, he

113

did for good reasons and under orders. He was paid, but only minimally, and in return he risked not only long terms of imprisonment but in some countries torture and death. He thought of Hean.

'. . . have just received the tragic news that Mr Meier has died in hospital without regaining consciousness. He leaves a widow and two children, still in their teens. To say that I share their horror and grief would be presumptuous of me, but I have no hesitation in stating that . . .'

Brenner could bear it no longer. He switched off the set, tears of rage running down his cheeks. 'Liar! Hypocrite! Pig!' he screamed soundlessly.

If Hean had been with him it would never have happened. Hean was the explosives expert. Hean would have used precisely the right amount, so that just Coyne's car would have been demolished. It was the lack of Hean's expertise that had resulted in the devastation and so many unnecessary tragedies.

Brenner accepted his responsibility. He had been afraid of crippling Coyne without killing him. As it was, through the merest chance, the man was unscathed and, because of his escape, attention was being showered on him. But not for long, Brenner swore. The next time he would take every care – and every risk – to ensure that Hector Coyne and only Hector Coyne would die.

*

Later that day Keith Dayton woke. It seemed to him that he had been drifting in and out of consciousness for hours. Now, for the first time, he was fully aware. He opened his eyes carefully.

He was in different surroundings; he was sure of that, at least. The furnishings and decorations were pleasant, with a large picture on one wall. The whole room gave the impression of being considerably less institutionalized than the last, but he assumed that he was still in some kind of hospital or nursing home. He could see a chart hanging on the bottom rail of the high narrow bed, and above his head a bottle, attached by a tube to a wide plaster on the back of his hand, was presumably

114

feeding him – or treating him, or drugging him – intravenously. His hand was sore.

He moved his head slowly from one side to the other until he was satisfied that for the moment he was alone. This was new. Usually, in his previous periods of consciousness, he had known there was a nurse close by, busying herself with him and his needs, or merely sitting and watching him.

Gently he raised himself. The bed had been arranged so that he could look out of the window, and the curtains hadn't yet been drawn. He could see sky and trees, and the top of an old stone wall. No roofs. No sounds of traffic. No sounds at all. No sense of subdued bustle and hustle in the building itself.

Clearly he was in the country as opposed to the town, and possibly in some private clinic. He tried to remember how he had been moved, and unexpectedly there came to him the picture of an aircraft taking off. He dismissed it as part of a dream, but he wondered if he were still in Germany – and if so in which part.

The door opened suddenly and a nurse came in. Dayton caught a glimpse of her blue and white uniform before he closed his eyes. She stood by the bed, looking down on him, and he made himself breathe steadily and lightly. He would trust no one at present. If he could become stronger and more clear-headed without them – whoever they were – suspecting any improvement, so much the better.

The nurse moved away and he heard the sigh of a cushion as she sat down. His mind wandered. He thought of Irena and remembered the last time he had spoken to her, but the memory was dim. He was aware of pain – pain, and that damned list of names and his inability to make Irena understand what she should do.

He thought of Dermot Piercey. Had Piercey got the list or not? And there were the other things – things that would have to be confessed. All he had revealed had been forced from him, but he was still ashamed. Suddenly, without warning, nightmare pictures began to chase themselves through his mind and he groaned aloud.

Immediately the nurse was beside him, bending over him, but soon he was quiet. For a little he slept. When he woke again he could hear soft music. Slowly and without moving his head he slitted his eyes and saw that the nurse had a transistor radio on the table by her. He listened with pleasure and began to doze.

He was startled by chimes – chimes well-known to him, those of Big Ben. Then, as a deep bell note faded into the background, a voice said, 'Six o'clock. BBC news. Good evening. This is James Shelton. This morning another apparently motiveless outrage occurred in London. A device attached to the car of Mr Hector Coyne, Parliamentary Under Secretary at the Department of Trade, exploded in the parking area of the block of flats in which he resides. Mr Coyne himself was unhurt but there were three deaths and a number of serious injuries. The dead have been identified as Mr Bernard Meier, whose car was parked next to Mr Coyne's, Mr John Hodgson, a porter at the block, who was moving Mr Coyne's car, and Mr George Yonge, an employee of a firm of furniture removers. No group has yet claimed responsibility . . .'

'No! No!' Involuntarily Dayton protested, attempting to sit up in bed.

Instantly the nurse turned off the radio and came to him. Pushing him gently back against his pillow, she said, 'It's all right, Mr Dayton. You're quite safe here. Quite safe.'

'Hector!' Dayton said hoarsely. 'And his name was on that –' He stopped. He told himself he must be careful. 'Who are you?' he demanded.

'I'm Nurse Benson, Mr Dayton. You've not seen me before because you've not been here long.'

'Where's here?'

'In England. In Kent, not far from Tunbridge Wells. You were flown home early today in an air ambulance. You were sedated for the journey so you probably don't remember much about it.'

There was a tap at the door and another nurse came in. Nurse Benson, Dayton thought, must have summoned assistance. He watched her murmuring instructions to the younger girl. Benson herself was in her forties, a plain thin-lipped woman with an air of authority and competence. She had spoken perfect English, but he had no intention of trusting her yet.

116

When she returned to his bedside, he said, 'Where do you come from, Nurse?'

'You mean originally? From Oxford, Mr Dayton.'

'You know the Mitre?'

'I know where it used to be. On the High.'

'And you used to go punting – along the Backs?'

'Mr Dayton, the Backs are in Cambridge.' Nurse Benson laughed. Her face lit with amusement, and she looked a quite different woman. She patted Dayton on the shoulder. 'You're home, Mr Dayton. In England. Believe me.'

Keith Dayton smiled wanly. Certainly he wanted to believe her, and his clumsy attempts to catch her out had failed. For the moment he would have to accept the situation. The effort he had already made had tired him to the point of exhaustion. He let the nurse change the bottle above his head and make him more comfortable. He swallowed the pills which her younger colleague brought and closed his eyes. He thought of Hector Coyne and wondered about the others on the list, the few of them whose names he could recall. Soon he slept.

TWELVE

An unmarked official car collected Ian Farling and then Dermot Piercey from their homes. It was early on Sunday morning and, as if by unspoken agreement, they exchanged no more than the briefest of greetings. Nor did they talk as the miles passed, though they were sitting together in the back. Piercey feigned sleep, and Farling stared out of the window.

Their driver, separated from them by a pane of double glass, paid them no attention. He listened to the cassette he had switched on as soon as he was out of central London, and drove purposefully and relentlessly. He was old enough to be the father of either of his passengers and he knew his job. He delivered them at the safe house five minutes ahead of time.

They were greeted by the operative in charge of the safe house, one Bill Gaunt, who found the doctor for them. The doctor was less welcoming. 'Pity you had to come down today,' he commented. 'You might have asked my advice. If you'd waited till tomorrow he'd have been a good deal more rested – and useful to you.'

'We don't work Sundays from choice,' said Piercey shortly. He had been disturbed by the news of the attack on Hector Coyne. He suspected that it might be connected with Dayton, though he couldn't imagine how, and he was afraid that if a second attempt on Coyne's life was made, Caroline might be involved. 'How *is* the patient?'

'I suppose he's better than expected,' the doctor admitted reluctantly. 'He bore the journey quite well and he's had a reasonable night's sleep.'

'Fine.' Piercey was still curt.

'But that doesn't mean he can stand a great deal,' the doctor cautioned. 'He's still very weak. Go gently. Take things in easy stages.'

'Right.' Piercey made no promises. He merely glanced from

the doctor to Gaunt. 'It's the usual set-up, I suppose. Perhaps you'd show us the way.'

Gaunt led them upstairs and into the room next to Dayton's. There were a couple of racks of sophisticated tape equipment – some of which, Piercey couldn't help thinking, might have come from Rossel's. Otherwise it was sparsely furnished with a couple of hard-back chairs, a small table and what appeared to be a wall mirror.

'Here we are,' Gaunt said. 'All wired for sound. You can hear everything that goes on next door and record it. You can do anything you like in here and he won't hear you. The mirror's one way and covers most of the room, so you can watch him too.'

While Farling tried the equipment, Piercey stood at the mirror and studied Dayton, who appeared to be asleep. Nurse Benson was reading a paperback. Her saw her put it down and go to the bedside as Dayton opened his eyes.

'The nurse will have to leave,' he said. 'I want no one in either of these rooms except Mr Farling and myself.'

The doctor demurred, but Piercey was insistent. If he judged it necessary he would ring for help and the medical staff could come running. But he would conduct the interview alone and in his own way. However, after a murmured word to Farling, he did allow the doctor to take him in to Dayton.

'Hello, Keith.'

'Dermot!'

In response to Piercey's gesture the doctor and the nurse reluctantly left the room, and Piercey pulled up the chair that the nurse had vacated. He smiled ruefully. 'Sorry about all this,' he said. 'It should never have happened.'

'Not your fault.' Dayton's obvious pleasure at the sight of Dermot Piercey was suddenly clouded. 'I – I tried, but – '

'That's all anyone can do,' Piercey said quickly. 'Now, listen, Keith. You're home and you're safe. Obviously there's a heap of questions I've got to ask you, but most of them can wait. First, let me relieve your mind. Irena, your wife – she's fine. She was desperately worried about you – we all were – but that doesn't matter any more. She sends you her love.' Only half a lie, he thought; she would have sent her love if she'd known it was possible.

'When . . .' Dayton began.

'When can you see her? Soon, I hope. This is a safe house, so it's a bit difficult, but we'll arrange it.'

'And Caro? Is she upset about this attack on Hector?'

'How did you know about that?' Piercey was startled.

'I heard it on Nurse Benson's radio last night.'

'I see.' Dayton was meant to be isolated. Discipline would have to be enforced.

'Coyne's name's on the list.'

'Ah.' Piercey was non-committal. 'Bauer gave you the list?'

'Yes, of course. I met him as planned.'

Dayton told his story slowly and laboriously, with pauses that grew longer as he became more exhausted. Piercey was patient and made no attempt to hurry him. Questions could wait.

'Stupid of me to phone Irena,' Dayton's mouth stretched into a kind of grin. 'I meant to phone the emergency number but I was at the end of my tether. Kept on half passing out.'

'But you managed to give Irena the list, Keith? That was a good effort.'

Dayton shook his head, not in denial of Piercey's comment, but in self-disgust. 'Maybe. But later I told them everything I knew. They banged me about. They wouldn't believe I was just – a courier and – and I was shit scared.'

'So would I have been. So would anyone.'

'Well, as you say, at least I got that list through, though I don't know what – ' Something in Piercey's expression made Dayton hesitate. 'Dermot,' he asked, 'Dermot, you *did* get the list? Irena passed it to you?'

It was Piercey's turn to hesitate. Then he said. 'No, Keith. I'm afraid she didn't.'

'Oh, God! Why not? I told her – At least I think I told her the – the phone number you gave me.'

As the potential implications of Piercey's words forced their way into his consciousness Dayton became agitated. He twisted in the bed and raised a hand, dislodging the drip tube and making the bottle above his head sway alarmingly. His words grew slurred and incomprehensible. Quickly Piercey rang the bell. Though he had intended to jolt Dayton, the man's reaction had been unexpectedly violent.

Doctor and nurse came running. Piercey withdrew from the room, ignoring them, and went next door where Farling greeted him with a sardonic grin.

'So what do you think?' Piercey asked.

'His story fits together. And he mentioned that list of his own accord, which he needn't have done. Even if we'd known of its existence, we couldn't necessarily have been sure he'd ever been given it. As far as Dayton's concerned, there's no reason for us to know the meeting ever took place. I'd say he was in the clear – except for the stuff we found in his filing cabinet. And there could be explanations for that.' Farling shrugged; doubts and reservations were routine in the trade.

Piercey nodded his agreement. 'What about Irena? If he managed to give her the list, why didn't she pass it on?'

'Ah, that's different. I'd guess she did pass it on – but to friend Casimir Sabik. And, what's more, if we question her about it, she'll swear blue murder Dayton was so incoherent on the phone that she couldn't understand a word he said.'

Piercey didn't contradict this assertion, but he wasn't entirely happy with the reasoning behind it. A tap on the door interrupted his thoughts. Nurse Benson said, 'He's asking for you again, Mr Piercey, sir. He's not too lucid, I'm afraid, but he won't settle till he's seen you. If you'd come, please.'

Without a glance at Farling, Piercey followed her. By now Dayton's face was grey, and his eyelids fluttered as if at any moment he might drift away from reality. When he saw Piercey he managed to produce a wan smile. He mumbled something, and Piercey bent over him, waving the nurse back.

'. . . ask Irena. I can't remember – the names.'

'Yes. All right, Keith. I will.' Once again Piercey hesitated. If he pressed too hard he might get nothing. On the other hand, if Irena refused to cooperate . . . It was impossible to judge the urgency of the matter. At last he asked gently, 'Tell me, when Bauer gave you this list what did he tell you about it?'

'Just – just that they were in danger. Wasn't time for more. And now – Hector!'

'Hector Coyne, yes,' Piercey was encouraging. 'Who else, Keith? Try to remember.'

'Mayberry. John Rossel. No one else I knew personally. Oh, and someone called Smith, I think.'

Dayton drew a long shuddering breath and his eyes closed. Piercey rose from his side. The interview was at an end.

*

That Sunday, Caroline and Irena lunched together, though it was a fairly silent meal. Both were depressed. Irena kept thinking of Keith, wondering where he was, what was going to happen to them, if they would ever be able to return to their normal, contented lives. Caroline's thoughts were mainly concerned with Hector Coyne. He had persuaded her to take back her engagement ring, but she remained beset by doubts.

It was a beautiful day, warm for the time of year, and they took their coffee out to the little paved garden, which the wings added to the house had transformed into a sun-trap. Irena passed Caroline the *Sunday Telegraph*.

'That's a good photograph of Hector, isn't it? Have you read the article on page five?'

'No, and frankly I don't want to. The other night I met the man who wrote it. He's a history professor of some kind and a great chum of Hector's.'

'You didn't like him?' Irena smiled; she didn't expect an answer. Then she was serious. 'Caro, it's all right now between you and Hector, isn't it?'

'Yes. I suppose so.'

Caroline finished her coffee quickly and got to her feet. She didn't want to discuss Hector. Restless, she wondered what to do with herself. Her eye caught a headline in the newspaper that lay on the garden table where she'd tossed it. Juxtaposed to Hector Coyne's photograph – purposely? she wondered – the headline read, *Left and Right to Clash at Rally: Police Prepared*.

Caroline grinned to herself. Her mind had been made up for her. She'd attend the 'Britain First' rally in Hyde Park that afternoon. It would infuriate Hector when she told him she'd been there – he'd consider it exactly the sort of occasion his wife-to-be should avoid – but she didn't give a damn. To be honest with herself, she was almost looking forward to the scene that would follow her confession. She said, 'I must go, Irena. I'm leaving you an awful mess in the kitchen. I'm sorry.'

'That's okay. I'm not doing anything particular.'

★

Caroline took a bus. She didn't want to risk her car, and anyway the roads around Marble Arch would either be closed by the police or clogged with traffic. With what she considered equal good sense she wore slacks and a sweater, and put only her door key, a handkerchief and some loose change in her pocket. With the crowd that was expected there were bound to be petty thieves around.

The 'Britain First' rally had been given a great deal of publicity. Though its stated purpose – to rouse the country to patriotic enthusiasm and self-awareness – sounded harmless, there was considerable opposition. 'Britain First' might be a good slogan, but not if it were interpreted as a pretext for the expression of every prejudice, racial, religious, social.

The minorities raised their voices. Words like Fascist, Jewboy, black scum were bandied about. The police, foreseeing trouble, had asked for a ban on the event, but the Home Secretary had refused their request. What he had done, however, was limit the march, so that it avoided Trafalgar Square and Whitehall, and passed as it were along the periphery of the centre of London.

In the event, the march itself was peaceful enough. The marchers were not numerous and were greatly outnumbered by their police escort and the accompanying spectators. They assembled in Regent's Park, marched south down Portland Place to Oxford Circus, then along Oxford Street to Marble Arch and the broad expanse of north-eastern Hyde Park, one of London's traditional sites for rallies. The column was headed by a contingent of young men in black shirts, who gave an impression of military precision. They were greeted by some derisive cheers and Nazi salutes as they marched, but on the whole the crowd was good-humoured.

The organizers had been allowed to erect a small platform on the grass beyond Speakers' Corner, and as soon as all the marchers had assembled the addresses began. There was a good deal of barracking, booing and a host of catcalls, but generally the scene remained peaceful. The senior police officer on duty began to wonder if he might dare to congratulate himself; it looked as if his fears had been unjustified.

Caroline, too, was pleased. She was enjoying her afternoon. The rally, of course, was a joke, something she refused to take seriously. She laughed at the more outrageous of the speakers and joined in the cries of 'Shame!' and 'Nazi!' with which their remarks were greeted. Her sympathies were with the barrackers, the objectors, rather than with the men on the platform and their black-shirted guards, and she failed to recognize the signs that the mood of the audience was changing.

It was hard to discern why this was happening. Perhaps the last speaker had been particularly arrogant and aggressive. Perhaps there were those in the crowd who wished to stir up trouble. Whatever the reason, the exchanges gradually took on an edge, the barracking became more abusive. Someone threw an apple core. A few people began to move away.

As the crowd shifted, Caroline caught sight of the man she'd met in Hector Coyne's flat before the dinner party on Friday evening. Hector had said he was a freelance journalist. She watched him with some interest. His name, she remembered was Steve; she'd not been told his surname.

It was by chance that she saw the next happening, and she didn't immediately understand its significance. As she watched, Steve put something to his mouth. The sun glinted on it and for a moment she thought it was a whistle. Only much later, when Dermot Piercey questioned her, would she realize that it was, of all things, a pea-shooter, but a pea-shooter adapted to shoot more than peas. Steve was pointing it directly at the neck of a police horse standing docilely a few feet away from him.

The next moment the horse gave a horrible whinny and reared, throwing its rider and knocking down a youth standing beside it. A woman fell under the flaying hooves. People screamed and scattered. And, as if they had been waiting for this signal, the whole crowd erupted.

Eggs spattered the speakers, and streaked the black shirts of their supporters. Then a brick caught one of the men on the platform on the side of the head and he toppled backwards like a target in a circus booth. More bricks flew, indiscriminately aimed, if aimed at all. In the general confusion some surged towards the platform, over-running it and seeking to destroy it, others did their best to move hastily out of what had rapidly become a danger area. Fights and scuffles broke out, many of them violent. The police intervened, and merely became embroiled. It was impossible to distinguish attacker from attacked, and they had little hope of restoring order without themselves resorting to violence.

By this time Caroline had decided that she must get away. Whatever all this represented – and she'd have to think about that later – the present battle wasn't hers. But she found herself boxed in, pushed here and there, hands pulling at her clothes. She stayed calm. She wasn't afraid – not until someone chopped her across the back of her knees and she fell.

On the ground she was immediately conscious of her vulnerability. Feet were trampling by her. A boot was coming down on her face. She screamed and managed to throw herself out of its reach. She fought to stand, but someone was lying across her left arm – and tugging at her engagement ring!

Caroline clenched her left fist, and with her right hand felt about her, searching for some purchase, some leverage to enable her to lift herself and pull her arm free. Her fingers closed around a half brick. She didn't know what she might have done with it. She scarcely realized what it was. In the event, whatever she had intended, she was frustrated.

'No, you don't!' Her wrist was seized. Fingers dug into her flesh. 'Drop it!'

She dropped the brick. She was aware of navy blue trousers and, as the police officer pulled her to her feet, she felt both anger and relief. The relief was short-lived. The officer, who had lost his helmet and already been subjected to kicks and punches in a scuffle, was not gentle. He twisted her arm up behind her back and, in spite of her protests, pushed her ahead of him, marching her through the thinning crowd to a police van.

'Get in, miss!'

'Why? What have I done?'

'Get in!'

It was useless to argue. Caroline, suddenly near to tears, climbed up the short steps into the van.

125

THIRTEEN

Not half an hour after Caroline had left for Hyde Park, the doorbell rang in the Hampstead house. Piercey and Farling stood on the doorstep. Behind them Irena saw a large black car, a driver at the wheel. The sight frightened her.

'Have you come to arrest me?' she demanded.

'I hope that won't be necessary, Mrs Dayton.'

'All we want is an exchange of information, Mrs Dayton.'

'Exchange of – ' Irena led the way into the sitting-room, then turned and faced them. 'How is my husband? Where is he? What have you done with him?'

'He's still alive, Mrs Dayton, though I doubt if it's any thanks to you.'

Irena stared at Piercey. She had no idea what he meant, but it was clearly an accusation. They were accusing her of harming Keith. How? When? Two ugly spots of red showed high on her pale cheeks. She swore at them in Polish.

'I'm sorry, but neither of us speak your language,' Piercey gestured to a chair, and automatically Irena sat in it. 'Mrs Dayton, you lied to us. You told us you'd not heard from your husband. In fact he telephoned you about midnight the Thursday before last, just before his presumed disappearance. He read you a list of names. We'd like that list, please.'

Irena swallowed hard. 'I – I don't know what you're talking about.'

Neither man said anything. They merely stared at her and waited. There was no sympathy in their expressions. Irena licked dry lips. They can't know, she thought. They must be guessing. I've told no one, no one except Cas. We'll all be fine as long as I keep on denying everything.

She said, 'What did you mean by saying Keith is *still* alive? Tell me the truth. Has he had a relapse?'

'Someone who knew he'd seen that list of names, someone who knew he was in hospital not far from Cologne, posed as a doctor and tried to kill him.' Piercey's voice was level and cold, and he went on immediately, before she had time to recover from the shock. 'Mrs Dayton, we now know that you *did* have that list. You've probably still got it. We need it. Your husband has given us some of the names. Coyne. Mayberry. Rossel. He couldn't remember them all. He said you would. He said he'd dictated them to you on the phone that night.'

'Keith?' Irena was by now hopelessly confused. She didn't know whether or not to believe them. Keith had told her to trust no one, especially Piercey, and the names Piercey had repeated were those she had mentioned to Cas. Had Piercey got them from Cas? She would trust Cas no longer. And she'd keep her own counsel. 'I've nothing to tell you,' she said, and added, 'When can I see my husband?'

Piercey and Farling exchanged glances. Farling knew what he would do, but the decision was up to Piercey. Piercey, who had already considered the possibility that Irena might try to bargain, didn't hesitate.

'Sometime. As soon as he's well enough, and as soon as you decide to cooperate.' He stood up abruptly. 'We'll be going now, Mrs Dayton, but I suggest you think over your position very carefully.'

'I will,' Irena said politely. But she was shaking as she shut the front door behind them. She felt physically sick, fearful for Keith and for herself.

★

Enough for a Sunday, Piercey thought, as later that evening he drove home to his flat. A couple of drinks while he grilled a steak and made a salad, then after supper he'd put his feet up and read. It was a pleasant prospect.

The telephone rang as he was taking the steak from the refrigerator. Drink in hand, he went to answer it. Having just left the office and with Weatherby away, he expected the caller to be either his family or a friend. He did not expect to find a police inspector on the line.

'I'm sorry to bother you, sir, but we have a young lady here at Rochester Row Police Station, a very persistent young lady, if I may say so. She claims to be your sister, Miss Deirdre Piercey.'

'I see,' Piercey said carefully. 'That surprises me. What's she doing there?'

'She was arrested this afternoon at the "British First" rally in Hyde Park, sir. We're still sorting out the possible charges, but they could include assault, offences against public order, resisting arrest, and so on.'

'Some of those are serious.'

'Yes, sir.'

Piercey was playing for time, trying to decide if the call was genuine or some kind of hoax. Whichever it was, he would have bet a year's pay that Deirdre was not in police custody. She lived in the country, and she would certainly have let him know if she was coming up to London. Add to that the fact that Mrs Mortimer – which was what his sister had been entitled to call herself for several years now – wouldn't have dreamed of going to a Hyde Park rally, and Piercey felt his bet was safe.

The voice on the phone was continuing, sounding more convincing with each word. 'It'll depend on the magistrate, sir, but for first offences I doubt if it'll mean more than a fine. However, the young lady has no means of identification on her and no money. I'm afraid she'll have to spend a night in the cells unless you can come along.'

'Okay, Inspector. I'll be there.'

Piercey set down the receiver. Then he checked with the phone book and called Rochester Row Station, asking for the inspector by name. He was put through at once and the voice was the same. He hung up quickly. At least it wasn't a hoax.

Slowly he finished his drink and considered the situation. Definitely not Deirdre. He reviewed his various girlfriends. None of them seemed likely, not as likely as Caroline Dayton. But he couldn't decide if this idea had occurred to him merely because these days his mind was apt to be preoccupied with thoughts of Caro. Anyhow, the way to find out was obvious.

He wondered if he should have supper first. It wouldn't do Miss Dayton, or whoever it was, any harm to spend a little more time in the hands of the police. But the steak no longer tempted him, and he settled for another drink and some bread and cheese.

At Rochester Row he asked the inspector if he might see his sister at once. 'Just to make sure it *is* her,' he said apologetically. 'My sister's not the kind of girl who'd normally go to such a rally, or make a fool of herself if she did. To be honest I find it difficult to understand how she ever came to get involved.'

The inspector had heard stories like this often enough and he remained unmoved, though he gave the necessary order. While they waited, he said, 'Perhaps you'd be good enough to identify yourself, sir.'

There was a pause while Piercey came to a decision. Then from his wallet he extracted a laminated card that was familiar to every senior police officer in Britain. The inspector studied it, verified the photograph and handed it back. He regarded Piercey with frank curiosity, but merely said, 'I see, sir. Does this mean that the young lady was . . .'

'Certainly not.' Piercey grinned ruefully. 'But you must admit it puts me in an embarrassing position. Did she actually assault anyone?'

The inspector shuffled through some papers. 'Not really, sir, not as far as we know. But she was caught with a half-brick in her hand. Mind you, I dare say there were a lot worse. It was a regular battle royal for a while. Several of my men ended up in hospital, and one of the police horses had to be put down because of its injuries.'

Piercey nodded his sympathy, which was genuine. He wished the constable who had been sent to fetch the supposed Deirdre would hurry. He was not enjoying himself, and he half-hoped that he would be faced with some strange girl or casual acquaintance whom he could leave to the inspector with a clear conscience. But he wasn't surprised when Caroline Dayton was brought in.

Caroline was very pale, and there was a bruise discolouring one cheekbone. Her sweater was torn and dirty. She carried her left arm at an awkward angle, as if it were causing her discomfort. Nevertheless, as she stood in front of the two men, not unlike an errant schoolgirl before her headmistress and housemistress, her chin was high in defiance, her mouth firm.

'Your sister, sir?' the inspector inquired.

Dermot Piercey, who had at first been moved by Caroline's appearance, was suddenly angry. She'd put him in an impossible and invidious position. He hated to think what Weatherby would have to say about it, for there was no doubt that Weatherby would have to be told; the police might be deceived, but not the General.

He avoided the lie direct. 'Inspector, I'm truly sorry. I must admit I'd like to say no. I'm not exactly proud of her at the moment, but . . .'

'All right, sir. We'll take it as a misunderstanding, shall we? The magistrate will be happy to have one less to deal with in the morning.'

The inspector got to his feet. It was late and he was tired. The rally had given him a lot of extra work, and he saw no point in making a mountain out of this particular molehill. He was prepared to do a fellow official a favour.

'Thank you,' Piercey said. 'Thank you very much. I'm most grateful, Inspector. I assure you we won't be bothering you again. And I mean that.'

'How I mean it!' he added to Caroline as they left the police station after Caroline's few possessions had been returned to her. 'The next time you get yourself arrested you can stay in jug, Miss Dayton. And I won't provide a character reference when you get to the dock.'

He took her by the arm to lead her across the road to his car, and involuntarily she gave a small gasp of pain. 'What is it?' he said, letting go of her.

'My arm,' Caroline said. 'It got – twisted.'

'By the police, I assume?' Piercey was sarcastic. 'Police brutality! And you picked up a brick to defend yourself.'

'No, it wasn't like that at all. I was knocked to the ground when I was trying to get out of the crowd and someone – I don't know who; I suppose he just saw his chance – someone started to pull off my engagement ring. I wasn't prepared to let it go and there was a sort of struggle. I never really knew I'd got a brick in my hand. Then the police arrived.'

'How fortunate! Otherwise Hector would have had to buy you another ring, wouldn't he?'

Piercey was ashamed of the remark as soon as he'd made it and Caroline didn't answer. He helped her into his car, shut the door on her and got behind the wheel. He didn't start the engine immediately, but sat, staring straight ahead of him, surprised at the violence of his feelings. He failed to notice that Caroline was herself on the point of tears, and after a minute he drove off.

'Tell me,' he said conversationally, 'just why did you get the police to call me? Why not Mr Coyne, or the Mayberrys?'

'Because – because I didn't want to give my real name. I was afraid a reporter might get hold of it. I wouldn't have minded so much for myself, but I knew it would all be tied in with Dad and there'd be more scandal that could harm him.'

'Which Mr Coyne wouldn't like?'

'No, he wouldn't! But that wasn't why!' Caroline drew a deep breath. 'Do you have to be so unpleasant about Hector?'

It was a question Dermot Piercey preferred not to consider. 'And Deirdre's name just popped into your head,' he said. 'And my address. My phone number.'

'A policeman found the number for me.' Caroline ignored the matter of the address, and the curiosity that after their first meeting had prompted her to look Piercey up in the phone book. 'I – I'm sorry.'

Piercey glanced sideways at her. 'We're on our way to Hampstead,' he said. 'Is that okay? Or would you rather go to the Mayberrys? Or see a doctor about your arm?'

'No, thanks. I don't need a doctor. Hampstead will be fine.'

At the Daytons' house Piercey helped her out of the car in silence, walked with her to the entrance to her flat and waited while she fitted her key into the lock. 'Are you sure you'll be all right?' he said at last.

'Quite sure.' Caroline hesitated. 'Come in and have a drink,' she said. 'I owe you that. I know I've been a bloody nuisance.'

It was Piercey's turn to hesitate, but he shook his head. 'I'm sorry, no. It's late and I've things to do.'

'Okay.' Caroline hid her disappointment. 'So I'll say good-night – and thanks!'

131

FOURTEEN

It was Manfred Brenner's experience that most people – guards, porters, security men, officials – were apt to be less suspicious and so less cautious early in the morning, rather than late at night. Given a peaked cap, something to carry and an air of purposefulness, it wasn't difficult to gain admission to most places at such a time.

It was, therefore, about a quarter to eight on Monday morning when Brenner, whistling cheerfully, strode through the main doors of Fairhaven Court in Marylebone. The big glass doors presented no problem for they were wide open; a woman in a flowered apron, her hair in curlers, was busy cleaning the hall. Brenner wished her good-morning and went straight to the lift that was waiting.

He knew where he was going, having made a careful reconnaissance of the building the previous Saturday, so he immediately put his finger on the button for the seventh floor. The flat he wanted was directly opposite the lift. He pressed the doorbell. This, he knew, was the tricky moment.

There was only a short delay before the door was flung open. A young man, with over-long fair hair and sleep in his eyes, looked inquiringly at Brenner. He was not, in fact, the man whom Brenner had expected, but he identified him instantly from the batch of photographs he had been shown in Zurich during his briefing. Noting the strong, muscular body that was obviously naked beneath its loosely-tied towelling robe, Brenner tensed.

'Packet for Mr Rossel,' he said, showing the parcel he carried. 'He'll have to sign for it.' He produced a small receipt pad from his pocket.

Indolently the young man turned away and shouted over his shoulder, 'John! Something you've got to sign for, love.'

John Rossel came through an archway which, Brenner guessed, led to the sitting-room of the flat. He too was wearing only a towelling robe. The relationship of the two men was self-evident, and it gave Brenner pause for satisfied reflection.

'What is it? What – ' Rossel stopped, mouth open.

His friend swung round, but by now Brenner was in the hall, the front door kicked shut behind him. He had dropped the packet and the pad and a pistol had appeared in his hand. He made no attempt to sound menacing – merely businesslike.

'Both of you, clasp your hands behind your neck and back slowly into the sitting-room,' he said. 'Don't try any tricks. I won't hesitate to shoot.'

'Now look here,' Rossel began. 'If it's money you want, you can have it, but – '

'Do as he says, John!'

Rossel complied, and the two men, followed by Brenner, moved slowly backwards into the sitting-room. Brenner allowed himself a swift glance around. A half-eaten breakfast lay on a table in front of the sofa. Music came softly from a pair of hi-fi speakers. The lighting was subdued, the curtains still drawn against the day. It was more or less what Brenner had expected to find, and it suited his purpose admirably. The presence of the younger man was an added bonus.

Rossel tried again. 'For God's sake, take what you want and clear out. We won't even call the police when you've gone. We swear it.' His voice was high with fear. 'Don't we, Steve?' he appealed.

'Sure. Pinch what you like, pal. But let me have a smoke.' Hands beginning to unclasp, Steve took a step towards a table on which stood an open box of cigarettes. It was also a step nearer to Brenner.

'Stay still, Mr Smith!'

'You know my name?' said Smith at once.

'You're Steve Smith. You and Mr Rossel are – associates.' Brenner nodded towards Rossel. He wanted them to admit their identities; mistakes must be avoided.

'Yes. So, what's it to you?'

Steve Smith didn't wait for an answer. He had already realized that Brenner was no ordinary thief, but a true professional. Unlike Rossel, who was at heart a coward, he seized the only chance he had. He ducked sideways, then flung himself at Brenner. Brenner shot him in the middle of the forehead.

'No,' Rossel said, unable to accept the evidence of his eyes. 'No, no!'

But Brenner was already on him. Knocking him to the ground with one savage blow, he thrust the gun into his mouth and, taking care to stand at arm's length, pulled the trigger.

Neither shot had been louder than the backfire of a car. Though the back of Rossel's head had been blown off, there was no blood or brain matter on Brenner's suit. Brenner wiped the gun on his handkerchief, carefully clasped Rossel's fingers round it, and let it drop. As he left the room he kicked over the table in front of the sofa. The scene was set to suggest a routine situation – a quarrel between two homosexuals ending in the murder of one and the suicide of the other.

Brenner picked up his packet and his pad and let himself out of the flat. He avoided the lift and ran down the stairs. The cleaning woman was no longer in the hall, and no one noticed him as he pushed through the glass doors of the building.

Minutes later he was getting into a tube train at Baker Street station. His pockets bulged a little, one with his peaked cap, the other with the packet. Otherwise he looked like any other white-collar worker on his way to his office job.

There were no seats available in the crowded train, but Brenner didn't mind. He clung to the strap above his head and merged into the bodies around him as they swayed with the motion of the train. He was pleased with himself. The assignment had been carried out perfectly, and he had achieved precisely twice as much as he had hoped for.

*

Casimir Sabik was making himself a late breakfast when there was a sharp knock on his door. The kettle was just on the boil and he made his tea. He was in no hurry to answer the knock; it would only be his landlady wanting the rent for his little basement apartment, or garden flat, as she insisted on calling it.

The knock came again, more insistently. 'All right, all right,' Sabik muttered. Wretched woman, he thought, why the hell can't she wait?

He was not in the best of moods. He had been pleased to be able to pass on the information he had gleaned from Irena Dayton, and had preened himself on the praise he had received for it. But he had been upset by the attack on Hector Coyne so soon afterwards. Though he didn't understand the connection, he was sure one existed, and secretly he was afraid – doubly so. The last thing he wanted was to be involved in a series of killings or assassinations. He had no wish to spend the rest of his life in an English prison. Nor, knowing the ruthlessness of his masters, did he wish to die.

The knocks on the door came again, louder now. Cursing, Sabik went to answer them. His landlady wasn't usually so persistent, but who else could it be? He peered through the little glass spy-hole that he had himself inserted in his door. He could see that there were two young men outside, and he took the precaution of opening the door on the chain.

'Yes?' he said inquiringly.

Piercey produced one of his identity cards, and explained his presence and that of Farling. 'We'd like a word with you, Mr Sabik, if we may. You are Casimir Sabik?'

'I am, yes,' said Sabik cautiously, through the gap. 'But I don't understand. Why should you – '

'Perhaps we might come in?'

Sabik hesitated. Then, 'Yes, of course, Mr Piercey. You must forgive me. An old man, you know, and there are so many villains around these days. I have to be careful.'

The caution was something he must keep in the forefront of his mind, Sabik thought, as he led them into his living-room. At least the delay at the door had given him a moment to think. He waved them to chairs.

'Now, what is it you want of me?' he asked formally.

'Information, Mr Sabik.' Piercey was bland. 'We're hoping you can help us about a matter that's highly confidential. We can trust you, I'm sure.'

'Mr Piercey. I'm a British citizen, and have been for many years. Though I'm Polish by birth, I love this country. I'd do anything for her. Certainly you can trust me.' Hoping he hadn't sounded too fulsome, Sabik leant forward. 'What is it you want?'

'You're a friend of Irena Kalak – Mrs Dayton, as she now is?'

'Yes, that's true.' Sabik nodded. 'I knew her in Warsaw in the old days. Though I don't see her too often, we are indeed friends.' Suddenly he allowed himself to sound anxious. 'It is because of Irena you are here? Poor woman, she has had so much trouble recently with her husband lost in Europe and – but I expect you know more about that than I do.'

Sabik had given Piercey a perfect opening, and he took it. 'Perhaps not, Mr Sabik. Perhaps not. As a confidant of Mrs Dayton's you may well be better informed.'

'It is to do with Mr Dayton, then?' Sabik gave a quick bright smile, hiding his nervousness.

'Indirectly,' Piercey said. 'We understand that when Mr Dayton was in Germany he tried to dictate a list of names over the phone to his wife. As he was injured at the time he only managed to give two or three before he collapsed. She told you this?'

'Yes,' Sabik said shortly. There was no point in denying it; they must have learnt it from Irena. 'She was terribly worried, as you can imagine, with Keith being so incoherent and obviously ill. She had no idea what he wanted of her. But I'm afraid I wasn't much use. Except as an old shoulder to cry on, of course.'

'Of course,' Farling agreed.

Piercey merely smiled. They waited for Sabik to continue, but the lengthening silence didn't appear to worry him. He merely looked at them expectantly; it was obvious they had underrated his acumen.

Finally Piercey said, 'That list of names must have been of great importance. It's a pity it's been lost.'

'Lost? But surely Keith will remember it, and since he's been found and is recovering . . .' Sabik left the sentence unfinished. He knew they were playing with him, but his only

136

option was to take part in the game. With sudden anxiety he said, 'Keith *is* getting better, isn't he?'

'Yes, but he was in a bad way the night of the phone call, and he'd only had a glimpse of the list. He can't remember.' Piercey shrugged. 'So, we're stymied.'

'Unless you can help, Mr Sabik,' Farling said quietly.

'Me? I only know what Irena told me,' Sabik said. 'Let me think. She mentioned Sir Peter Mayberry and John Rossel – Rossel's is the firm Keith works for – and – and Hector Coyne, the MP.'

The last was added quickly, but Sabik saw the two officials glance at each other, and knew he had made a tactical error. Coyne's was the name he should have given first. It had been all over television, and spread across the Sunday newspapers, and it should have been uppermost in his mind.

'Was your controller pleased to learn that Irena Dayton knew only three names?' Piercey asked conversationally.

'My controller? What? I – I don't know what you mean.'

'Oh come, Mr Sabik, don't let's fence. As soon as you left Mrs Dayton's you passed on what she'd told you,' Farling said.

'Who's your contact, your controller, Mr Sabik?' Piercey pressed him.

'You've made a great mistake. I don't have any contact, any controller.' Sabik had begun to sweat. He rose to his feet, and made a show of indignation. 'Mr Piercey, what are you talking about? You've no right to burst in here, making all these accusations and bullying an old man. You're no better than the Gestapo. If you don't go at once I shall complain to my MP.'

'Perhaps he's on your famous hit list, like Hector Coyne.' Farling laughed. 'Sit down, Mr Sabik, and don't be silly. We're all professionals.'

'Just why do your masters want these people eliminated?' Piercey demanded. 'Tell us, Mr Sabik, and please don't waste our time with more pretences.'

'But I don't know! I don't!' Sabik's façade collapsed; his protestations constituted an admission. He had spoken the truth but he was sure they wouldn't believe him. 'You can't tie me in with any killings. I've never in my life tried to kill anyone.'

'Oh, we know that, Mr Sabik. But it seems to us you've been passing on information that's made murders – or attempted murders – necessary and possible.' Piercey's voice was cold. 'Let's take Hector Coyne, for example. Why does Moscow Centre want him dead?'

There was a pause. Then, 'I don't know,' Sabik said slowly.

'You mean you won't tell us.' They were getting nowhere, Piercey thought; it was time to apply pressure. 'Okay, Mr Sabik. We hoped you'd cooperate with us, but if you prefer not to, it's your choice. However, I should warn you that we've more than enough evidence to have you arrested and charged under the Official Secrets Act.'

Sabik looked down at his hands clasped in his lap. 'What – what for? What evidence?' he said slowly, taking care to keep his voice uncertain.

Farling cited several examples of information that had been passed by the Pole to his Soviet contacts. Sabik listened attentively, his face expressionless; he was surprised how much the British knew of his dealings with the Russians, and prayed they knew no more.

'Shall I go on?' Farling asked.

'That should be enough,' Piercey said. 'I'm sure Mr Sabik has the picture and appreciates the options. It could be a term in prison, Mr Sabik – most uncomfortable at your age, I should have thought. Or perhaps a quiet deportation – after we'd taken care to let your controller know that you'd been playing a double game, let's say. Or there are one or two other alternatives. Which shall it be, Mr Sabik, one of these – or a little cooperation?'

Sabik didn't like the way Piercey was watching him. He buried his face in his hands, a gesture that caused Dermot Piercey to smile inwardly. The Pole drew great, shuddering breaths, which were genuine enough, and forced himself to think hard. His problems were not as simple and clear-cut as the Brits seemed to believe, but when at last he raised his head he had made his choice.

138

'Gentlemen,' he said. 'I'll tell you everything I can but, as you must know, I'm no one of importance. The Russians don't take me into their confidence.'

'But you've got some idea why they want to get rid of Coyne and Rossel and Mayberry?' Piercey spoke with more assurance than he felt.

'I don't, Mr Piercey. Please believe me.' Sabik ran his fingers through his grey hair. 'I'd tell you the answer if I knew it. All I do know is that there was a sudden interest in Keith Dayton about the time he disappeared, and because of my friendship with Irena I was ordered to report on – on the family.'

'Perhaps you could make a guess?' Farling suggested.

Sabik had recovered some of his composure, and he shrugged. 'If I knew some of the other names it might help.'

'It might help us too,' Farling agreed.

'I'm sorry,' Sabik said.

Piercey, who hadn't spoken for a minute or two, got to his feet. 'Well, if you can't help us, Mr Sabik, we shall leave you,' he said briskly.

'Yes, but – but what is to happen to me? I've done my best to help you. I swear I have,' Sabik pleaded.

'We'll have to see.' Piercey was non-committal. 'Anyway, we know where we can find you. Meanwhile, take my advice, Mr Sabik. Stay quietly at home, and in no circumstances try to contact your Soviet friends. Understood?'

The Pole bowed his head. He understood only too well. He was, as it were, on probation – and probation of a kind unknown to the British Courts. Every move he made would be noted. He must take no risks – no risks at all. Nevertheless . . .

He saw the two men out, and watched them climb the stairs from the basement. As soon as they were out of sight, he moved quickly. He shut the door, put up the chain and hurried to a small desk to find paper and pen. He wrote without pause – a brief note explaining that he was unwell and would be unable to keep an appointment to play chess.

Sabik was smiling as he signed his name. The man to whom he addressed the letter would know how to interpret it, but if it were intercepted – which was by no means unlikely – it should appear harmless. He often did play chess with the addressee, and the appointment was a genuine one.

He sealed the envelope and put on a stamp. He was just in time. There was another knock on the door. Now it was his landlady, and for once he was glad to see her. He paid the rent and explained that he had the beginnings of a cold. She said she would be happy to post a letter for him. He thanked her profusely.

So much for young Messrs Piercey and Farling, he thought as he went back to the kitchen. He threw away the cold tea and the hard toast, and started to make a fresh breakfast. He decided to scramble himself some eggs – to celebrate. The outlook was less than perfect, but it was considerably better than had seemed possible half an hour earlier.

It was lucky for his peace of mind that he couldn't hear Piercey's comment to Farling as they drove away.

'That man,' said Piercey, 'is not to be trusted. He's hiding something, and it's not his Moscow connection. He admitted to that readily enough. But there's something else, and he values it dearly.'

FIFTEEN

The old man who had done his best to ensure that British intelligence should be appraised of the danger facing the ten people he had named was pacing his salon and cursing. How could the damned Brits be so inefficient? The warning had been passed to them at great risk to his own good name and that of his family. Yet, as far as he could judge, it had been completely ignored.

He had had great difficulty in not showing his chagrin when his son-in-law had informed him of what was being hailed as a triumphant operation – an operation that could more than compensate for several failures. The previous day, in a single attack, Manfred Brenner had eliminated not only John Rossel, but Steve Smith as well. And Smith, it had been feared, would be hard to track down – perhaps the most difficult of the targets.

He didn't give a damn for Coyne or Rossel or Smith, the old man thought angrily. He wished them all dead. But in the abortive attempt on Coyne's life, more innocents had been killed. And if, instead of Smith, some innocent girl, some neighbour or friend, even a child – yes, even a child – had been in Rossel's flat, there could have been another completely pointless killing. Young David Gorey over again – and this in spite of his warning!

Why hadn't the British taken action, he asked himself. Keith Dayton had managed to survive the attempt on his life in that German hospital, and by now he must have passed on the information that Bauer had given him. By now the Brits must know the names of those marked down for assassination. Why then had they done nothing?

His son-in-law had told him of the plot to discredit Dayton by planting communist material and espionage apparatus in his house. He had forced himself to laugh, but the news had disturbed him, though at the time he had comforted himself with the assurance that the British authorities were not so stupid as to accept such a simple trick at its face value. Still, he wondered. An alternative was that Bauer had been interrupted before he could tell Dayton all he knew.

Either way the old man decided that there was no action he could take. He stopped pacing and stood beside the grand piano, staring sadly at the silver-framed photograph of his own David. His son-in-law, who had obviously guessed something of the part he had already played, had given him an implicit warning that further interference would not be tolerated. So all he could do was hope; maybe the British would eventually come to their senses and act.

*

Although John Rossel and Steve Smith had been killed early on Monday morning, their bodies were not found until the following day. Beryl Ackley, Rossel's secretary, was the first to become perturbed.

Beryl Ackley was a competent girl, which was fortunate as Rossel's staff was small and she was often left on her own to deal with the business of the company. Yesterday she had coped well, answering any inquiries that she could, and otherwise assuring callers that Rossel would be in later. But Rossel had not come in. He had apparently cut a luncheon without excuse, and failed to keep an appointment with the Commercial Attaché at the Danish Embassy. The telephones at his flat and his country cottage remained unanswered. Beryl Ackley left the office in the evening totally nonplussed. This was a new situation. Normally Rossel kept her informed of his movements.

On Tuesday morning, when Rossel again failed to appear at his office, Miss Ackley phoned Hector Coyne. She knew him of course, as a director of the firm as well as one of Rossel's personal friends. There was, however, no reply and after some hesitation she tried Sir Peter Mayberry. She was relieved when he answered.

'What am I to do, Sir Peter?' she asked. 'Mr Rossel has three important engagements today.'

'Take the initiative and cancel them,' Mayberry said promptly. 'Say he's been taken ill. Luckily, Mr Coyne's here at my house. So not to worry. We'll consider the position and be in touch with you as soon as we've found out what's happened. That's the best I can suggest for the moment. All right?'

'Yes, Sir Peter. Thank you.' At least the responsibility was in other hands. 'And I'll let you know if I hear anything.'

'Good girl!' Mayberry said heartily.

He put down the receiver and stared at himself in the ornate Victorian mirror that hung on the wall above the phone in his study. What he saw didn't please him. His usually florid face was mottled, two frownmarks were digging deep creases between his eyes and his shoulders sagged. He cursed savagely. Then, straightening himself with an effort, he returned to his drawing room.

As he entered Patricia threw down the magazine Coyne had just handed back to her. 'Peter! I was showing Hector. Yet another photograph of the beautiful Rebecca! You can't get away from the damned girl. The daughter of the Israeli Ambassador, next Sunday's bride-to-be of our Foreign Secretary's son. Wedding of the year and all that!' Patricia practically spat the words. 'Wretched little Jewess. She's not half as lovely as Caroline, is she, Hector?'

'No, indeed.' Coyne's smile was sardonic. He glanced at Mayberry and his expression changed. 'Peter, what is it? What's wrong?'

'Rossel's disappeared,' Mayberry said bluntly.

'Christ!' Coyne said. 'That's all we need. When?'

Patricia's violet eyes were wide. 'John Rossel – disappeared? You mean – like Keith? Or has he just decamped with the company funds?'

The men ignored her. Mayberry relayed what he knew to Coyne. This was little enough, but Patricia appreciated how shaken they both were. Out of proportion, she thought.

'Isn't it possible he's sick and his phone's out of order?' she said. 'I don't think he knows his neighbours at all well, and anyway they could be away, or he mightn't want to drag himself out of bed.'

'There's a porter always on duty,' Coyne pointed out.

'But he'd not necessarily need to go to John's flat.' Patricia shrugged. 'Why don't I call on him on my way to Caroline's? At least we'll have taken some positive action.'

It was more action than Patricia Mayberry had bargained for. Forty minutes later, accompanied by the day porter at Fairhaven Court whom she had persuaded to produce his master key, she found the bodies of John Rossel and Steve Smith.

It wasn't long before the news reached Special Branch and General Weatherby. An alert had gone out for any information, obviously important or seemingly meaningless, concerning the firm of Rossel & Company, and the routine, for once, worked well.

'The first impression is of a quarrel between lovers,' Weatherby said, 'and conceivably that might be the explanation. But it would be stretching coincidence. Coyne – now Rossel. There's no way we can put off warning Mayberry. He'll have to be given protection, if he'll accept it. Coyne's refused so far, but he might change his mind now. No mention of any list, though. For public consumption the line we take is that it's an inexplicable vendetta against the firm and its directors. That should keep the media happy, though I hope it doesn't re-arouse their interest in Dayton. If necessary we'll cook up a disaffected ex-employee, or something.'

Piercey nodded. 'What about this chap with Rossel, sir. It was odd he had no means of identification at all.'

'Yes. But we can't read too much into that. He may be irrelevant. Rossel could have picked him up anywhere. A bar. A pub. A public lavatory.' The General wrinkled his nose. 'We'll know before long. There'll be a retouched picture of his face on television and in the evening paper. Someone will recognize him and come forward.'

In the event Weatherby was only partly right. Many people that evening recognized Steve Smith's photograph or description, but few of them were prepared to admit it. Some had met him in bars or discos, and others had seen him at the rally on Sunday, or picketing somewhere or at some fringe political meeting. Most decided it was in their own best interests not to bother the police. The few that did volunteer information were of little help.

Nevertheless, by evening the police – and Weatherby – had learnt a certain amount. They knew, for instance, the name by which Rossel's companion in death was known – Steve Smith. Weatherby, seizing on the name and remembering that Dayton had mentioned a Smith as being on the list, at once demanded that a copy of the dead man's photograph be shown to Mayberry and Coyne. This was done, but neither admitted to recognizing it. Nor did Beryl Ackley, who was unsure whether to be grieved by Rossel's death, or indignant at its sexual implications.

When it emerged that Steve Smith was in fact a far left militant, who was believed to live in an insalubrious area of Notting Hill in north-east London, Weatherby began to doubt whether this could be the man named on the list. This Smith simply didn't fit the pattern. Alternatively, Weatherby told himself, he'd got the whole thing wrong and had better rethink the problem – urgently.

*

There was no reason for anyone to make a special effort to ensure that Caroline Dayton saw Steve Smith's photograph. She spent the morning shopping and pottering in her flat. It was after twelve when she went in to the studio, where Irena had been occupied with a sitter. The two women lunched together in amicable silence. Caroline explained her bruised face and her stiff arm as the result of a fall from a pair of steps. Neither of them thought of turning on the lunch-time news.

Thus Caroline didn't hear of John Rossel's death until Peter Mayberry telephoned late in the afternoon. He gave the barest of details, and referred to Steve Smith not by name but only as someone who was 'apparently a friend of John's'. Though she had never particularly liked Rossel she was shocked, as she admitted to Irena when she went into the studio to tell her the news.

145

'Peter wants me to keep Ma company for the evening and spend the night there. He has to go to the House, and he doesn't like the idea of her being alone. She's being very brave, he says.' Caroline permitted herself a wry grin. 'But naturally she's shaken. She's not used to finding corpses.'

'Who is?' Irena said, and hoped the remark didn't sound unkind. If anything she was more shocked than Caroline and, in the light of that list, and the names she herself had given to Cas, she was frightened. She tried to sound casual. 'I hope you had no plans for the evening, Caro?'

'I was meant to be going to a birthday party – one of my bridesmaids-to-be – but I'd already called it off. I wasn't prepared to go with my face like this. She'd have been as catty as hell about it, and I'd have felt sick.'

Irena laughed. 'Why a bridesmaid, if you don't like her?'

'Need you ask? She wasn't my choice.' Caroline sighed. 'If I'd known what a business getting married was I'd have stayed a spinster for life. However, I must go.' She kissed Irena. 'Good night, my dear. You'll be all right?'

'Oh yes. Good night. And take care. Give Patricia my – my sympathy.'

'I will,' Caroline promised.

Patricia, however, showed little interest. Caroline found her lying on the sofa, looking beautiful but disconsolate. A novel was discarded on the floor, a box of chocolates stood on the table beside her and her forehead was adorned with a handkerchief soaked in cologne. Given a good old-fashioned bottle of smelling salts and the picture of a Victorian heroine would be complete, Caroline thought dispassionately, though Patricia lacked the meekness needed for such a role.

'Is that why you've been so long?' she said sharply when Caroline gave her Irena's message. 'Gossiping with that woman when I needed you. You're always fussing over her these days, Caroline. Don't you realize what I've been through? It wasn't just finding poor John and his friend – that was ghastly enough – but afterwards the police never stopped asking questions, though it was perfectly obvious to me what had happened.'

'What do you mean?'

'Well, you know what John was like.' Patricia made a

dismissive gesture. 'Mind you, when I first went into the room I thought it was a girl with him. Long fair hair down to the shoulders, but his robe was open and . . .'

Caroline listened; she had no choice. She wondered if Patricia was right, if Rossel had died in a lovers' quarrel. She would have liked to believe it. But after the attack on Hector and the trouble her father had been in, it seemed highly unlikely.

'Turn on the TV and let's hear the news,' Patricia said at last. 'Maybe by now they've discovered who John's boyfriend was. Evidently he had no means of identification on him. And pour me a whisky, there's a dear. I know it's early, but I need it.'

'Okay.' Caroline did as she was asked.

By the time she had poured the drink and sat down again, the news had begun. The lead item was the death of John Rossel, and the apparent murder of his unknown companion, whose name had not yet been released to the media. The police were still seeking information about him.

Caroline sat up with a jerk and stared in disbelief at the face on the screen. She had recognized it instantly. Steve! Steve – She'd never known his surname. But he was the man she'd met in Hector's flat, whom she'd seen again at the 'Britain First' rally, whom she'd connected with the start of the riot. She drew a quick breath between her teeth.

She said, 'Hector knows that man. He told me he was a freelance reporter, but – '

'Hector knows him? My dear, are you sure?' Patricia was startled.

'Yes.' Caroline didn't elaborate.

'Well, in that case there's no need for you to do anything about it,' said Patricia firmly. 'Hector will have told the police what's necessary. Incidentally, Peter said he'd probably bring Hector in for a nightcap if they get away from the House reasonably early.'

'Good,' Caroline said absently, and wondered if she meant it. She hadn't seen Hector since Saturday, though they had spoken on the telephone, and their relationship was still slightly strained by their quarrel.

The men, in fact, didn't appear. At half past ten Patricia

147

decided to go to bed. She said she was exhausted, and there was some truth in her statement; she was far from stupid and she disliked the way events around her seemed to be getting out of control. Caroline, glad of the excuse, said good-night, and went up to the room that was always kept ready for her.

She undressed and got into bed. For a while she listened to the radio. Then she tried to sleep, but her brain was much too active. Thoughts of Rossel and Steve, Hector, Dermot Piercey, her father and Irena, Peter Mayberry and Patricia chased each other inconsequentially through her mind. Patterns formed and reformed before her eyes. She turned from one side to the other, unable to get comfortable. She dozed and woke, and dozed again.

Shortly after midnight a tap on her door brought her fully awake. She started up in bed and turned on the light. Hector Coyne came softly into the room.

'Hello, darling. I'm sorry. I shouldn't have woken you. But I don't seem to have seen you for days, let alone made love to you.' He sat on the side of the bed and drew her to him. He kissed her lightly, then stroked the side of her face. 'What on earth have you been doing to yourself?' he said, seeing her bruise.

'I fell off a step ladder, but it's nothing.' Caroline pulled herself up into a sitting position. 'Hector – that man I met in your flat last Friday – Steve. He was John Rossel's boyfriend, wasn't he? Have you told the police yet?'

Hector Coyne paused, and Caroline was tempted to mention the second time she had seen Steve, though that would have meant admitting her presence at the 'Britain First' rally. Then Coyne said bluntly, 'No, I lied to them. And if necessary you must lie too, Caroline.'

'Me? Why? Why should I lie?' Caroline was aghast.

'Listen, darling, and don't be angry.' Coyne spoke gently, persuasively. 'It really is desperately unfortunate that this should have happened just now. First there's this business of your father, then someone blows up my car – maybe that was meant for Meier, but I'm getting the publicity – and now John Rossel. The PM's working up for a Cabinet reshuffle, and I won't stand a chance in hell if I'm associated with Steve Smith.

So when the police showed me a photograph of him I denied all knowledge. Don't you understand?'

'I suppose so, but . . .'

'It's almost true, Caro. I scarcely knew the man. I don't think I'd met him more than twice. I was furious last Friday when you found him in my flat. John had sent him around to collect some papers connected with the firm. It was too bad of John. He usually kept his private life very private.'

Caroline didn't know how far to believe Coyne. He didn't sound as if he were lying, and anyway he could have no reason for lying to her, but she couldn't stifle her doubts. She asked, '*Was* Steve a freelance journalist?'

'I don't know. That's what John told me.' Coyne shrugged. 'Darling, it's nothing to do with us. The police know his name by now, and they'll trace him without our help. Promise me you'll forget you ever saw the bloody man. Please, for my sake, Caro.'

Caroline nodded. She couldn't refuse him. 'All right, Hector. I promise.'

'Thank you, darling.'

Coyne hid his relief. He kissed her and began to caress her. Almost at once she felt herself aroused, but she pushed him away.

'No, Hector. It's been such an awful day, and I'm exhausted.' As she spoke, Caroline heard in her own voice the intonations of her mother and was ashamed. 'I'm sorry,' she said. 'Tomorrow.'

Coyne didn't insist. He gave her a quick kiss and slid off the bed. 'All right, darling. Tomorrow. We'll treat ourselves to a splendid dinner and make a night of it. Incidentally, when's Irena going to produce that photograph of you?'

'Soon, I hope.'

'Good.' Coyne smiled at her. 'Bless you, darling. Sleep well.'

'Good-night, Hector.'

Thankfully Caroline watched the door close behind him. She plumped up her pillow, put out the light and tried to relax. But it was dawn before she slept.

149

SIXTEEN

Hector Coyne had refused personal police protection, partly because he had no confidence in its efficacy and partly because he felt it might circumscribe his movements.

Nevertheless, Coyne was prepared to be practical. He accepted advice on reasonable precautions and agreed to a minimal police presence at Wilton Mansions, in the shape of officers on duty at the front and the rear of the building twenty-four hours a day. If nothing else, this arrangement at least gave some degree of comfort to the more nervous of the block's tenants.

In general, it was Coyne's intention to continue to behave as normally as possible. The morning after his appeal to Caroline, he set off for a committee meeting at the House. Leaving Wilton Mansions, he greeted the police officer standing beside the front door, and waved in the direction of two men who had just got out of a car.

'That's Hector Coyne, the MP someone tried to blow up last Saturday.' The older of the two men, who was a member of the firm of agents that managed Wilton Mansions, shook his head in disgust. 'An unpleasant affair!' he said.

'He lives in this block? I didn't realize.' His companion, Manfred Brenner, allowed anxiety to show. 'Mr Spear, I'm not certain that . . .'

The agent hastened to reassure him. 'There's absolutely no danger, sir. The porters are on the alert, as you can imagine, and we have a police guard night and day. No one would be so stupid as to return for a second attempt here.'

'No, I suppose not.' Brenner smiled. 'But – is the apartment you're about to show me near Mr Coyne's?'

'It's on a different floor,' Spear said quickly. 'You won't be neighbours. Actually, the flat you're considering is directly above Mr Coyne. You wouldn't object to that, would you, sir?'

'No,' Brenner agreed. 'Especially as I gather furnished apartments in this part of London aren't all that easy to find.'

'They're certainly not.' Spear nodded to the police officer, and motioned to Brenner to go ahead of him into the hall as the porter held the door open for them. In the lift, he said, 'As I told you, Mrs Avery, who owns this flat, has been called away unexpectedly. Her daughter in New York is ill, and she's gone to stay with her for a while. She asked me to rent the flat for three months, with a possible further option. I take it that would be agreeable to you?'

'Fine,' Brenner said.

He wanted to laugh. It was an unexpected stroke of luck that any apartment in Wilton Mansions was available, and its location within the block could be a considerable bonus. He had called on the agents – their name was on a board outside the building – on the off-chance that he might learn something of value. What he was delighted to hear was that one of the apartments was actually for short-term rent. He would have taken it sight unseen, but knew this was not sensible; it would be unwise to appear over-eager.

'Here we are,' the agent said, flinging open the front door of a flat on the fourth floor. 'I'm sure you'll like it, sir. I know it's expensive, but it's beautifully furnished and equipped, and Mrs Avery has left absolutely everything – linen, china, everything, even some bottles in the liquor cabinet! She's merely locked one cupboard with personal things like clothes.'

Brenner nodded. He was studying the locks on the front door, and the evidence of an alarm system. 'She's a careful lady, I'm glad to see,' he said. 'Or do you provide all your apartments with such protection, Mr Spear?'

'Most people add to the standard arrangements,' Spear admitted. 'You can't be too careful. I regret to say it, but there are a great many burglaries in London.'

'In all big cities, these days,' Brenner said magnanimously. 'Even in my native Austria, alas.'

Spear showed him around the flat, and Brenner noted the layout and feigned an interest in the various amenities. He admired everything, and only casually reverted to questions of security, such as the frequency with which the night porters

151

did their rounds. He had failed once, and was determined not to fail again through lack of care in planning.

He stepped through the french windows of the sitting-room on to a small balcony, and looked about him. Below was a quiet London square with mature plane trees. There were a few pedestrians, the occasional car, and children playing in the central garden. In the middle of the night it would be dead. He could have wished for nothing better.

'If you can accommodate me over one or two matters, Mr Spear, I'll take the apartment,' he said. 'First, the rent – '

Spear held up his hand. 'I'm sorry, sir, but the answer has to be no. Mrs Avery left me no room for negotiation.' He spoke regretfully. 'I know it's exorbitant. I told Mrs Avery so, but she was adamant.'

'That's not what I was going to say, Mr Spear.' Brenner smiled disarmingly. 'My Austrian firm will raise no financial objection. The point is possession. I dislike hotels – even the best – and I should prefer to move in right now – today. I realize this is unusual, but I'll give you cash for the rest of this month, and a cheque for the remaining two. The other matter is references, which I'm sure Mrs Avery will require. In Vienna it would be simple, but here I'm less well-known and I would like to ask my business colleagues before giving you their names; it's only courteous. Would you mind a delay?'

As he spoke Brenner took a thick wallet from his inside breast pocket and held it in his hand. He looked at Spear expectantly and confidently. The agent's hesitation was minimal; he had already lost two good prospects over the rent.

'Whatever's convenient for you, sir,' he said. 'I'll get the agreement drawn up at once.'

And later that morning Manfred Brenner was explaining to the receptionist at his hotel that he was forced to leave London on a business trip. He hoped to be back tomorrow, but couldn't be certain; in any case, he would keep his room. The doorman stowed his luggage – a suitcase and a briefcase – in a taxi, and he told the driver loudly to take him to Victoria Station. Here he went in through the main forecourt, suitcase in one hand and briefcase in the other. Some minutes later he was catching a second taxi at the side entrance in Buckingham Palace Road.

At Wilton Mansions, as Herr Gustav Brandt, he was welcomed by the head porter to whom the agent had introduced
him earlier, and escorted to the lifts. He was grinning broadly
as he opened the door of the apartment. Before anything else,
he thought, he deserved a drink, and he regarded Mrs Avery's
well-stocked cabinet with satisfaction.

★

Hector Coyne and Caroline dined at a restaurant in Chelsea,
which had opened recently but already become a cult, packed
every night in spite of astronomical prices. Coyne, however,
had had no difficulty in making a reservation, even at the last
minute. His name was sufficient to ensure them a corner table.

While Caroline studied the menu Coyne ordered champagne.
It was one of the things that Caroline liked about him; when
he took her out he didn't stint. But champagne? 'What are we
celebrating, Hector?' she said.

'The fact that I'm still alive when I could so easily be dead.
Don't you think that's worth a celebration, darling?'

'Of course.'

'And the fact that we've made up our first lovers' quarrel.'

Caroline smiled, and returned her attention to the menu. She
had no wish to rehash their disagreement. She didn't want to
think of it. She was determined to enjoy the evening, and in the
event this wasn't difficult. The food was excellent, the service
unobtrusive and Hector laid himself out to be charming and
entertaining. It was some while since she had felt so close to him.

They were back at Wilton Mansions by eleven. The police
officer saluted them as they went in, and they met the night
porter crossing the hall, about to start the first of his rounds.

'Everything all right?' Coyne asked.

'Yes, sir. No trouble. But, as you said, we're not really
expecting any more, are we? Just taking a few extra precautions.'

'Fine. Good-night.'

'Good-night, sir. Good-night, Miss Dayton.'

As they entered the flat Coyne turned on the lights in the
hall and the sitting-room. In the room above Brenner, sitting

153

in semi-darkness by his window, saw the sudden brightness and knew his quarry had returned. Then the curtains below were drawn and the light outside faded.

'A night-cap, darling? Help you to keep awake,' Coyne said.

'You mean I'll need one, Hector?'

Hector Coyne laughed. 'I hope not. But we'll take a bottle with us – for the intervals.'

'Lovely,' Caroline said, and meant it.

Over dinner Coyne had drunk two-thirds of their champagne, but Caroline had had sufficient to make her feel happy and relaxed. She was in a mood to welcome Hector's lovemaking. It was some hours before they slept.

Coyne was the first to wake. He had no idea what had disturbed him, but he was instantly alert. Carefully he disentangled himself from Caroline and sat up. He was conscious of his heart thumping against his ribs. He listened hard, and he was almost convinced he had been mistaken when his ear caught an alien sound, and he knew without doubt that someone was in the flat.

Cautiously Coyne slid his legs over the side of the bed. It might be an ordinary thief, but with the notoriety that Wilton Mansions had achieved in the last few days and the police presence nearby it seemed improbable. No. Here again was his would-be assassin. Hector Coyne felt his adrenalin begin to flow. He didn't give the sleeping Caroline a thought.

He acted quickly. Sliding open the drawer of his bedside table he took from it the heavy service revolver that had belonged to his father and should have been returned to the War Office years ago. It was loaded and he knew how to use it. Pulling a robe around his body he crouched beside the bed. He had little time to wait.

The bedroom door was flung back. A beam of light shone on the tumbled bedclothes where he should have been lying. Caroline woke, sat up. 'What – ' she began, choking off her words as two guns fired almost simultaneously. A bullet ripped into the mattress beside her and she screamed.

Brenner had been slow. The half-empty bed and the naked girl had startled him. He had assumed that Coyne, in the aftermath of the car bomb attack, would conduct any affairs elsewhere. Too late, he realized what a fool he'd been.

Coyne's shot had been wild, but it had found its mark. The bullet ploughed into Brenner's right side, causing him to drop his pistol. Now he had few options. Aware that the sound of the shots – particularly that of Coyne's heavy revolver – plus the girl's scream, were likely to raise the alarm, he slammed the bedroom door behind him and fled.

His original plan had been to allow Hector Coyne one moment of terror before shooting him. Then he had intended to let himself out of the front door of the flat, and run up the stairs to his own rented apartment. A few hours later, in the morning, he would walk out of Wilton Mansions – an ordinary tenant, a businessman, briefcase in hand. And in the briefcase, apart from a few personal articles, would be the pair of rubber-soled sneakers and the black shirt he was wearing, his pistol, and the nylon ladder by means of which he had climbed down to Coyne's balcony. With luck, Coyne's body wouldn't have been found for some hours, at least, and by the time any possible connection with 'Herr Gustav Brandt' had been suggested, Brandt would have disappeared.

Such plans, however, were worthless. Coyne had survived, and he himself was wounded, possibly seriously, and probably not thinking straight. He needed help fast, but his first priority must be to put a safe distance between himself and Wilton Mansions. Almost without realizing it he found himself running down the stairs. The immediate problem was to escape from the building, and here luck was with him. There was no one in the rear hall, no difficulty in opening the door to the car park from the inside. As he did so, the thin moonlight gave him a glimpse of a policeman's helmet.

Brenner hesitated, wondering why the alarm had not yet been raised. Then he slipped out of the entry and, like a shadow, lost himself among the cars. Minutes later he was walking along a street. When he came to a drain he stopped and, taking the rolled nylon ladder from his pocket, thrust it between the iron slats. Now – apart from his appearance and his wound – there was nothing to connect him with the attack on Hector Coyne. And, not fifty yards away, stood a phone box.

Suddenly he thought of Keith Dayton, and the parallel between himself and Dayton, both wounded by gunfire, both

155

seeking help and seeing it in a public telephone, made him grin wryly. Both unlucky, he might have added, because when he reached the phone he found it had been vandalized. He leant against the glass wall of the box, pressing his hand to his side to ease the pain, fighting for strength to continue.

Eventually he managed a few further yards, but only to collapse in the doorway of a small grocer's shop. Here he was found soon afterwards by a roving police patrol car. At first they thought he was drunk, but as soon as the wound was discovered he was rushed to hospital. The doctor on emergency duty decided on an immediate operation.

*

'It's all right. The bugger's gone,' Coyne said, returning to the bedroom. He was breathing hard and his eyes were bright. 'And he won't be back! I winged him!'

'You shot him?'

'Yes. Why not? He came to kill me, didn't he?'

'I – I suppose so.'

Caroline was sitting up in bed, clutching a blanket round herself to stop shivering. She wasn't exactly afraid. Everything had happened too quickly for her to feel real fear, but she was shocked. Nor did Hector's behaviour reassure her. He stood in the middle of the room waving his gun in triumph, and his robe fell from his shoulders to disclose between his legs a large erection.

'I wish I'd killed the bastard. I could always have said I was defending you against the bloody Jewboy.'

'Hector! You don't know he was a Jew. You don't know who he was. And anyway why aren't you calling the police? He may be still in the building.'

'I doubt it. He'll have slipped through those damned guards going out, as he did getting in. A lot of use they are! What we need's a properly trained force. Then we wouldn't have scum like that wandering around.'

'Hector, we must tell them, and the night porter.'

'We are not going to tell anyone, Caroline. We're saying nothing about this little episode. Nothing, Caro darling, to anyone. You understand?'

156

'But why not?'

'Because I say so. Because I don't want any more fuss. Because we've better things to do.' Coyne thrust the gun into the drawer of the bedside table and got into bed. 'Come on, darling. I want you!'

'No! Hector, please no!' She tried to push him away.

'You didn't say that earlier. You're not going to be a difficult wife, are you, darling? Giving just when it suits you? You'll make me wish I was marrying that delectable little Rebecca your mother was talking about.' Coyne spluttered with laughter, seemingly half-drunk with satisfaction at his victory over the intruder. 'My God, the wedding of the year! Come on, Caro, let's have the screw of the year.'

Caroline struggled, only to desist when she found her movements excited Hector even more. There were things she could have done to fight him off, but she couldn't bring herself to attack him. After all, she had loved him. She had promised to marry him. She lay unresisting beneath him and let him take her, brutally and impersonally, as if she'd been a whore. Biting her lips to prevent herself from crying out as he hurt her, she vowed that this would be the last time.

Fortunately for Caroline, Coyne soon exhausted himself. He rolled off her, murmured something she didn't catch, and almost at once was asleep. Caroline waited. When she was sure he wouldn't wake, she got quietly out of bed, collected her clothes and went to the bathroom. She was bruised, and bleeding a little. Fighting back her tears, she washed and dressed. Her first impulse was to avoid a scene by fleeing from the flat, but she told herself not to be stupid. Instead, she went into the kitchen and made herself a pot of tea and, surprised at her hunger, some buttered toast.

By the time she had finished her impromptu breakfast she had reached a decision. She fetched a piece of paper and an envelope from Hector's desk in the sitting-room, and wrote him a note, enclosing her engagement ring. She left the sealed envelope in the middle of the kitchen table.

Outside it was beginning to grow light, but she realized that her handbag was still by the bed, and went quietly to collect it. As she did so, Coyne stretched and yawned. 'You're an angel, Caro,' he said. 'Kiss me.' He put out an arm to pull her down, but didn't protest when she evaded him.

'I must be off. I've a hair appointment at nine,' she said.

'Okay, darling.' He let her get to the door before he said, 'Caro, about last night . . .'

God! thought Caroline, here comes the apology. What do I do now? 'Yes?' she said coldly.

'Don't forget what you promised!' It was an order. 'No mention of that bloody Jewboy.'

Caroline's temper flared. No kind of apology, but . . . 'Why the hell do you keep on calling him that? You've no idea who . . .'

'No, perhaps not. But it's a general term of opprobrium, so it's applicable enough.' Coyne smiled at her. 'He intended to kill me, darling. You too, probably.'

'I see,' said Caroline flatly.

'But it's our secret,' Coyne insisted. 'You won't forget?'

'I shan't forget anything, Hector. It – all of it – was traumatic. Goodbye.'

*

Soon after Caroline left Wilton Mansions a flight from Brussels landed at Heathrow. Among the passengers was a man of medium height and slight build. He was fair with blue eyes, and he affected an air of weariness as if he were burdened with many problems. He was in his middle thirties, and he could have been taken for, say, a schoolmaster who disliked his work but was stuck with it. According to his Belgian passport his name was Pierre de Beaune.

He had no trouble with immigration. He was in London, he said with a smile that showed perfect white teeth, for a week's holiday. While he waited for his single bag, he made for a telephone.

Beryl Ackley answered. 'I'm sorry,' she said, 'but Mr Rossel isn't – isn't available. He was . . .'

'Perhaps I could help you, sir.'

The voice was suave, but it had broken in too quickly. Its owner must have been listening on the line. De Beaune sensed danger.

'Can you tell me when Mr Rossel will be available?' he asked.

'No, I'm not sure I can, sir, but if you'd give me your name and tell me where we can contact you . . .'

'Oh, I won't put you to that trouble.' In his turn de Beaune was equally suave. 'I'll call again later. Many thanks. Goodbye.'

Thoughtfully de Beaune put down the receiver. He collected his bag from the carousel and passed through customs without incident. In the arrivals hall he found another phone and tried Rossel's home number; it was always possible the man had been taken ill. An answering machine asked him to leave his name, phone number and any message, but he didn't take advantage of this opportunity. He was convinced now that something had gone wrong.

His agreement had been with John Rossel. It had been fully understood that Rossel wasn't speaking for himself alone, but no other names had been mentioned. Now de Beaune was in something of a quandary. Rossel had promised to be in his office this morning, but clearly was not there. What was he, de Beaune, to do?

He could go home and forget the whole thing. He had kept his part of the bargain and come to London on the appointed day. As he'd been paid half his fee in advance he wouldn't be out of pocket. But he considered himself a professional, and he disliked the idea of abandoning an undertaking.

Though Rossel had given him the minimum of information, de Beaune had followed his usual practice and made inquiries of his own. He knew far more than Rossel suspected about Rossel & Company and its activities, and he had wondered about the other directors.

Hector Coyne was still in bed when de Beaune tried his number. He was surprised, but immediately alert.

'Monsieur de Beaune, I thought everything had been completed,' he said. 'Except for the last payment, of course, and that's not in question. I can't imagine why you should contact me.'

'You prefer that I go home, Monsieur Coyne?'

'No. Certainly not.'

'Then we meet.'

Pierre de Beaune issued his instructions, and meekly Hector Coyne agreed.

SEVENTEEN

The death of John Rossel, following the attack on Hector Coyne, forced General Weatherby to a decision. It was vital to learn more about this damned list and, since Dayton had been unable to come up with any further names, his wife must be persuaded to disgorge it. Why she was so reluctant to do so, the General could only speculate, but maybe a carefully arranged confrontation between Keith and Irena Dayton would bring matters to a head.

As a result, Piercey and Farling again found themselves on the Daytons' Hampstead doorstep.

'Hello, Mrs Dayton. This time we've come with good news,' Piercey said cheerfully.

Irena looked at them in disbelief. 'What is it now?' she said.

'Mrs Dayton, Keith's in what we call a "safe house" in England. He's been flown from West Germany. He stood up to the journey quite well and, if you'll come with us, we'll take you to him now.'

'What?' Irena's face registered a range of emotions from joy to suspicion. She couldn't refuse – she didn't want to refuse, but . . . 'I shall have to leave a note for Caroline,' she said, 'to tell her where I've gone.'

'Of course.' Piercey grinned. 'But you needn't worry, Mrs Dayton. We'll bring you back safely.'

*

'Irena! Darling!' Keith Dayton held out his arms.

The doctor who had escorted Irena to Keith's room obeyed Dermot Piercey's instructions and left immediately. Dayton was alone with his wife. For a split second Irena hesitated, then she ran to the bed. Taking care not to hurt him, she embraced her husband, covering his face with kisses.

'My darling, my love!' Overcome with emotion, Irena burst into Polish.

'It's all right, Irena. Everything's all right now.' Keith stroked her hair.

In the adjoining room Piercey and Farling watched and listened. They weren't embarrassed at witnessing the meeting between the Daytons; it was an essential part of their plan. But neither of them was a voyeur from choice, and they were glad when Dayton gently pushed Irena away.

'The list,' he said. 'Irena, when I phoned you from Germany I gave you a list of names. At least I tried to. And a phone number for you to call. What did you do?'

'Keith, I didn't know what to do. I'm sorry, darling, but your voice kept fading and you weren't coherent; I couldn't understand half you said. I never got any phone number.'

'But the list itself,' Dayton insisted. 'You got some of the names, Irena?'

'Yes. All of them. There were ten. I have them safe, darling.'

'Thank God for that. You must give them to Piercey at once.'

'Piercey?' Irena was disbelieving. 'Are you sure, Keith? What's he done to make you say that? Look, Keith, on the phone you told me to trust no one, especially not Piercey. Now you want him to have the list. Are you ill, Keith? Or has he been threatening you – us – somehow?'

Keith Dayton stared at his wife. He felt incapable of providing a long explanation. The emotions of their meeting, brief though it had been, had exhausted him. He said, slowly and carefully, 'Irena, I was bringing that list to Dermot – for the Foreign Office. I wanted you to give it to him. It's my fault; I wasn't clear. But everything must be put right now, darling. Give Dermot Piercey the list.'

'Yes, Keith, yes.' Irena struggled to reassure him. 'I will.'

It can't be true, she thought. It was all a mess – and some of it was due to her. Perhaps she couldn't be blamed for having misunderstood Keith that dreadful night, but she ought never to have confided in Cas, and there was still the damning evidence found in the filing cabinet to be explained. She couldn't tell Keith about that now. Through her tears Irena looked down at her husband. His eyes were shut and he seemed to have fallen asleep. She bent forward and kissed him softly.

There was a tap at the door and Nurse Benson,who had been summoned by Piercey, came in. 'Mrs Dayton, your husband has had enough for the moment. I must ask you to leave.'

'Yes. I understand.'

Another nurse was waiting in the corridor. She took Irena downstairs and along to a sitting-room. Piercey and Farling were there and, to her surprise, so was a table laid for tea. Sandwiches and cake, bone china and silver. The incongruity of the situation made her want to laugh or cry – she didn't know which. The nurse left the three of them alone.

Piercey waved her to an armchair. 'Mrs Dayton, you've seen your husband, and been able to talk to him a little.'

'Yes,' Irena said. 'Thank you.' She watched Farling place a small table beside her, bring her tea, offer her sandwiches. She was thirsty, but she couldn't face eating. She said, 'Mr Piercey – ' and then she realized she didn't know how to begin.

Piercey made it easy for her. 'Now you've talked to Keith, Mrs Dayton, is there anything you'd like to add to what you told us before?' he asked gently.

Irena shook her head, but in bewilderment, not negation. She said, 'Mr Piercey, I'm sorry . . . Please try to understand.'

Words tumbled from her mouth, and this time they told the truth. Piercey and Farling were an attentive audience. They didn't interrupt, but waited until she had finished.

Then Piercey said, 'As usual there are a few questions, Mrs Dayton.' He gave a wry grin. 'First, where is the copy you made of this list? We need it as soon as possible.'

'I'll give it to you now, if you'll let me have a pair of scissors or a knife and I may go to a cloakroom.'

'What?'

The expression on Piercey's face cheered Irena. She smiled faintly. 'I've been keeping it sewn into my bras,' she explained.

Piercey nodded resignedly. 'And you've told no one about it except Sabik?'

'I gave him three names only, as I said, and since then –

162

with Hector Coyne and Rossel – it's been like a nightmare. I've not known what to do.'

'Did you suspect Sabik was a communist – a minor communist agent?' Farling asked.

'No. And I still find it hard to accept. He suffered badly under the communists in Poland.'

'Could he have planted the stuff we found in your husband's filing cabinet?'

'You mean, was he the man that night, the one who knocked over the flowers?'

'Yes. Or would it have been possible at any other time?'

'At no other time, no. I don't think so. He could have been the intruder, I suppose. But – you mean you do believe they were planted?'

Piercey didn't answer. There were a few more questions. They made her finish her tea and persuaded her to eat a little. Then the young nurse who had brought her downstairs took her to a cloakroom.

'Well, Weatherby should be pleased,' Farling said as the women left the room. 'We really seem to be getting places at last.'

'Let's hope so.' Piercey was more doubtful. 'Irena gives Sabik three names and swears to him that's all she knows. Sabik passes the information on to his pals, and they go into action. Dayton's attacked and Rossel's killed. It can't conceivably be coincidence.'

They were interrupted by Irena's return with a small piece of crumpled paper. Piercey glanced at it, and passed it to Farling without comment.

'What now?' Farling asked.

'Back to London – and some research,' Piercey said.

'Mr Piercey, do I have to come with you?' Irena said at once. 'Please let me stay. I'm sure Keith would like me to,' she pleaded.

Piercey reached a decision quickly. 'Very well, Mrs Dayton, you may stay overnight. I expect Nurse Benson can find you everything you need. But you must not leave this house and you may make no phone calls. We'll be in touch tomorrow. Agreed?'

'Oh yes, and thank you.'

Piercey shrugged as Nurse Benson took her away. 'I think we owe Keith Dayton that, at least,' he said to Farling.

He hoped Weatherby wouldn't disagree. He cogitated for a moment whether their success – their so far limited success – constituted a crisis and warranted a phone call before they left the safe house, but decided against disturbing the General's weekend. They might well know a good deal more by tomorrow morning, when a full report was due.

★

'Well,' said Farling once they were alone in their car, the glass pane separating them from the driver. 'I suppose it's some kind of hit-list.'

'I suppose so,' said Piercey. 'But why, in heaven's name, would Moscow want to eliminate Coyne, Mayberry, Rossel – and the rest of them? What have they got in common that would make them candidates for assassination?'

'The ones I've heard of – you could say they were right-wing, establishment types,' Farling suggested. 'With the exception of Steve Smith, of course.'

'You could,' Piercey agreed. 'But I don't see anyone of major importance. I can think of a hundred others who'd be better targets from Moscow Centre's point of view.'

Together they examined the list again. Though a few of those included were people of some eminence whose deaths might have merited a leading obit in *The Times*, the others would have had to be content with a paragraph, if they were mentioned at all. Some neither Piercey nor Farling had ever heard of. Three of the men were concerned with Rossel's firm, but apart from that there was no immediately apparent connection between any of them – they weren't even all males.

Back in their office Dermot Piercey and Ian Farling worked hard for several hours. When the right inquiries were made there was no lack of unexciting information concerning the people on the list.

Pausing to stretch and stifle a yawn, Farling said, 'Any ideas now, Dermot?'

'Not a one,' Piercey admitted. 'I dare say we could make a chart connecting A with B and B with C until we'd intertwined the whole lot – except for our friend Steve, of course – but apart from the fact that they all seem to be Brits I can't see that as a bunch they have anything positive in common.'

'Nor can I.' Farling pointedly looked at his watch.

'We'll call it a day, then,' Piercey said, taking the hint. 'But we'd better get in early to put something together for Weatherby.'

*

For years General Sir Christopher Weatherby's wife had been trying to break him of the habit of pulling at his shaggy eyebrows, but he still reverted to the gesture in moments of extreme stress or irritation. Now was such a moment. He had leafed through the report prepared for him by Piercey and Farling, and listened to their briefing. He regarded the crumpled list of names with a jaundiced eye. He had hoped to learn so much, but in reality had learnt little. All he had was what seemed to be some kind of totally irrational hit-list.

'Do you think there's any chance that as Dayton improves he may be able to remember any more of what Bauer said, other than that these people are in danger?' he asked.

Piercey shook his head. 'I don't think so, sir. Dayton was clear that that was all Bauer *did* say.'

'Which pretty well leaves us with Sabik, who may not know what it's about any more than we do,' Weatherby ruminated. 'And even if he does, he'll deny it.'

Farling said, 'Sir, there are the people actually on the list. Isn't it possible they may have some idea why they're there? I know Hector Coyne hasn't been able to come up with any reason for the attack on him, but some of the others might help.'

'They might.' Weatherby was reluctant. The fewer who were aware of the list the better, he thought. He knew how quickly rumours could spread, and grow in the spreading. Once the existence of a hit-list became known, God knew what might follow. Accusations. Denials. A diplomatic incident. Scandal. The media would leap at it.

165

'But before we tackle them, we'll have another go at Sabik,' he said finally. 'We'll get Special Branch to pull him in. We've enough on him to make things unpleasant, if we choose. Meanwhile I've an appointment with the PM at eleven o'clock.'

Weatherby sighed. He would have to decide whether or not to mention the list; the third man on it was a relation, albeit not a close one, of the Prime Minister's. Nevertheless, it would bring up the problem of protection, and even with the cooperation of the presumed target, this could never be totally effective. On the other hand, if he kept quiet about the list, and . . . The idea of enforced early retirement was unappealing.

'We'll have another meeting this evening,' he said, hoping he didn't sound as ineffectual as he felt.

EIGHTEEN

Caroline arrived home only seconds before the official black limousine drew up at the front door. Irena emerged and, as she waved to the driver, Caroline realized she was alone. Caroline ran to her, momentarily disappointed that Dermot Piercey wasn't with her.

'Irena? What is it? Where have you been?'

'Hello, Caro. Didn't you see the note I left you?'

'No. I – I spent the night with Hector. I've just got back. What's happened?'

'Believe it or not, I've been in the country somewhere in Kent, visiting Keith. I'm so happy. They've brought him back to England, to what they call a safe house, and he's getting better. Oh, Caro, it was wonderful to see him, to talk to him.' Irena's face was bright with remembered pleasure.

'Yes. It must have been. I envy you. I wish to God . . .'

Caroline's voice was tight, and Irena glanced at her shrewdly. The bruise on her cheek had faded to a dirty smudge, but she was pale and there were dark circles under her eyes. She looked tense and unhappy. Even the good news of her father hadn't noticeably cheered her.

Irena said, 'Let's go in. We'll make some coffee and I'll tell you all about it.'

'That would be great.' Caroline made an effort to sound genuinely pleased. 'I could do with something to eat, too. It's a long time since I had breakfast.'

Irena chatted as she made coffee, boiled an egg and buttered toast. In fact, apart from Keith's condition, she had very little she could disclose. Piercey had warned her not to mention the list, or anything connected with it. She must keep her own counsel on that subject.

'Is everything straightened out then?' Caroline asked absently as Irena began to repeat herself.

Irena hesitated, frowning. 'You mean about Keith? I don't know. I think they still have doubts. They certainly didn't confide in me.' She hurried on, wanting to forget her lingering worries, at least for the moment. 'But they were kind and considerate. Piercey even gave me permission to stay the night.'

Caroline nodded. She finished her egg and, like a child, pushed the plate away from her. Irena would be full of sympathy if she were told about Hector, but she wouldn't understand the unease – the fears, even – that he had created. Caroline scarcely understood them herself. She wondered if Dermot Piercey . . .

'Did Dad say anything about Mr Piercey?' she asked abruptly.

The question surprised Irena. She paused, then. 'Not really,' she prevaricated, 'but – but I would trust Piercey now.' When Caroline made no reply, she said hesitatingly, 'Caro, is something the matter?'

Caroline shook her head. 'No. Not really. But I'm not going to marry Hector.'

'You've quarrelled again?' Irena asked tentatively.

'No, not exactly. But I can't marry him. I was in love with him once, but I'm not any more. I don't even like him now.' Caroline chose her words carefully. 'I think I've known for some time, but I let myself be persuaded. I should have had more sense.' She grinned ruefully. 'You'll support me, won't you, Irena? I dropped by and told mother and she's furious. She refuses to believe me.'

'Of course I'll support you, Caro, if you've quite decided. And so will Keith,' Irena said. 'I'm not sure he ever wanted Hector as a son-in-law anyway.'

'Thanks.' Caroline smiled, and lapsed into silence. She was thinking of Dermot Piercey. She needed help and advice and, in the circumstances, surely he was the obvious choice.

*

Patricia Mayberry opened the front door to Coyne herself. She was startled by his appearance. His face was grim and even his

168

clothes looked less elegant than usual, as if they were somehow reflecting his mental stress.

'My poor dear Hector,' Patricia said. 'I saw you from the window. Come in. Come in. You must be distraught. I would be myself, except that I can't really believe it.'

'What do you mean? *You* can't believe it.' Coyne was brusque to the point of rudeness. 'You don't know anything about it. Where's Peter?'

'Upstairs in his study. But he can't help you.' Patricia was nonplussed by Coyne's behaviour, but she continued to be placatory. 'He's never had any influence over her. Not that I've got much. She's a wicked girl.'

'What on earth are you talking about, Patricia?' Coyne was halfway up the stairs but he stopped and stared down at her. Because of de Beaune's demand to meet with him he had been forced to hurry from his flat, and had failed to notice Caroline's envelope in the kitchen.

'Caroline, of course. What else? I know she says she won't marry you and the wedding's off, but I'm sure she doesn't mean it. She wouldn't be such a fool.' Patricia produced one of the wide-eyed smiles that nearly always achieved her purposes. 'Hector, my dear, you'll forgive her, won't you? It's just pre-marriage nerves.'

Coyne nodded. At that moment he didn't give a damn for Caroline, providing she kept her mouth shut about . . . He ran on up the stairs and strode into Peter Mayberry's study without knocking. Mayberry, who was just finishing a call to his stockbroker, said a hurried goodbye and regarded Coyne with some distaste. He expected everyone, including Patricia, to respect his privacy.

'What on earth's the matter, Hector? Surely it's not . . .'

'Caroline. Good God, no! I'll deal with that later. It's Rossel.'

'Rossel! What about Rossel?'

'It seems the arrangement was that when de Beaune arrived in London today he'd contact Rossel and they'd finalize their business – but Rossel wasn't available, of course.' Coyne flung himself into a chair. 'So he called me, just like that, as a director of Rossel's.'

'But he wasn't meant to know that we . . .' Mayberry had

forgotten his earlier annoyance. He was alarmed. 'Hector, what did you say to him? I hope you denied all knowledge of – of whatever arrangements he'd made with John.'

'Certainly not. It was impossible. De Beaune had been told, or he'd guessed, much too much. No, I had to do what he wanted.' Coyne spoke through gritted teeth. 'I picked him up at Heathrow and took him for a drive. Obviously I didn't want to be seen with him in public, and that seemed the best idea. We talked as I drove.'

'But what about? Hector, you didn't mention me, did you?'

Coyne's glance was disdainful. 'No, Peter, I didn't mention you, but I'm sure he knows of you. He's not to be underrated.'

'You think he might try blackmail?'

'No. He had the nerve to – to set my mind at rest on that score. He said his business wouldn't last a day if clients couldn't rely on his discretion.' Coyne winced at the memory; de Beaune had treated him with scant respect. Indeed, it was many years since he'd been made to feel so inadequate, so inferior, so amateurish almost, and to be humiliated by a man such as de Beaune had doubled the insult. 'But clearly he knows a great deal more about Rossel's – and about us – than we thought, and that's not pleasant, is it?'

Mayberry fidgeted in his chair. 'You should have cancelled the whole thing, Hector. Paid him the rest of his – his fee, if he insisted.'

'And then what? Wait for another God-sent opportunity like next weekend?' Coyne was disgusted. He failed to understand Mayberry's attitude; he'd expected him to have more guts. After all, he'd not had to deal with de Beaune personally. 'We'll never get such a chance again, Peter. All those lovely birds in one basket!' His lips parted in a mirthless smile. 'We couldn't turn down the opportunity. Not now everything's laid on.'

'If everything's laid on, what the hell did de Beaune want? Why didn't he just go ahead and do his job?'

'You won't believe it. I had difficulty in believing it myself. But Rossel's briefing hadn't been specific enough.' Coyne shook his head. 'Rossel had omitted the main point. De Beaune hadn't been told the – er – the targets.'

'Christ!' Mayberry said. 'Hadn't de Beaune asked before?'

'No. He was quite indifferent. Extraordinary, isn't it? He said it didn't matter, but naturally he had to know now.'

'So it's all settled, then?'

'Yes,' Coyne agreed. He couldn't explain to Mayberry how he felt, how de Beaune had both excited and revolted him.

*

Miss Sherwood didn't smile at Piercey and Farling as they came into her office. She merely bowed her immaculate grey head and gestured towards General Weatherby's door before returning to the work on her desk.

The two men exchanged glances. Piercey gave a minute shrug and suppressed a rueful grin; Farling grimaced in reply. Miss Sherwood's attitude was always a good barometer by which to gauge the General's mood, and it seemed that at present all was not set fair.

The barometer hadn't failed. For a moment the General regarded them coldly, as if they were a couple of private soldiers on a charge. But Weatherby himself was looking old and worn, and any amusement the younger men might have felt faded when his tired eyes met theirs. Then he made an obvious mental effort and waved them to chairs.

'I take it that neither of you reads *The Times* with care. You don't study what in my youth was called the "despatched" column?'

'Not usually, sir,' Piercey answered for both of them.

'I recommend it. For instance, today's issue contains notices of two deaths. Mrs Hamon-Smythe – ' The General glanced up and saw that both Piercey and Farling had realized the significance of the name. 'Mrs Hamon-Smythe died in her sleep some time last Saturday night at her home near Brighton. Presumably – and at present it's only a presumption – it was heart failure. She was seventy years old, but everyone thought she'd last another ten. She was very active on all sorts of committees, and often on radio and television, as you know. A woman of some influence – and on that damned list, of course!'

'It might have been a natural death, sir.' Farling made the obvious comment. 'At her age it wouldn't be unreasonable.'

'Agreed,' said Weatherby. 'But what gives me pause for thought is that early on Monday morning further along the coast Lord Lynwood met with an accident, as a result of which he subsequently died.'

'What sort of accident?' Piercey asked promptly.

'Apparently he fell over a cliff while he was out walking his dog.' The General paused. 'The key word is "apparently". Anyway, the details of both deaths are what you and Ian are going to investigate, Dermot. Lynwood and the Hamon-Smythe woman. I want preliminary reports on my desk by tomorrow morning. I've already made sure there'll be full autopsies, and the local police have been told you'll be with them. Five and Special Branch are aware of our interest, naturally.' Weatherby held up an admonitory hand as Piercey seemed about to speak. 'Dig deep – as deep as you can. Remember: out of the list of ten that Dayton got through to us, four are already dead, and it could easily have been five.'

'True, sir,' said Farling. 'But, apart from Coyne, they're all speculation. Have we any proof that Rossel and Smith were – '

'Yes, we have,' said the General angrily. 'If you were up to date with the reports on your desk you'd know that whoever killed Rossel and Smith made a mistake when he set the scene. He didn't know that Rossel was left-handed.' Weatherby turned to Piercey, who was frowning. 'Something worrying you, Dermot?'

'Sir, it's a question of timing. If you're right, we seem to have two assassins.'

Weatherby nodded, relaxing at last. 'Ah, you've finally taken that in. It seems highly improbable – though perhaps physically possible – that one man killed all four of them. We've got to narrow down the times of death to know for sure. That's part of your job. And if there are two killers . . .'

The General allowed the silence to lengthen. He wasn't heightening the drama of the moment. He was lost in thought, and his thoughts were not pleasant. They were reflected in his face, and neither Piercey nor Farling would have dared to break his obvious concentration. They waited patiently until the buzz of the intercom relieved them of their unease.

'I've had the Prime Minister's office on the line, General.' Miss Sherwood's voice was even. 'I'm afraid your first opportunity to see the PM will be late Friday afternoon. He left half an hour ago for an EEC meeting in Brussels.'

A slow smile spread across Weatherby's face. 'Thank you, Pamela,' he said; he rarely used her first name. 'Thank you very much. Bring in coffee now, please – for one.'

'We've had a slight reprieve,' he said, looking from Piercey to Farling. 'I can't report to the PM if he's not here. But it's only a respite. If anyone else from that list dies or is attacked in any fashion before I see the PM, I shall probably be for the chop. And I doubt if my successor would do more than put you out to grass in the Registry or some other dull corner.' The General relapsed into unaccustomed jargon. 'So, get with it. See what you can do. In the meantime, Five and the SB will give full protection to the others on the list, and you'll have all the back-up you need. Though I doubt if that'll help,' he remarked reflectively. 'What we need are some constructive ideas.'

'Yes, sir,' Piercey and Farling said in unison.

Miss Sherwood brought in the coffee tray, and Weatherby nodded his dismissal. They were at the door when he added, 'Sabik has been brought in and questioned without any result. He seems happy to admit to his piddling little betrayals to the Russians, but that's no help. Otherwise he whines about being a poor old Pole, tempted by the money Moscow offered. He didn't ring true to his interrogators, and he doesn't to me, though I'm not sure why. The reports ought to be on your desk by now.'

'Is he being charged, sir?' Piercey asked.

'Not at present. He's been allowed to go, but he's under surveillance, though I suspect he's too cunning to lead us anywhere.'

Weatherby bit morosely into a biscuit. He had little hope that Piercey or Farling would achieve anything of value, and none of his other sources were being of any help. This affair of Rossel & Company – if it was an affair of Rossel & Company

– was proving extraordinarily involved. Clearly something was odd about the concern, but it could easily be mere financial shenanigans without any bearing on the main issues. After all, more than half the names on the list had no connection with Rossel's. But then the list was a most curious conglomeration of disparate characters.

General Weatherby rose to his feet as Miss Sherwood came in to collect his tray and remind him of an appointment with the Foreign Secretary. He sighed heavily, wondering how he would fill his days if the PM asked for his resignation. Golf and gardening had never appealed to him, and good works he left to his wife, who wouldn't take kindly to having him around the house all the time. Life, he thought, was going to become extremely difficult unless he – or his staff – could pull something out of the hat.

*

'Which shall I take?' Farling asked, as together they went to their own offices. 'Lord Lynwood or Mrs Hamon-Smythe?'

'Whichever you want, Ian.'

Farling raised his eyebrows. He had put the question as a formality, assuming that his superior would want to go after Lynwood's so-called 'accident'; the old girl's death seemed to hold no promise. He said, 'Okay, if you're indifferent, I'll take His Lordship.'

'Fine!' Piercey hid his amusement; he'd guessed what Farling's choice would be. Personally he saw little hope of anything useful emerging from either assignment, and there was a point he hadn't mentioned: he had an uncle in Brighton. 'We'll compare notes this evening then, Ian. Good luck.'

Farling didn't believe in luck except as a reward for hard work. He was a conscientious officer and he did what he could with reference books and on the phone before he left for the south coast. Once there he made his number with the local police, took advantage of their knowledge and then, in the guise of a newspaper reporter, set off on some leg-work of his own. The results weren't commensurate with his efforts.

Lynwood had been a rich, powerful landowner, with many

174

influential directorships and seats on several important official and semi-official bodies. From time to time he had been asked to advise the Government on economic matters. He had been generally liked and, as far as could be determined, had no enemies and no worries. But all this was public knowledge; it would certainly already be known to Weatherby. It was also public knowledge, at least in the surrounding area, that every morning Lord Lynwood took his dogs for a walk along the cliff-tops adjoining his land.

On the previous Monday he had fallen, or jumped, or been pushed, over the edge. The dogs had raised the alarm and the body had been found quickly, so that the time of death had been established with some accuracy. There were no signs of struggle on the cliff-top, and no evidence that his death had been other than the result of an accident – a stumble, a sudden giddiness, an over-exuberant dog.

So, Farling reflected as he drove back to London, he hadn't ruled out an attack, but he'd found no evidence to support one. To judge from the timing, however, if Lynwood had been deliberately killed, his murderer could not also have killed Rossel and Smith. This was a poor result from a hard day's work, Farling thought bitterly, and not one that would bring joy to General Weatherby.

For his part, Dermot Piercey had had a good day, though in terms of gathering information he had achieved no more than Farling. Unlike Lord Lynwood, Gertrude Hamon-Smythe seemed to have been unpopular in her neighbourhood. She was variously described as 'bossy beyond words', 'interfering', 'a crazy old witch', 'a damned Nazi'. But there was no scintilla of evidence to suggest that she had not died naturally and peacefully in her sleep.

Piercey took the opportunity to lunch with his uncle, a retired doctor. A widower, he was always glad to see his nephew and, while they ate the ample meal his housekeeper provided, they exchanged family gossip. It was not until they were drinking coffee that he inquired what Piercey was doing in Brighton.

'Don't tell me if you'd rather not,' he added hastily, knowing something of Piercey's work.

'Well, for your ears only, I've been looking into the death of a Mrs Hamon-Smythe,' he said.

'That old hag! She should have been put away years ago. She was mad!' The doctor was vehement, surprisingly so. 'Not certifiable perhaps, but mad nevertheless. I attended her once when her own doctor was away and – can you believe it? – she had a photograph of Hitler in her bedroom, autographed, too. She told me proudly that she'd bought it at an auction in Vienna.'

Dermot Piercey laughed. 'No, that's the first I've heard of that, but I had gathered she was pretty eccentric.'

'Eccentric! She was a menace! Only a whiff that someone might have mild leftish views, and she'd do her best to get them removed from whatever job they held. The woman was stuffed with prejudice.' The doctor shook his head in disgust. 'She even disinherited her son because he married a girl she disapproved of. In fact, I met the girl. She was charming and intelligent, but she happened to have a Jewish mother, and that was enough for Mrs Hamon-Smythe.'

'Not your favourite person, Mrs Hamon-Smythe, obviously,' Piercey commented.

'Not on your life. She wasn't only mad, she was bad!'

Dermot Piercey was impressed. He knew his uncle to be a broad-minded, compassionate man, and never before had he heard him condemn anyone so whole-heartedly. Clearly, Gertrude Hamon-Smythe had been a most unpleasant woman. But that single fact, Piercey ruminated as he in turn made his way back to London, was unlikely to satisfy General Weatherby as the only outcome of a day's investigation.

NINETEEN

'Answer, damn you! Answer!' Caroline said to her telephone. She could hear the instrument ringing in Dermot Piercey's flat.

She had been trying to get hold of Piercey for the better part of the day, but without success. It was now almost seven o'clock in the evening and she was becoming annoyed. Worse, she was beginning to doubt whether the action she proposed to take was for the best.

There was a sudden click on the line and an impatient voice said, 'Hello! Hello!'

'Dermot! At last. Where have you been? I've been ringing and ringing.'

'I've had a day at the seaside.'

'What? This is Caro – Caroline Dayton.'

'That I'd guessed. And if you've got yourself arrested again I'm not interested. I just wish you a comfortable cell.'

'Generous of you! As it happens the police aren't after me at the moment. I'm at home, in my Hampstead flat and . . .' Her voice had altered, lost its bantering tone and become serious. 'Dermot, I need to talk to you. It's important.'

'What about?'

'I don't think I should tell you on the phone.' She spaced her words. 'But it *is* important.'

'To you or to me?'

'To both of us.'

'Okay. If you mean what I think you do, Farling and I will be along in the morning. Is that convenient?'

Caroline drew a deep breath. She didn't know if he was being deliberately obtuse, or if he really didn't want to meet her alone. 'No,' she said. 'It's not convenient. I don't want to be officially interrogated. I want to talk to you, by yourself, as soon as possible. Please, Dermot.'

'Look, I've just got in. I want a drink and some supper.'

'Would you rather I came to you?'

'No!' It was an emphatic negative.

'Then come here. There's plenty to drink and I'll make you supper. But please come, Dermot.'

'All right,' Piercey said finally, sounding resigned and ungracious, but in reality wishing that the proposed visit didn't give him so much pleasurable anticipation. 'I'll be along shortly.'

'Thank you,' said Caroline meekly, and meant it, glad that she was now committed to telling Piercey what she knew and feared, regardless of any promises to Hector Coyne.

Nevertheless, when Piercey arrived almost an hour later, she felt surprisingly nervous. Nor did his manner help. He accepted a drink, but at first made it clear that he considered this to be a duty call rather than a social visit.

'Well,' he said while Caroline was still fussing with the drinks. 'What's the mystery? Is it something to do with your father?'

'No, I don't think so. Not directly, at any rate.' Somehow, with Dermot Piercey sitting there and waiting for an explanation, what she had to say seemed of little relevance, if not plain stupid. She took a long swallow of gin and threw herself into an armchair opposite him. 'There are two things, really,' she said, 'both sort of connected with Hector.'

'Your fiancé, yes.' Piercey's voice was level, his smile cynical.

'Not any more. I've told him, and my family, that the wedding's off.'

Piercey swirled the whisky in his glass, watching the amber liquid change colour. Outside, after a fine day, the sky had clouded over and suddenly rain lashed against the windows. The momentary violence covered Piercey's silence. By the time it subsided he had his feelings well under control.

'And now you've told me,' he said, for want of better words.

'Yes.' Caroline brushed his remark aside. 'The first thing is about this Steve Smith,' she said. 'I met him, once, in Hector's flat, and I saw him again at that "Britain First" rally last Sunday.'

'You're sure it was Steve Smith, Rossel's boyfriend?' Piercey was intrigued; he remembered that Coyne had denied all knowledge of Smith.

'Positive,' Caroline explained the circumstances. 'I know Hector lied to the police – he didn't want the publicity – but that's understandable, isn't it?' she concluded.

'Yes,' Piercey admitted.

Indeed, he did appreciate Coyne's point of view. No MP would want to be associated with such an unsavoury murder-cum-suicide. As for Smith, his part in the rally as described by Caroline was consistent with what was known of the man. What didn't fit, what never had fitted, was his name on that wretched hit-list.

Then Caroline said, 'I think Hector lied to *me*, too. I don't believe he and Smith were the – the casual acquaintances he told me. It's terribly difficult to say why, but I got the impression they were doing business together that evening, and I – I'd interrupted them.'

Business together? Piercey frowned, then sniffed. 'Something's burning,' he said absently.

'Oh God!' Caroline ran for the kitchen, calling to him over her shoulder to help himself to another drink.

Piercey stood up, went to the side table and unscrewed the top of the whisky bottle. He was standing there, bottle in hand, deep in thought, when Caroline returned.

'No damage done,' she said. She stared at him, and laughed. 'A penny for them . . .'

Piercey regarded her seriously. 'My thoughts could be worth a whole lot more than a penny. Tell me. You say that at the rally you saw Steve Smith put something to his mouth and then the trouble erupted. It could have been a pea shooter adapted to take a little metal pellet – a most effective weapon to startle a horse and start a riot. Did you see him later?'

'No. I didn't have much chance, I suppose, but no, I didn't see him. Why do you ask?'

'He's got a reputation for being a left-wing activist, but somehow he never gets himself arrested. I wondered if he could be a paid agitator, an *agent provocateur* if you like, working for the right,' Piercey said slowly, and thought that, if this were so, it would explain a great deal.

'Working for Hector and – and John Rossel?' Caroline had grasped the point almost too quickly.

'Not necessarily.' Piercey brought his drink back to his chair. 'I'd hate to make such an accusation without evidence, especially against an eminent member of the House.'

Caroline looked at him sharply, but Piercey's face was hidden in his glass. 'I wouldn't put it past him,' she said. 'He's a strange man. I hadn't realized how strange till quite recently.'

Remembering the previous night, Caroline pursed her lips as if she had tasted something bitter. She was still physically sore from Coyne's violence and, paradoxically, ashamed of what he had done to her. She didn't want to tell Piercey about it.

She said, 'If you've finished your drink, Dermot, supper's ready.'

'Thanks.'

He had noticed the tautness in her voice when she'd spoken of Coyne just then, and he knew she had more to tell him, but he didn't press her. He went to the table, set intimately for two at the far end of the room, and lit the candles while she brought in the food. The avocado was followed by a casserole, fresh fruit and cheese, with a bottle of good claret. It was a simple meal, but excellent and appropriate, and he appreciated the trouble she had taken to produce it at such short notice.

When he complimented her, Caroline said, 'One of the few useful things I learnt at my expensive Swiss finishing school was to cook, but the ingredients you owe mostly to Irena. I raided her kitchen.'

'How is she?' Piercey asked.

'Much happier now Dad's in England and getting better, but still worried about him being under some kind of cloud – some suspicion. Dermot . . .' Caroline leant across the table towards him. 'Please, may I tell her she has no cause to worry, that Dad's in the clear? He is, isn't he?'

Piercey hesitated. 'It's all more complicated than you know,' he said. 'Irena . . .'

'You surely don't suspect Irena of anything?'

'No. Nor your father. Not now,' Piercey admitted. Then he grinned. 'Okay, Caro, tell her, but for God's sake impress on her that she mustn't mention it to a soul. That goes for you too. Otherwise you'll get me sacked, or worse.'

'Bless you!' Caroline said, and gave him a radiant smile, which suddenly faded. 'I'll bring coffee. I – I guess you know I've more to tell you.'

Dermot Piercey waited. He was aware that, whatever was to come, Caroline found it difficult or unpleasant to explain. He wondered if perhaps she was already regretting her break with Coyne, and the doubt made him less responsive than he might have been.

As Caroline carried in the coffee, he said, 'How's Coyne taken your *démarche* – about your engagement, I mean?'

'I don't know. I've not seen him since – ' Caroline concentrated on pouring the coffee, but Piercey's question had given her the opening she needed. She said, 'Look, Dermot, it was like this. Last night Hector took me out to dinner and I went back to his flat with him.' She saw Piercey's expression and continued angrily. 'Don't be Victorian. I'm not promiscuous, if that's what you're thinking. After all, we were engaged. And there's only been Hector and a boy in Switzerland, years ago, when I was seventeen and I wanted to know how it was.'

'And how was it?'

'Uncomfortable and unsatisfactory, if *you* want to know.'

Dermot Piercey laughed, and the tension between them was broken. Caroline gave him the facts, as she knew them, about the intruder and the attack on Coyne the previous night. She couldn't have had a more attentive audience and, when she had finished, Piercey's questions came fast.

Would she recognize the would-be assassin again? Was she sure the man was wounded? Did Coyne usually keep a gun beside his bed? Why didn't he want to report the attack? Her answers to most of these and similar questions were either 'No', or 'I don't know', and thus highly unsatisfactory to Piercey.

'And what did Coyne do after the chap had gone?' he asked at last, almost desperately. 'Did you spend the rest of the night arguing about whether to call the police, or did he just come back to bed and go to sleep?'

'He raped me,' Caroline said simply.

'What?'

Caroline nodded, unwilling to repeat the word. Instead, she tried to explain. She said, 'He seemed to be hyped up. The attack and the fact that he'd shot the man made him terribly – terribly excited.'

Dermot Piercey stared at her, appalled. The knuckles of his hands where he gripped the arms of his chair grew white. Then he pulled himself together and said, 'My dear, I'm sorry. But it's a – a well-known syndrome, you know. After extreme excitement – You must have heard of athletes and boxers and all that.'

'Of course,' said Caroline. 'I've tried to make allowances, but Hector kept on saying things like, "I winged the Jewboy" and – '

'The Jewboy?' Piercey interrupted. 'You mean Coyne identified the man?'

'No. He was using the word Jewboy as what he called a "term of opprobrium". He was usually careful in public, but I know he hated Jews. I've heard him make dreadful remarks about the Foreign Secretary and he's always saying it's time something was done to stop the country being run by Jews.' Caroline heaved a sigh. 'It wasn't just last night. I must have been mad to think I could ever be happy married to him.'

'Well, it's over now, Caro,' Piercey said, adding anxiously. 'You're all right, aren't you?'

'Yes, I'm all right, Dermot.' She smiled at him. 'As you say, it's over, ended – completely. And I'm better still now I've told you about it.'

'I'm glad of that.' Reluctantly Piercey got to his feet. An idea had been forming in his mind and he knew there were things he had to do.

'Must you go?' Caroline was startled. 'It's still early.'

'I'm sorry, but I've some unfinished work. I'd much rather stay, believe me.'

'Okay.'

She didn't argue, but saw him to the door. He looked at her

182

a little doubtfully as he thanked her for the supper. She said, 'Another night, perhaps,' and, reading her expression, he caught her in his arms and kissed her.

*

The night nurse made her rounds and stood for some moments by Manfred Brenner's bed. The operation had been simple and successful, the bullet had been removed and the patient was well out of his anaesthetic, sleeping peacefully. One she needn't worry about, the nurse thought, and wondered who he was, this man who had been shot and left for dying in the street earlier that day. She shrugged her shoulders: that was a problem for the police, when they returned to question him.

As he heard the rustle of her departing skirts, Brenner slowly opened his eyes. In fact, he had awakened some while ago, and had at once guessed where he was and what had happened. Instinctively, to avoid awkward questions, he had given no indication of consciousness.

Now he moved his body gently under the bedclothes, trying to assess how much strength he had. From the position of the bandages on his body it looked as if the bullet had gone between his ribs and his right arm, injuring both in the process, but the size of the dressings suggested that he'd been lucky and Coyne had done him no great harm. Inch by inch he lifted himself into a sitting position.

He knew it was vital to escape from the hospital. He couldn't continue to feign unconsciousness indefinitely, and he was in no position to face police enquiries. Pushing back the bedclothes, he swung his legs to the floor and stood up. Gingerly he took a few steps, relieved to find that he could walk unsteadily but without too much pain.

The first problem was clothes. He was wearing only a standard surgical gown which opened indecently all the way down the back. He wouldn't get far in that, certainly not in the street, he thought, and a wry grin turned into a grimace as he moved indiscreetly.

At least the lights in the ward made movement simple and by chance his bed was close to the door, the night nurse busy

183

with a distant case. Brenner made slow and unnoticed progress, managing to collect a dressing-gown and a pair of slippers on the way. By the time he got to the corridor he was any ambulant patient in search of a lavatory. He passed a hurrying nurse, a couple of porters pushing a trolley on which lay a still form, a doctor speaking into a wall phone. No one paid him the slightest attention. He was lucky when he reached the lifts. An empty car arrived almost immediately and he descended to the ground floor.

Here there was more activity, people moving purposefully, and no unattended patients in robes and slippers. A nurse sitting at a desk looked at him curiously as he shuffled past her. He thought she was going to call after him, but a colleague hurried up and distracted her. Brenner was at a loss. He had got so far but, dressed as he was and without money, he couldn't leave the hospital. He realized he had made a mistake; he had acted too precipitously.

Already, after relatively little exertion, he was exhausted and in a cold sweat. He suspected that this was the result of anaesthesia rather than his wound, but he knew he had to rest and reconsider. He took a side corridor at random and leant against the wall. Then, slowly, eyes shut, he slid down until he was in a half-sitting position on the ground.

Here he was found, semi-conscious, as Dermot Piercey arrived at the hospital.

*

After leaving Caroline, Piercey had wasted no time. He had gone straight to his office and the telephone, and it hadn't been difficult to discover that in the early hours of the morning a man with a gunshot wound had been found in a shop doorway a short distance from Wilton Mansions and taken to the nearest casualty department. It was more difficult to deal with the hospital's bureaucracy, but Piercey's credentials, aided by Brenner's obvious attempt to get away, proved sufficient.

Brenner was moved to a private room, and an orderly established by his bedside until Special Branch officers could take over. Meanwhile, Piercey was shown the clothes that the patient had worn when he was brought in; they had been kept in a locker in the ward office. There were Brenner's dark trousers and sweater, his rubber-soled sneakers and the contents of his pockets, a handkerchief, a couple of keys, a small purse containing money, but nothing to identify him. Nor was the sight of Brenner's still form any use.

It wasn't until the nurse who had been on duty in the recovery room after the operation to remove Brenner's bullet was brought to him, that Piercey learnt anything of value.

Questioned about her patient, she said, as an afterthought, 'I think he's Jewish. Like me. He doesn't look it particularly, but he muttered as he was drifting into sleep after coming round from the anaesthetic. I didn't really catch what he was saying but, whatever it was, it was in Hebrew.'

TWENTY

'The Israelis,' General Weatherby said meditatively. He seemed rather less surprised than Piercey had expected, but he added, 'Aren't you rather jumping to conclusions, Dermot?'

'I don't think so, sir. It's only a theory, admittedly, but the pieces fit together, and in my opinion it's worth pursuing.'

'Pursue it then.' Weatherby pulled at his right eyebrow. 'Expound it for me.'

It was nine o'clock the next morning. Dermot Piercey hadn't been to bed. Having ensured that Brenner wouldn't have another opportunity to escape, Piercey had returned to his office. There he had spent the rest of the night once more going through the files of the ten people on the list, and waking a variety of others irritatingly early with phone calls. He was now convinced in his own mind, but uncertain about convincing the General.

Brushing a hand across tired eyes, he began: 'First, the background. In the last year or two there has undoubtedly been a growth of anti-Semitism in this country, with obvious political overtones. It's been reflected both in big events and in ludicrously small ones, from the fire bomb thrown into that synagogue in south London to some girl who complained to the Race Relations Board that her colleagues in the office made fun of her big nose. Sir, if only half what Rabbi Richler has brought to public attention is true, we have reason to be ashamed, if not seriously worried. What's more, someone thought what he was saying important enough to try to shut him up – hence the attack that ended in the death of Aaron Kaufmann.'

'As far as I know,' Weatherby said as Piercey stopped, 'the police have got nowhere either with the synagogue fire or with

186

Kaufmann's murder. All they can say is that rumours in the underworld suggest they were both the work of left-wing extremists, possibly Libyans, possibly home-grown.'

'Or possibly this chap Steve Smith, sir. Anyway, it's easy to start rumours.'

'How right you are.' Weatherby nodded. 'Go on.'

'Any growth of anti-Semitism in a foreign country is of concern to Israel. Apart from the moral aspects, it can affect a multitude of things, political support and cooperation, arms deals, general trade, the ordinary give and take between nations well-disposed to each other. Developments of this sort in the UK would be viewed with particular sadness, because the British have always had a reputation for generosity towards the Jews.'

'Agreed, but you can't suggest that our present Government is anti-Israel, Dermot.'

'On the contrary, sir. Our Foreign Secretary's Jewish himself, as you know. A lot of people believe he'll be the next Prime Minister – a worthy successor to Disraeli. But I've been going through the files again and I've made some other enquiries and . . .' Piercey paused for emphasis. 'Sir, I'm as good as certain there's not a single person on that list of ten who doesn't consider a Jewish cabinet minister, let alone Prime Minister, a disaster for the country.'

'Possibly not.' Weatherby, who had been listening intently, was frowning. 'Nor would they be the only ones. There's always prejudice; you can't legislate against it – though they try these days, it seems.'

'Sir, the Israelis are fully aware of that.' Piercey was now speaking fast and urgently. 'But I'm talking about more than mere prejudice. Suppose the Israelis discovered there was a conspiracy among a small group of influential people in the UK to oppose Jews in every sense, to block their progress, to bring the more successful of them into disrepute and in extreme cases to kill them. Then what would you expect them to do?'

'Inform the authorities here, naturally.' Weatherby raised his hand as Piercey opened his mouth to object. 'I know, Dermot. The next question is what would we do, and the probable answer to that is damn all, unless specific accusations could be made. Even then – I don't know. We'd bear the situation in mind, of course, but if the people said to be involved were beyond reproach, as it were . . .'

'The Israelis aren't people to take things lying down, sir. They don't turn the other cheek. And, as I said before, their national interests could be affected in a variety of practical ways.'

'That wouldn't justify Mossad sending operatives into the UK to eradicate British citizens, which is what I gather you're suggesting, Dermot.'

Piercey said firmly, 'Justified or not, sir, that *is* what I'm suggesting. I think that at first they intended the deaths to appear accidental, so there'd be no question of harming relations between them and us. But once they thought we had that famous list they decided to risk overt violence, and hope we'd blame Moscow.'

'Which we did,' Weatherby said. 'Not unreasonably our thoughts tend to turn in that direction, and in this case we were encouraged. There was a certain spread of disinformation, for instance – the suspicion thrown on Keith Dayton, and the fact that Casimir Sabik was a known communist agent.'

'Yes, indeed, sir.' Piercey was encouraged by the General's seeming acceptance of what he had been saying. 'And it was easy to forget that Sabik was also a Jew. I suspect that when the chips are down he's more Jew than communist.'

'It could be. It might account for his behaviour.' Weatherby was interrupted by the burr of one of his telephones. 'Yes,' he said, and listened for some minutes. 'Yes,' he said again. 'Thank you.'

He put down the receiver and turned to Piercey. 'News, Dermot,' he said. 'Special Branch have been busy. A photograph of your hospital chum was recognized at Wilton Mansions as a new tenant. Yesterday, one Herr Gustav Brandt rented the flat directly above Hector Coyne's for three months. He paid cash in advance and moved in at once, references to follow. He claimed to be an Austrian, here on business, who disliked hotels and was anxious to get out of the one he was staying in. Possible hotels are being checked, of course, but that's a big job.'

'And he'll have registered under another name, for sure.'

'I expect so. I'll send Ian Farling around to Wilton Mansions, and to Brandt's hotel when it's traced.' Weatherby was thinking quickly, organizing. 'This is what I want you to do. Go to the safe house and . . .'

The instructions were succinct, but detailed. When it was clear the General had finished, Piercey got to his feet. 'What about Hector Coyne, sir,' he said, 'and Mayberry and the rest of them on the list?'

'They're either getting protection or are under surveillance, whichever you like to call it. Have you had a chance to study the reports on Coyne? No? Well, yesterday morning, after failing to inform anyone of the excitements the night before, he shot out of Wilton Mansions, drove fast to Heathrow and picked up an incoming passenger. They didn't shake hands when they met and they didn't seem particularly friendly. Coyne then took him for a fairly long drive before dropping him at Charing Cross. The team had enough sense to split into two. The new chap took a taxi to the Savoy and registered as Pierre de Beaune. He's said to be a businessman from Belgium, and we've already telexed Brussels.'

Weatherby flicked on his intercom and asked Miss Sherwood to send for Ian Farling, and Piercey knew he was dismissed. As his fingers closed round the door knob, the General added, 'By the way, Dermot, there's something else you won't have seen.' He grinned. 'I should probably have told you before. An unconfirmed but interesting report's come in. One of our sources in Israel says that a certain so-called "hit-list" has been sent to the British from Tel Aviv, of all places. Does that make you feel better?'

Typical, thought Piercey, typical of the General to keep the clincher till last. 'It certainly does, sir,' he said. 'But why? Could someone in the know have had a crisis of conscience – a wife perhaps or a girlfriend – someone who didn't like the idea of such killings?'

Weatherby gave no answer. He was reaching for a phone, his mind apparently already elsewhere. Nevertheless, Piercey, as he passed through Miss Sherwood's domain and went along the corridor to his own office, was smiling to himself with satisfaction.

★

Brenner woke to find himself in a moving vehicle. Its equipment identified it as an ambulance, but when Brenner gently shifted his position he found his wrists cuffed to the side of the stretcher upon which he lay. And the man sitting opposite him was no ordinary doctor. Beneath his neat grey jacket was a small and ominous bulge.

To relieve his feelings Brenner groaned as if in physical pain. He tried to remember how he had come to be here, driving at speed through what he assumed to be the English countryside, but he could remember nothing from the time he collapsed in the hospital corridor. A little more luck, he thought bitterly, and he might have got away. As it was . . .

He saw almost nothing of the house to which he was brought. He was conscious of gravel crunching beneath the wheels of the ambulance, and he guessed they were travelling up a long driveway. Then the vehicle stopped, the doors at the back were thrown open, his stretcher was lifted and carried inside. There was a wide hall, with a lift. It could have been a nursing home, but to Brenner it didn't smell right.

No one spoke to him, but his handcuffs were released and he was settled in bed in a room, pleasantly furnished and decorated, with a picture on one wall. The man who had accompanied him in the ambulance stayed watching him from a corner until another man in a white coat, whom Brenner assumed to be a doctor, appeared with a uniformed nurse and gave him a medical examination in near-silence. It was professional, but completely impersonal. Neither of them smiled at him or showed any concern for him. They treated him like an object they were assessing; they would have shown more regard for a dog. Brenner found it disturbing.

Until now he himself had asked no questions and made no attempt at communication, but when the nurse prepared his arm for an injection he protested. 'Who are you?' he said.

190

'What are you doing? Why are you treating me like a – a . . .'

He failed to find a suitable simile, and his attempt to bluster petered out. No attention had been paid to his words, in any case. The needle jabbed into his vein and he waited passively for another long period of unconsciousness. To his surprise, though he began to feel relaxed, there was no sense of drowsiness, of floating into nothingness. Rather he had a sense of anticipation, as if he were about to enjoy whatever was to happen.

The doctor and the nurse left the room and immediately the man from the ambulance returned. This time he pulled up a chair by the bed and produced a note book.

'Name. Rank. Serial number,' he said in a flat, businesslike voice.

It was on the tip of Brenner's tongue to respond with the truth, but he stopped himself in time. 'Brenner. Manfred Brenner,' he said firmly.

'Not Gustav Brandt today?' Again the question was expressionless.

'No. I don't know what – ' He must be careful, watch his tongue, Brenner told himself. Obviously he'd been drugged, but he must cling to his cover. 'I am Herr Manfred Brenner, an art dealer from Zurich. I am in London on business, and I demand to know what – '

'Where are you staying in London, Herr Brenner?'

Brenner gave the name of his hotel, and his interrogator smiled thinly. Dermot Piercey, listening and watching in the adjoining room, would pass on this item of information and save the police time and trouble. The interview was going well. So-called 'truth' drugs weren't necessary – just simple tranquillizers and a sophisticated interrogation technique.

'I shall call you David.'

'That's not my name.'

'Address me as sir! Do you understand?'

'Yes – sir,' Brenner replied reluctantly.

'Why did you rent a flat in Wilton Mansions under the name of Gustav Brandt?'

'I didn't.'

'Herr Brenner-Brandt, you've been recognized from a photograph. Why did you try to kill Hector Coyne?'

'I don't know what you're talking about.'

'Sir!'

'Sir.' Brenner glared. 'Why the hell should I call you sir?'

'Because in a very real sense you're under my command. I can do what I like with you. You're a long way from your country, David, and once they know we've got you, their immediate reaction will be to forget you. So bear that in mind, and let's start again. What's your name? What are you called by your family and friends, if you've got any?'

The interrogation continued. Question after question beat on Brenner. Sometimes they formed a sequence, sometimes they seemed to have no apparent connection. Sometimes Brenner answered truthfully, sometimes he lied. But it was a carefully planned interview, and many of his lies were revealing.

As time passed Brenner became more and more exhausted, the shooting, the operation and the drugs all having their effect. He closed his eyes. He yearned to sleep. The interrogator stretched as if he too were feeling the strain, and in the next room Piercey said to Keith Dayton, 'Now! You know what to do.'

'For God's sake, must I?'

'Yes, Keith. Sorry, but it's the simplest way.'

The interrogator heard the door open and, without turning his head, said, 'You remember Keith Dayton, don't you, David?'

Brenner opened his eyes, for the moment too shocked to speak. He looked up at the man he and Hean had left for dead in a burning car miles away in Germany. He waited, not knowing what was to come next.

Dayton acted swiftly. He pulled back the bedclothes, exposing the dressing on Brenner's right side. Then, avoiding Brenner's gaze, he clenched his fist and drove it into Brenner's body just above the wound. Brenner screamed and let flow a torrent of words, half oath, half prayer – and all in Hebrew.

The interrogator nodded his thanks, but Dayton was already staggering out of the room. The action he'd been forced to take had recalled his own nightmare in the German woods and he felt physically sick. Nurse Benson had to help him to his room, his only desire at that moment to forget what had just happened.

Piercey, watching through the one-way glass, felt no such compunction. Dayton's cooperation had been unpleasant but necessary. He dismissed it from his mind. The interrogation had begun again, remorselessly. Brenner was breathing hard, his face contorted with pain, and it was not always easy to hear what he said. Piercey had to listen closely.

'So you're a Jew, are you, David?'

'Yes.' There was no point in denying it, Brenner thought. The Brits knew; he was surprised how much they knew, even things he hadn't known himself – how Hean had died, for instance.

'An Israeli, born and bred? A proper Sabra?'

'Yes,' Brenner said. His father had been Russian, his mother German, but he himself had been born in a kibbutz. 'Yes,' he repeated, 'A proper Sabra, and proud of it.'

'Bully for you!' the interrogator said.

The expression was unfamiliar to Brenner and he frowned. He waited for the next question. The pain in his side was acute, and he brushed beads of perspiration from his upper lip. He wanted to cry, 'Hurry! Get on with it! Let's be done!' But, to his surprise, his questioner was standing up, preparing to depart.

'Okay,' he said, quite casually. 'Thanks.'

Five minutes later, as Brenner was enjoying the sensation of being alone, no longer harried by questions, Dermot Piercey came into the room. He was carrying a tray with coffee, a glass of water and two pills.

'Pills first,' he said. 'They're pain-killers. Very effective. You must be feeling like hell,' he added sympathetically as Brenner obediently held out a hand for the glass.

Brenner swallowed the pills, while Piercey poured them each a mug of coffee. Piercey watched him drink thirstily, and asked if he would like something to eat. Brenner shook his head

Piercey grinned at him. 'I'm in the British Foreign Office,' he said, 'and we need your help. Your country and mine are in a quandary.' He saw Brenner frown again, and explained, 'To put it simply, we've got a problem. It seems that here we have been allowing an anti-Jewish conspiracy to go on under our noses, and you've been sending in hit-men to eliminate the conspirators. Obviously this has got to stop. Too many innocent people have already been killed.'

Brenner's pain had eased and his mind could focus again; the pills must have contained more than just pain-killer. He studied Piercey with interest. This, he knew, was the soft sell that invariably followed the hard on occasions like this.

'What do you want to know – sir?' he said.

'No need to call me sir,' Piercey said. 'I serve my country much as you serve yours.'

'Oh yes.' Brenner was sarcastic. 'What do you want to know? The details of my assignments?'

'Not really.' Piercey's voice hardened. 'My friend, we've got enough on you already to put you down for the rest of your life and, though they may not be Gulags, British prisons can be pretty unpleasant places. I don't think you'd enjoy them. However, you're lucky. You've got a chance. We might be prepared to send you home.'

'Home – to Israel? On what conditions?'

'That will depend on your people – on whoever's running this operation. We'd like to come to some agreement with them, but to achieve that we need to know who to deal with, here in London and in Israel.'

'I can't tell you. I don't know. I'm not a high-up. I just get orders and obey them.' Brenner shrugged. 'I don't ask questions.'

'You must have contacts – a controller, at least.'

Brenner was silent. He thought of days and months and years in a cold British prison, of never seeing Israel again, of Hean dead, of the smug Cultural Attaché at the London embassy. If he were sent home, blown and burnt-out, he knew the best he could hope for was a routine office job. But would that be so bad? He was becoming sick of killing, and lately he'd been making mistakes; his nerve was beginning to go. That bastard at the embassy would send in an adverse report on him, but still – Perhaps it really was time he came in from the field.

'All right,' he said finally. 'It isn't a lot, but I'll give you what I know.'

★

'The General's gone to lunch,' Miss Sherwood said.

'Already? It's only just past twelve,' Piercey said. Elated by what he had learnt from the Israeli he had telephoned the office immediately. 'When will he be back?'

'I'm not sure, but he has a meeting with Sir Rupert at half past five. He said he'd like to see you and Mr Farling before that – probably around four.'

'And I'd like to see him,' Piercey said. The Director-General of M15 was an acid man, apt to criticize rather than cooperate, especially if he felt that anyone had been poaching on his territory. The last thing Piercey wanted was for his own Chief to go into a meeting with his opposite number unbriefed on the latest developments.

'Well, you'll have to wait till then, Mr Piercey. Goodbye.'

'Goodbye, Miss Sherwood,' Piercey said, though he'd already heard the click as she replaced her receiver.

He was surprised that he hadn't been given a contact number. Surely in the present circumstances Weatherby would have wanted him to keep in touch. He wondered what the old man could be up to. Twelve till four was an exceedingly long lunch hour, and Miss Sherwood had been oddly reticent.

It never occurred to Piercey, among his many speculations, that General Sir Christopher Weatherby had invited himself to lunch in the country with a member of his old school.

★

Weatherby did not enjoy his lunch. The food and wine were excellent, his hostess charming, but he found it hard to concentrate on conversation so far removed from his present preoccupations. The Arts Council and a new variety of Alpine plant seemed totally irrelevant. His host didn't help either; he was distrait and taciturn, as if he had a premonition of what was

195

to come. Chris Weatherby didn't unexpectedly invite himself to lunch without a purpose.

Now, the meal over, the two men were in the library, and Weatherby was enjoying himself even less. He hated to see a grown man cry. He went and stood at the window, staring at the rolling English parkland that stretched before him, and he waited for the *crise de nerfs* to end. When at last the sobs ceased, to be replaced by sniffs and nose-blowings, he turned around.

'Pull yourself together, Hugh,' he said brutally. 'I've no time to spare.'

'But what in God's name should I do, Chris? Stephanie – the children – I got out when I realized what Coyne and some of the others were doing. I swear – '

'Tell me all you know. From the beginning.'

'I've no idea how it began, whose idea it was originally, but a few of us were getting fed up. The bloody Jews seemed to be running the country, and we decided to take action before it was too late.' For a moment he glared at Weatherby through blood-shot eyes, and he added aggressively. 'I still think we were right – at that point.'

'Go on!' Weatherby showed no sympathy.

'There were twelve of us.'

Weatherby's expression didn't change, though the number had startled him. He listened to the names. Nine of them were no surprise; they were on that damned list. Three were new to him, though he recognized them as eminent individuals, all of whom had died in the last six months, two of apparent heart attacks, and one blown up in his boat with his small grandson. The Israelis, he thought angrily, had been more successful than he had realized.

'What about Steve Smith?' he asked.

'He – he wasn't one of us. Rossel found him somewhere and .we – we used him. There were some things . . .'

'Such as fire-bombing a synagogue? Things you wouldn't be prepared to carry out yourselves?' Weatherby's voice was harsh.

'I knew nothing about that till afterwards. I swear to God, I didn't. You must believe me, Chris. I hate violence. This started out as a propaganda campaign, and when I found what it had developed into I was sick, literally, and I wanted out. I told Coyne I wouldn't be a party to – to killings and suchlike.'

'And what did he say?'

'He called me a coward, and he threatened me if I opened my mouth. There was an almighty row. Some others, like Lynwood, felt as I did, but there was a hard core – Coyne and Rossel and Gertrude Hamon-Smythe and, to a lesser extent perhaps, Mayberry. They said we could please ourselves, but they wouldn't stop.'

Clearly, he found it a relief to confess. He continued to talk, and it was half an hour before Weatherby got up to take his leave. He had learnt a certain amount about human nature, but little of value except that over the years Rossel & Company had been used as a cover for a variety of semi-illegal undertakings – the repayment of favours, handing out bribes, odd imports.

'For instance,' his host said as they went into the hall, 'I don't know if it's important, Chris, but I met Mayberry in our club the other day and he let slip that Rossel had made a large payment to a chap in Belgium recently. I got the impression it could be for some anti-Jew thing, but he shut up when he remembered I wasn't with them any more.'

'And that's all he told you?' Weatherby said calmly, though he had instantly thought of Hector Coyne meeting a man called de Beaune off a Brussels flight.

'Yes. I didn't ask questions. I didn't want to know.'

'Right. Thanks for the lunch. Say goodbye to Stephanie for me. And don't forget,' Weatherby paused outside the front door and added in a low voice, 'no mention of this talk of ours, or you'll end up in jail.'

His host nodded; he couldn't bring himself to speak. But Weatherby was well satisfied.

TWENTY-ONE

By the time Weatherby had reached his office and been briefed by Dermot Piercey, it was clear to him that, if suitable action was to be taken, all the appropriate authorities had to be informed. The result, as always, was a series of meetings, involving in this case himself as Chief of the SIS, the Director-General of the Security Service, the Foreign Office and the police, including the Special Branch. The trouble was that, also as always, the interests of the various agencies diverged.

The Commissioner of the Metropolitan Police, after some initial hesitation, seemed to feel that sufficient evidence existed to arrest the surviving 'conspirators', as the meetings came to refer to those on the so-called hit-list. This, he argued, would have the double advantage of protecting them from further attempts on their lives as well as subjecting them to the full force of the law.

The Home Office disagreed, insisting that the evidence against them was inadequate and that, distinguished people as they were, they might be questioned but not held. Sir Rupert, the Director-General of 'Five', who considered that Weatherby had overstepped his authority and seriously encroached on MI5's territory, agreed. His approach was to play down the whole affair, and he was none too pleased when Weatherby pointed out that in all probability at least one member of Mossad's death squad was still at large and operating in England. This remark of Weatherby's also upset the FCO, whose main immediate interest seemed to be to avoid an international incident that might prejudice long-term relations with Israel.

As the meetings continued Weatherby grew increasingly dour. He wanted action rather than talk, but not spectacular or overt action, such as that advocated by the Police Commissioner. This, he feared, might spark off further violence from one, if not both, of the groups involved, and achieve little of significance.

He urged that surveillance of the six people remaining on the hit-list should be intensified, both for their own protection and possibly to secure further evidence. Special care should be taken over Hector Coyne and Peter Mayberry. These two, he believed, were the extremists among the remaining conspirators, though he doubted whether bringing cases against them would be ultimately possible or even desirable. The others, if approached at the right moment, warned and threatened, might wittingly or unwittingly provide valuable information.

Pierre de Beaune was another conceivable source, though there was still a chance he was irrelevant. The Belgian authorities had nothing against him. He was said to be a bachelor, obviously rich, and a frequent traveller. But, during the three years he had lived in Brussels, he'd not picked up so much as a parking ticket. Nevertheless, Weatherby insisted, his relationship with Coyne must be investigated. Neither should Sabik be forgotten; his exact position in the affair had not yet been established with any certainty.

'That's my opinion,' he said finally. Then, turning to the FCO representative, 'When we've assembled all the data we can, that will be the moment to confront the Israelis, both through your channels by calling in the Ambassador and his so-called Cultural Attaché to deliver a formal diplomatic protest and extract any further information they may have, and through my own channels direct to Mossad.'

Eventually Weatherby won support for his proposals, though on the whole it was grudging support. Sir Rupert finally agreed, urging discretion, and after a glance at his Commissioner the Head of Special Branch nodded a reluctant assent. The FCO and the Home Office followed suit, adding as a warning that the views of the Prime Minister, still in Brussels, had not yet been ascertained.

The net result of all this activity in high-ceilinged Whitehall rooms, now much less smoke-filled than once they would have been, was that nothing of consequence was achieved until after the Prime Minister's return on Friday evening. Thirty-six hours were wasted.

True, Pierre de Beaune was questioned. He had expressed surprise but had been co-operative. He said he had come to London because he was considering putting money into Rossel & Company but, on hearing from Hector Coyne of John Rossel's tragic death, had decided against the investment, and was now merely enjoying a few days holiday. His explanation was plausible and, though surveillance had continued, it was allowed to relax – and relax to such an extent that de Beaune apparently found no difficulty in checking out of the Savoy, mentioning to the Head Porter that he was going to stay with friends in the country, and promptly disappearing.

It was not until late on Saturday morning, after the PM had had a fierce off the record interview with the conspirator to whom he was related, that an attempt was made to take more positive action. Two men called on Sir Peter Mayberry, showed their credentials and asked him to accompany them to the Foreign Office. Mayberry demurred, saying he had a luncheon appointment. They insisted, but would give no reason. He still refused, blustered, pretended anger, but it was clear to the visitors that he was fearful. Patricia joined the argument and was extremely rude. The two men ignored her.

'All right,' Mayberry said at last. 'I suppose I'd better go. God knows what it's about, but I shan't be long.' Turning his back he embraced Patricia with more than his usual warmth and whispered, 'Tell Coyne to call it off.'

Patricia gave no sign that she had heard, but as soon as the front door closed behind her husband she went to the phone. She told Coyne what had happened and delivered the message. 'Hector, what does it mean?' she demanded. 'It was as if they were arresting Peter.'

'Nonsense, Patricia. It's probably just some flap or other. Perhaps Peter's secretary's turned out to be a spy.'

'Hector, it's no joking matter!' Patricia's temper rose. 'For Christ's sake, what's going on? What is it that's got to be called off? Hector . . .'

There was a click on the line as she was cut off. She immediately dialled again. She could hear the ringing tone, but Coyne didn't answer. He was much too busy. His emergency bag was always packed. Now he collected some other essentials, took the money that he kept ready in his safe and went down to his car, missing by less than five minutes the two men who came to request his presence at a meeting at the FCO. He drove out to Heathrow and once again luck was on his side: a truck stalled on the Hammersmith overpass and impeded his surveillance team. He left his car in the long-term parking area, and took the courtesy bus to Terminal One.

He phoned the Savoy to be told that de Beaune had gone, and left no forwarding address. It was an unpleasant surprise, for it meant he had no control of events. He could only wait and see. At least he wouldn't have a long wait, Coyne told himself grimly; either de Beaune had returned to Brussels and abandoned his undertaking, or tomorrow the Jews would have something to remember.

Coyne found himself shaking, from fear or excitement or both. He told himself to keep his head, avoid panic. If things turned out badly, his first idea – to dash off abroad – might be considered tantamount to a confession of his involvement. The alternative was to lose himself in the English countryside for a day or two until the situation was clearer. What was more, he knew just the place: an ex-girlfriend owed him a favour. He took the airport bus to Victoria Station, then a taxi, then a train. When enquiries came to be made, no one remembered him.

★

The next day, Sunday, dawned fair and fine. It was the day when, in what the media called the wedding of the year, Rebecca, the beautiful daughter of the Israeli Ambassador to the Court of St James's, was to become the bride of the British Foreign Secretary's handsome son. A big gathering of public figures was always a nightmare for the security forces, and on this occasion every precaution had been intensified. Search teams and sniffer dogs had been at work since first light, the arrangements scrutinized in the utmost detail, police and security men were omnipresent.

Outwardly it was a day of celebration. First the couple were united in a ceremony to which only families and close friends were invited. Then there was a reception in the ballroom of a

Park Lane hotel. If there were any underlying tensions, few of those present seemed aware of it.

The bride was surrounded by admirers. Her groom chatted happily with friends. Her parents were calm, smiling, apparently at ease. The Foreign Secretary, his usual agreeable self, moved among the guests, affairs of state appearing to weigh lightly on his shoulders for the moment. Champagne flowed. Voices rose. Laughter grew louder. It was a good party – all the better because word had been passed around that there were to be no speeches.

Dermot Piercey was not enjoying himself, however. Originally, when he had received his invitation, he had looked forward to the reception, but General Weatherby's orders to keep his eyes open and not drink too much had had a dampening effect. Nor were they easy orders to obey. A variety of people engaged him in conversation, waiters constantly proffered their wares. He couldn't stand with his back against a wall and watch; the security men, doing just that, were obvious. He was a guest, and he had to act like one.

'You're not listening, Mr Piercey,' an attractive girl said accusingly.

'Indeed I am.' Piercey grinned at her. 'But there's so much noise, it's difficult to hear.'

She gave him a pitying look; that was the sort of excuse her father would use. 'I was saying – ' she began.

'Ah, here's the cake.' Piercey interrupted.

The girl shook her head and drifted away. Escorted by the maître d'hôtel a large trolley bearing a magnificent five-tier cake was being trundled to one end of the room by two beaming chefs in tall white hats. The wedding party gathered round. The maître d' handed the bride a silver knife. The noise level abated. Attention focused on the newly-married couple. What happened next was totally unexpected.

The small thud of the explosion was scarcely louder than the release of a champagne cork, badly drawn. There was even scattered laughter at the sound. Then those near to the cake began to choke and cough as acrid smoke filled the air. There was another soft plop. More smoke, spreading rapidly. Someone screamed. Someone else shouted, 'Fire!'

People made for the exits, pushing and thrusting, some trying to protect wives and friends, others conscious only of their own safety. A few shouts for calm were ignored. There was a crash as a tray of glasses was knocked from a waiter's hands. One man, terrified, used a bottle to clear his passage.

Afterwards Dermot Piercey was unable to remember what had alerted him. Like everyone else he had watched the cake brought in by the smiling chefs, but out of the corner of his eye he had caught sight of a waiter at a table nearby. The man was beginning to open a bottle of champagne, back turned. There should have been nothing odd about that, but the action seemed to Piercey suddenly surreptitious. The next moment came the smoke.

Piercey had no chance of preventing the catastrophe, but at least he knew its source. Holding his breath, a handkerchief pressed to his face, he went for the waiter. The man had pulled what seemed to be a soft rubber protective mask over his eyes and nose and mouth. Any doubts in Piercey's mind evaporated instantly at the unreal sight.

As the confusion grew, everyone was bent on escaping from the fumes, though the occasional individual kept his head. The Foreign Secretary, for instance, regardless of his own safety, had leapt on to a table and was trying to still the panic. His son hurried his bride and his new in-laws to a corner of the room. The security officers struggled to preserve some kind of order. In doing so, however, their protective tasks were temporarily forgotten. Only Dermot Piercey realized the truth – the smoke, the seeming fire was merely a cover for an assassination attempt, and the Foreign Secretary seemed the primary target.

Choking as smoke filled his lungs, Piercey shouted a warning, but it went unheeded. He and the pseudo-waiter reached the Foreign Secretary's table simultaneously. The man in the mask produced a small pistol. A gas gun, Piercey's mind registered. Then he flung himself at the would-be assassin and tackled him low, flinging out one arm to strike the pistol from the man's fist. Intent on his aim, the man was taken by surprise and he and Piercey crashed to the ground together, the table and the wedding cake falling on top of them. The Foreign Secretary jumped safely to the floor, and the gun skittered away as two security men, more perceptive than their colleagues, reached the scene and hurried the politician away to safety.

Regardless of what was happening above and around them Piercey and the assassin continued to fight desperately. Piercey managed to pull off his opponent's mask, but momentarily he had released his grip. As the police and other officers belatedly realized what was happening and began to move, he saw the man's arm come up and caught a glimpse of the champagne bottle before it descended on his skull.

★

Five people died in the shambles of that wedding reception; all were Jewish. An elderly lady and a child were trampled to death. A counsellor for the Israeli Embassy, attempting to open a window, was knocked through it and fell to the pavement below. A middle-aged man had a fatal heart attack. A security officer, who should have known better, picked up the unfamiliar weapon and, searching for the safety catch, released a cloud of cyanide gas in his own face.

Many others received cuts from broken glass or were bruised and shocked. And in the confusion Pierre de Beaune escaped from the hotel. But his primary purpose – to kill the Foreign Secretary, as well as anyone else within range – was not achieved. The Foreign Secretary, the Israeli Ambassador and their immediate families, including the bride and groom, were all unscathed.

The public was shocked by the news, and appalled by the pictures shown on television later that evening. And, though he would never have wished it, public outrage gave the Israeli Ambassador some additional leverage in the discussion which took place at Number Ten the next day.

The Prime Minister himself took charge; he feared that the Foreign Secretary's judgement might be impaired by his close personal involvement. There were of course accusations and counter-accusations, but the PM was firm. He would not have Mossad operating in his country. The Ambassador, horrified at Weatherby's revelations of some of their activities during the last few months in England, could only express regret. But he also insisted that Israel deplored the recent and increasing attacks on the Jewish community in Britain – not least this latest outrage.

On one point, however, there was complete assent. The less publicity the better. If the full facts became known, the Israelis would be condemned for the actions of their agents, and the British blamed for their ignorance of an anti-Jewish conspiracy in the midst of their own Establishment. In the circumstances, it wasn't hard to come to terms.

A few days later de Beaune left the country. Questioned at Heathrow he swore he had been staying with a friend and had not been in London on the day of the wedding. The friend, soon to follow him to Europe, confirmed this over the phone, but Dermot Piercey – at the airport with Weatherby and Farling to watch de Beaune's departure – had a final comment.

'That's the man I struggled with,' he said to Weatherby. 'But I suppose a clever defence barrister would make me out a liar.'

Weatherby nodded. 'Best to let him go, as we agreed. We've no real evidence against him, not without Coyne. But our Belgian colleagues will be looking out for him. Okay, Dermot. Off you go. Ian will drive you home.'

'Thank you, sir.'

Obediently Piercey let Farling take him by the arm. Apart from a slight tendency to giddiness and a large discolouring bruise on his forehead he was fine, but he wasn't about to refuse a week's sick leave – especially a week such as this promised to be. Irena had said she would lend him the Daytons' cottage, and Caro had insisted on coming to look after him. Piercey smiled as he recalled Irena's explanation – obviously cooked up with Caro – that Keith would soon be home, and anyway photographic commitments would keep her in London. He intended to enjoy the week. And – who knew – a week together in the confines of a cottage could have long-term implications (as an official report might put it) for Caro and himself. Others could sort out the rest of the muddle.

In fact, much of the muddle had already been cleared up.

Piercey knew why the General was still waiting at Heathrow. He wanted the satisfaction of seeing the El Al jet take off for Ben Gurion International at Tel Aviv, happy in the knowledge that on board were the Cultural Attaché from the Israeli Embassy, posted home without warning, and, seated together, Casimir Sabik and the man who had been known as Manfred Brenner. There had been furious arguments about Brenner, but finally it was decided that there was no alternative but to let him go.

And that left the British conspirators. Those who survived, Piercey thought, as Farling drove along the M4 towards London, had got off better than they deserved. Threatened with disgrace, if not worse, they had all sworn to watch their future behaviour and to keep their mouths shut. The PM had dealt with Peter Mayberry himself. Piercey wondered if Patricia would stick by a husband forced to retire to private life, and guessed that she wouldn't.

Hector Coyne was the fly in the ointment. He had disappeared, and the best efforts of the police and the Security Service had been unable to trace him since he left his car in a Heathrow car park. If he were suddenly to surface somewhere and start to tell his story, the entire situation might change and the whole careful cover-up collapse.

Once more the old man stood at the long window and looked down into the square below. It was evening in Tel Aviv, and again he was thinking of death, the death of enemies – and of innocents. There was a knock at the door and he turned and looked up enquiringly as his son-in-law came into the salon.

'It's all over,' the younger man said. 'More or less success-fully. Those whom the British call the conspirators have been eliminated or rendered harmless, and we've come out of the affair better than we might have done. In the end, when they'd got over their rhetoric, the Brits were cooperative. They don't like scandals in high places.'

'Who does, Moshe?'

'Who indeed?' There was irony behind the words. Moshe Seinan had had little difficulty in persuading his colleagues that the matter of the hit-list and how it had reached British hands should not be pursued. 'You're glad it's over,' he said; it wasn't a question.

'Yes. Too many people have been killed and hurt, innocents many of them. It's not right we should have caused this.'

'So we should stand by and let Jews be persecuted? Is that right? Is it right to allow a friendly country to be turned against us by a group of – of racist right-wing fanatics?'

'No, of course not,' the old man replied sadly.

'We've no need to apologize. We knew of this conspiracy in Britain, but we couldn't prove it. Direct action was the only – '

'The only option? Maybe, Moshe, but . . . Oh, Moshe, let's agree to disagree. You are young and I am old, and death means more to me, perhaps – especially the death of children.'

'Your David – and David Gorey?'

'Naturally.' The old man paused. 'You say it's over. That means at last you know what happened to Coyne.'

'Yes, that's what I came to tell you. Coyne is dead. He got out of England on the Hook of Holland ferry. Heaven knows where he hoped to go after that – to South Africa, perhaps. Anyway, he didn't make it. It was rough and there were few people on deck. Our man saw Coyne standing by the rail – '

'Our man? We had a man on Coyne?' The old man said sharply. 'But Mossad swore to withdraw from Britain.'

Moshe Seinan smiled. 'He was the last – and he was withdrawing. But he had made sure he withdrew with Coyne, whom it seemed the Brits had failed to trace.'

The old man stared. 'And we . . . That was a mistake, a mistake, Moshe. The British won't forgive us. We gave our word. We should have – '

'We did nothing – nothing. One moment Hector Coyne was on deck, the next he was in the sea.'

'He jumped?'

'Jumped? No, no. He was pushed – but not by our man. The Brits aren't stupid, any more than we are. Weatherby – General Sir Christopher Weatherby – is a cunning devil.'

The old man sighed and made a gesture of dismissal. He went to the grand piano and picked up the silver-framed photograph of his son. He stared at it as the light faded. At least he had done his bit – his best. He had no regrets about sending that list and yet – Was his conscience clear? Or would it always, he wondered, be burdened by guilt, his own and that of others?